OFFICIAL STATS

NAME:	Mike Gerard
VITALS:	6 feet tall, rugged, broad shouldered, mesmerizing dark eyes and to-die-for athletic build.
OCCUPATION:	Police detective
SPECIALTY:	Protecting women in jeopardy and arresting bad guys.
OBJECTIVE:	To find a caring woman to fill his lonely days—and nights.

Dear Harlequin Intrigue Reader,

The holidays are upon us again. This year, remember to give yourself a gift—the gift of great romantic suspense from Harlequin Intrigue!

In the exciting conclusion to TEXAS CONFIDENTIAL, *The Outsider's Redemption* (#593) by Joanna Wayne, Cody Gannon must make a life-and-death decision. Should he trust his fellow agents even though there may be a traitor among their ranks? Or should he trust Sarah Rand, a pregnant single mother-to-be, who may be as deadly as she is beautiful?

Another of THE SUTTON BABIES is on the way, in *Lullaby and Goodnight* (#594) by Susan Kearney. When Rafe Sutton learns Rhianna McCloud is about to have his baby, his honor demands that he protect her from a determined and mysterious stalker. But Rafe must also discover the stalker's connection to the Sutton family—before it's too late!

An unlikely partnership is forged in *To Die For* (#595) by Sharon Green. Tanda Grail is determined to find her brother's killer. Detective Mike Gerard doesn't want a woman distracting him while on a case. But when push comes to shove, is it Mike's desire to catch a killer that propels him, or his desire for Tanda?

First-time Harlequin Intrigue author Morgan Hayes makes her debut with *Tall, Dark and Wanted* (#596). Policewoman Molly Sparling refuses to believe Mitch Drake is dead. Her former flame and love of her life is missing from Witness Protection, but her superior tracking skills find him hiding out. While the cop in her wants to bring him in, the woman in her wants him to trust her. But Mitch just plain wants her back....

Wishing you the happiest of holidays from all of us at Harlequin Intrigue!

Sincerely,

Denise O'Sullivan
Associate Senior Editor
Harlequin Intrigue

TO DIE FOR
SHARON GREEN

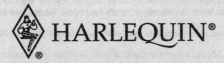

HARLEQUIN®

TORONTO • NEW YORK • LONDON
AMSTERDAM • PARIS • SYDNEY • HAMBURG
STOCKHOLM • ATHENS • TOKYO • MILAN • MADRID
PRAGUE • WARSAW • BUDAPEST • AUCKLAND

ISBN 0-373-22595-4

TO DIE FOR

Copyright © 2000 by Sharon Green

This edition published by arrangement with Harlequin Books S.A.

® and TM are trademarks of the publisher. Trademarks indicated with ® are registered in the United States Patent and Trademark Office, the Canadian Trade Marks Office and in other countries.

Visit us at www.eHarlequin.com

Printed in U.S.A.

ABOUT THE AUTHOR

Sharon Green was born and raised in Brooklyn, New York, attended New York University and graduated with a B.A. in English and a minor in government. She is the proud mother of three sons, Andy, Brian and Curtis. She has worked for AT&T as a shareowner correspondent, then as an all-around assistant in a construction company, then sold bar steel for an import firm. She left that job as assistant sales manager. She has been writing full-time since 1984.

Her hobbies include knitting, crocheting, Tae Kwon Do, fencing, archery, shooting, jigsaw puzzles, logic problems, math problems, *not* cooking.

She is a well-known science fiction author and has written thirty-eight novels in four different subgenres.

She makes her home in Franklin, Tennessee.

Books by Sharon Green

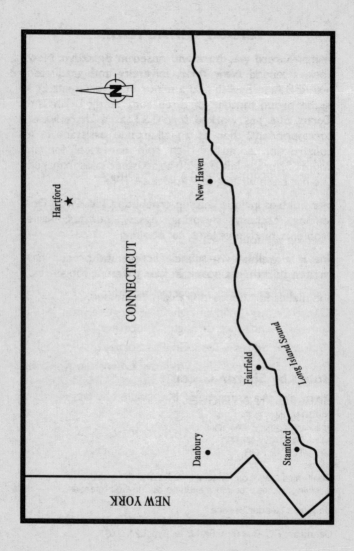

CAST OF CHARACTERS

Mike Gerard—A detective lieutenant working to capture a serial killer before any more innocent lives are claimed.

Tanda Grail—She had ties to three of the murder victims. How long would it be before the murderer decided Tanda should be a victim herself?

Don Grail—The first murder victim and Tanda's estranged brother. Could a mysterious key hold the answer to his death?

Roger Saxon—A private investigator hired by Tanda to find her brother's killer, he never expected he'd become the fourth victim.

Rena Foreman—The police sergeant who was replaced on the murder cases by Mike.

Larry Othar—Rena's detective partner.

Oscar Relling—Victim right after Roger Saxon, someone Tanda met through her brother.

Arthur Weddoes—Don Grail's attorney.

Richard Draper, Miles Rayburn, Lawrence Ransom, Jocelyn Geroux, Howard Ullman, and Mark King—Members of a group being blackmailed by the serial killer.

For Pamela Crippen Adams,
without whom this book couldn't have been written.

Chapter One

It was raining when Lieutenant Mike Gerard got to the motel, but rain in August doesn't come down cold even in Connecticut. Stuffy was what it was, making it uncomfortable to wear a raincoat. But the uniformed cops from the units already on the scene were in raincoats, one way of picking them out from the crowd of gapers they were keeping back.

"Sergeant Renquist is inside waiting for you, Lieutenant," one of the uniforms told him as he got out of his car. "He's pretty sure it's another one."

"Make sure you keep the press away until the lab people are finished," Mike said, ignoring the rain. "They almost mucked up the last murder scene, and I don't want it happening again."

The man nodded and turned back to help the others with the crowd, leaving Mike to enter the motel unit alone. Once inside, though, he was no longer alone. The forensics team was already there in the usual mob, working over every inch of the room.

"The body's over here, Mike," Art Renquist called. The room's bed stood to the left and Art was just beyond it, looking down at what lay on the floor. Art looked as rumpled and tired as Mike felt, and the extra ten years of age Art carried made his appearance that much worse for wear. Mike circled the unmade bed, and joined Art's inspection.

"The doc thinks he'll find the same twelve stab wounds," Art told him, gesturing to the bloody corpse. "And if that letter opener isn't one of the set, then I'm Santa Claus. Once we get the note loose, we'll be able to compare the handwriting."

Mike nodded as he stared at the corpse, sickened more by the implications than by the terrible sight. This was the fifth victim murdered in the same way, which once again confirmed that there was a psychopath on the loose. Whoever the perpetrator was, he left precisely twelve stab wounds in the body, then attached a note to it by putting a letter opener through the note and into one of the wounds.

"'From your secret admirer,'" Mike muttered, wondering for the thousandth time what that meant. It had been printed in awkward block letters on all of the notes, set off by the presence of the letter opener. The opener was silver-bladed and gold-handled, a meaningless design in black on the gold handle, a shocking-pink ribbon tied just below the handle. The letter openers looked as though they should be given to friends as inexpensive gifts, not left in a handful of dead bodies.

"The victim's name was Roger Saxon, but he registered day before yesterday as Roger Brown," Art said, consulting a small notebook. "According to the ID in his wallet, he was a private detective from New York. But there's nothing to say he was here on business. Since it's Sunday we can't check with his office, so that'll have to wait until tomorrow."

"How about his cash?" Mike asked, turning away from the body. "Is it still in his wallet, or missing?"

"Gone, just like with the other victims," Art answered with a humorless smile. "Aren't you glad they dumped this on you when the fourth body turned up? That'll teach you to be the best cop in the state.''

"Cut the bullshit," Mike answered with a grimace. "I was lucky a few months ago, and that's the way my report read. I think the chief is hoping I'll get lucky a second time, because if we don't get this psychopath soon, *he* could be out of a job."

"And we'll be on the unemployment line right along with him," Art grumbled. "Why would somebody who kills like this take whatever cash his victim has? He's not trying to make it look like a robbery, or he'd take watches and jewelry and credit cards too. What could he possibly be doing?"

"He's trying to tell us who he is," Mike said, having spent a lot of time considering the point. "It's probably the best clue we have, but we haven't been able to read it. Once we do—"

"Excuse me, Lieutenant, but there's a lady outside who says she has to talk to you," a uniformed officer interrupted suddenly. "She said to tell you she knows the victim."

"If she isn't a reporter, you can bring her in," Mike said as he looked around. "I'll talk to her over there near the television set, where the lab crew has already finished."

The officer nodded and went back out into the rain, and Art put a hand on Mike's sleeve.

"I wish you the best of luck, buddy," he said with a grin that was too worried to look amused. "If this is the break we've been waiting for, take pity on all of us and don't blow it."

"Art, he said she knew the victim, not the murderer," Mike pointed out with a shake of his head. "Try to take it easy, will you? We'll catch him, and *before* we all get tossed out."

"Try to make that 'before the next body,'" Art suggested, looking at him with haunted eyes. "Five of these is five too many, and don't forget that one was a woman. I don't think I could take another one like that."

Mike watched Art walk away, finally understanding what was really bothering him. It had taken Art two bad marriages and a lot of years before he found a woman to be in love with. Since they were dealing with a crazy, the next victim could be anyone at all and women weren't safe. Art was picturing himself arriving at a crime scene to find the woman he loved as the victim.

There's something to be said for being alone, Mike thought as he moved to the area near the TV. Usually the loneliness was a black gap in his life dating back even before the divorce, but every now and then it was shaded with relief.

"Excuse me, but are you Lieutenant Gerard?" a low, pleasant voice asked, pulling him out of his thoughts. "The officer said I was to talk to a Lieutenant Gerard."

"That's me," Mike acknowledged, turning to look down at the woman who had just come in carrying an umbrella. She was somewhere in her mid- to late-twenties, with dark blond hair and gray eyes. Jeans and a T-shirt covered a good figure, and she would have been prettier if her face hadn't looked so drawn. "You told the officer that you knew the victim?"

"More than that," she said, guilt clear in the gray gaze coming up at him. "I hired him, so his being dead is my fault. There's no law to hold me responsible, but there should be. There should be."

She brought one hand up to cover her mouth, the gesture holding off the hysteria that obviously wanted to claim her. Mike moved forward quickly to put a comforting arm around her, impressed in spite of himself. Instead of hesitating, she'd immediately come forward with what she knew. Most people would have tried to hide their connection, hoping at the same time to bury their feelings of guilt.

"Why don't you and I go and get ourselves some coffee at the diner next door?" Mike suggested after a moment, then began to urge the young woman back toward the door. "Once we're comfortable, you can tell me all about it."

There was no resistance as he guided the woman out and away from the crowd of onlookers. Happily the media hadn't gotten here yet, so he and the woman were able to walk quietly to the diner only a few feet beyond the motel.

"Okay, let's start from the beginning," Mike said once they were seated in a booth. "What's your name, and why did you hire a private detective?"

"My name is Tanda Grail," the woman answered, running a hand through her hair. "If the name sounds familiar to you, it should. My brother Don was the first victim of that maniac."

Mike hid his surprise, but not his interest. Don Grail had been found dead a week earlier in his rental car, starting the chain of bodies that hadn't yet stopped. Mike had only been working the case since the fourth victim, which was why he hadn't recognized the first victim's sister.

"And you hired a private detective because the police weren't getting anywhere with finding your brother's murderer," Mike suggested. As a guess it was the next thing to a certainty, and Tanda looked at him with defiant gray eyes.

"It's been a whole week and the bodies just keep piling up," she challenged, bleakness behind the defiant tone. "After the third body was found I knew you would never catch the killer, so I went shopping for someone who might. Saxon's agency was recommended to me by a friend, so I called them. After explaining that they couldn't do anything to interfere with the police investigation, they sent Saxon to look around. After being here

only a day and a half he called me last night to say he
discovered something totally unexpected, and would give
me a full report this morning. When I got here and saw
all those police cars…''

"You knew that someone had noticed his discovering
that 'something unexpected,'" Mike finished when she
didn't. Frustration was climbing high and trying to
smother him, but losing his temper would have been a
waste of time. "I wish to hell people would learn to call
the police first and their favorite gossip partners second.
The morgue would have a lot fewer bodies that way."

"We were supposed to talk to the police together," she
offered, at least having the decency to look embarrassed.
"That way he would not be acting behind my back, and
I'd be there to explain why he was here. The agency said
police departments don't like having private investigations
into cases they're working on."

"But we do enjoy being given leads when we're at a
dead end," Mike said, trying to sound a bit more reasonable. The woman had lost her brother, after all. "Was
there anything else Saxon told you last night? Any comment at any time, no matter how unrelated it sounded?
Did he keep any files, take any notes?"

"He had a file with the newspaper articles on each of
the murders," she said. "I supplied that, and the first day
he was here he double-checked the papers to be sure I
hadn't missed anything. He kept a small notebook, where
he wrote down directions and things."

"And about what he told you?" Mike prompted, leaning on the table with both arms. "Is there anything you
can add to what you've already said?"

"Saxon laughed and said it was the purest kind of
luck." The frown on her face was one of concentration,
and somehow, Mike noticed, the expression made her
look unexpectedly attractive. "Saxon said if it had been
anyone else who was sent here—well, the implication was

no one else would have spotted what he did. What I don't understand is how he could have let the murderer get close enough to kill him. He didn't strike me as a stupid man, so how did it happen?''

''There are any number of reasons why he made the mistake,'' Mike said, glad to see that she was already shaking off the guilt. ''Even professionals get caught by surprise, especially if they underestimate their quarry. Saxon seemed to be a fairly big man, and almost certainly believed he could take care of himself. If you depend on greater size or even superior ability when dealing with a psychopath, you need to have your head examined. Ready for that coffee yet?''

''Yes, as a matter of fact I am,'' she answered, giving him a tentative smile. ''I still feel responsible for Roger's death, but you've made it a little easier for me. Thank you, Lieutenant Gerard.''

''Call me Mike,'' he said, gesturing to a waitress for two of something to drink. When the woman held up the coffeepot Mike nodded, then looked at Tanda again. ''I can understand how impatient you felt, but now there's a way for you to help. Are you willing?''

''Of course,'' Tanda agreed with raised eyebrows. ''No matter what you happen to ask for in the way of that help, I'll give it if I can. I was willing long before this.''

''But before this we didn't have something for you to be willing about,'' Mike countered, leaning back to let the waitress put a cup in front of him. Once they both had coffee and the woman was gone, he continued, ''Roger Saxon saw something while he was here that turned him into a victim. Aside from the murderer, you're the only one who knows where he went. Will you help me to retrace his movements?''

''Try and stop me,'' she said, now looking doggedly determined. ''But what about the second half of the problem? From what Roger said, it was something he originally learned elsewhere that gave him the real hint. How do we find out what that something was?''

''I do that finding out, by contacting his agency,'' Mike answered quickly. Tanda was faster at understanding than he'd thought she'd be, and he was pleasantly surprised. ''We'll certainly have to go back years in his life, and simply hope we get lucky. If the incident wasn't something he was publicly involved in…''

''We may never find it,'' she summed up glumly when he let the sentence trail off. ''But retracing his movements could give us a clue about what to look for, so let's get started with that. When he got here day before yesterday, he registered at the motel then called for directions out to my place. He showed up about half an hour after the call.''

''Where is your place?'' Mike asked, pulling out his notebook and a pen. ''Close enough so that he might have stopped somewhere on the way?''

''Not really,'' Tanda replied. ''I have a place on Old Stage Road, and for me it's only a fifteen-minute drive. For a stranger to find it you can add at least five minutes to that first fifteen, and another five if he didn't leave the instant he hung up. If he stopped somewhere, it had to be on the way and at a place where he could be in and out.''

''I'll drive it myself, and look for any possible stopping places,'' Mike said, making a note. ''How long did he stay?''

''About an hour or so,'' Tanda estimated as she tasted her coffee. ''I gave him the file of newspaper articles, and then he questioned me about my brother. It was the logical place to start, and I was expecting it. He also asked if I recognized any of the other victims from their pictures in the newspaper, and I said I didn't.''

''And what did he ask about your brother?'' Mike said. ''Try to remember as many of the questions as you can.''

''Since my brother lived out of state, he asked how long

he'd been here," Tanda said, now staring down at her coffee cup. "I said Don got here August first, just the way he always does. He's come back every August first for the last five years as a vacation of sorts, I guess. Then Roger asked me why my brother hadn't been staying with me. That was when I had to admit I wouldn't have let Don stay with me."

Mike watched her as she fell silent, remembering reading parts of the statement she'd made when her brother's body had first been found. It would have been nice if Mike could have spared her the need to go through the whole thing again, but Tanda Grail seemed determined not to hide anything at all.

"Don—Don wasn't what you would call a nice person," she groped, raising her gaze again as she tried to explain the condemnation. "When I was very young I adored my big brother, just the way everyone else seemed to. He had a charm about him that most people found irresistible. I think I must have been one of the first to notice that he used the charm to use people. You know, to get out of chores or have favors done for him?"

Mike nodded in answer to the question. He'd known people like that, just as everyone did.

"Our mother never did see through him, but Dad finally did," Tanda continued. "There was some sort of trouble with the police, and when Dad brought Don home there was a big fight. Don kept insisting he was innocent, Mom supported him, Dad yelled that Don had been caught in the act. All Dad wanted Don to do was admit his guilt and show something in the way of remorse, I think. It didn't happen, because the only thing Don was sorry about was the fact that he'd been caught."

She paused to sip her coffee again, and then she shook her head.

"When I got home from school the next day, Don was gone. He'd taken the emergency money Mom kept in a jar behind the preserves, and had left with as many of his clothes as he could stuff into a single valise. It was obvious why he'd left, but Mom insisted he'd done it to keep from being railroaded. Not only did Dad lose the bail money he'd posted, but Mom made him offer money as reparation to the people accusing Don. If he hadn't made the reparation, then the people involved wouldn't have dropped the complaint against Don, and Don would have been a wanted man wherever he went.''

''And it never occurred to your mother that if you're innocent you stay and fight,'' Mike couldn't help remarking. ''Especially if your family is willing to stand behind you.''

''It wasn't entirely Mom's fault,'' Tanda answered wearily. ''Don never let her see the ugly side of him. All she knew was that Don was her son and she loved him. Mom kept insisting she understood why Don had disappeared like that, but he hadn't even left her a note to say goodbye. When more and more time went by and there wasn't a single word from him, she must have begun to suspect the truth. It made her grieve herself to death.''

Mike could see the anger in Tanda, remembered anger that was still strong. It made the cop in him stir uneasily, but he didn't interrupt.

''Dad took her death hard, and when Don finally came back—three years after the day he disappeared—Dad refused even to see Don.'' Tanda had taken a deep breath, and it seemed to have calmed her. ''My big brother had apparently done very well for himself, and everything about him screamed money. He seemed to think we would welcome him back as soon as he paid for any inconvenience he might have caused…

''Well, Dad refused to talk to him, but I didn't,'' Tanda stated, defiance clear in her eyes again. ''First I made him come up with the money Dad had thrown away getting him free of all charges, and then I told Don what I thought of him. Don didn't stay for the whole speech—I guess the truth made him too uncomfortable—and although he was here the whole month, he never tried to come back to the house. It must have finally gotten through that we didn't want to know him.''

"But now you're trying to find the person who killed your brother," Mike pointed out. "Are you doing it out of respect for your mother's memory, or is there another reason?"

"My dad died less than a year ago," Tanda said, now toying with her coffee cup. "I wouldn't have gotten in touch with Don even if I'd known where he was, so I was shocked when he showed up for the funeral. He paid for everything, mourned alone, then left again without even trying to speak to me. He seemed...quieter than usual, somehow changed, and when he came back at the beginning of this month he sent a note asking me to have dinner with him.''

"And you went," Mike said, knowing it for a fact. "Did you find out if he really was changed?"

"Maybe I was kidding myself," she answered with a shrug and a sigh. "All I know is that his practiced charm wasn't beating me over the head any longer, and what he wanted to talk about was our time as kids. I found out in passing that he was a widower, and I hadn't even known he'd been married. I think it had finally come to him that he and I were the last of the family, and he was trying to make things right between us.''

"But before he could do it he was killed," Mike summed up, finally understanding. "He might not have been serious about it, but now you'll never know."

"But I *will* know who killed him," she said, staring at Mike fiercely. "It's a final gesture I owe my brother, even if he wasn't serious. What else can I tell you?"

"How about the details of your own whereabouts?" Mike said, taking advantage of the moment. "Saxon called you last night, and arranged to see you in person this morning. What time did he call, and where were you from then until you got here?''

''He called about seven-thirty last night,'' she said, again frowning in thought. ''I went to bed early, and was out by four this morning to track fugitives.''

''To do what?'' Mike asked, looking up from his notebook to blink at her. ''You couldn't have said what I thought you did.''

''Oh, we weren't tracking real fugitives,'' she answered with a laugh that brightened her whole face. ''It's what the exercise is called, and I usually have friends doing the remote part. Teddy went first this morning, and she performed beautifully.''

''It's obvious that I'm missing something here,'' Mike said, still staring. ''Who is Teddy, and what sort of exercises were you doing?''

''I thought you knew,'' Tanda said with a smile replacing the laugh. ''I raise and train bloodhounds, and right now Teddy is my star pupil. Yesterday afternoon one of my friends laid a trail through Rimsdale Mall, visiting certain prearranged stores before leaving by a specified exit. At four this morning Teddy followed that trail, and found every stop her quarry had made. Doing the tracking with no one around is to keep onlookers from getting upset.''

''But you said the trail was laid yesterday afternoon,'' Mike protested. ''Since the mall doesn't close until 9:00 p.m., how could there still be a trail after so many people have walked over it? There'd be nothing left to follow.''

''For you and me, maybe, but not for a really good bloodhound,'' Tanda corrected with amusement. ''Teddy's father once followed a trail that was laid through a site that was about to be used for a three-day Renaissance fair. He wasn't put on the trail until the fair was over, but he still had no trouble. Very often the hardest part is to train your tracker to follow the trail, not shortcut to the end of it. If the trail is too short and the person being tracked is standing at the end of it, that's what happens."

"That's something I'd like to see someday," Mike said, seriously fascinated. "So you were out this morning tracking fugitives. Was there anyone with you?"

"Only Teddy and Masher," Tanda admitted, losing her amusement. "They may be good trackers, but they lack something as witnesses. I hadn't realized that I could end up being a suspect."

"Right now I'm only collecting information," Mike soothed, surprised to find that he *didn't* consider Tanda a suspect. "Since your own movements can't be confirmed, let's go back to Saxon's. You told him all about your brother, and then what did he do?"

"He asked about where Don had been staying, then wanted directions to the local newspaper office," Tanda responded. "I told him about Don's house, but I don't know if he went to look at it."

"That's the house your brother bought and renovated five years ago?" Mike asked, remembering the reference to it in the case file. "I understand that he put a lot of money into the place, but only lived in it one month out of the year. Do you have any idea why he did that?"

"None," she admitted. "It certainly wasn't for the purpose of being close to Dad and me. We were never invited out to see the house. I understand he bought the place longer than five years ago, but didn't do the renovations until then. Whatever, he didn't even mention it at dinner."

"Well, I think this is enough to get started with," Mike said, closing his notebook. "I should have more information later today, and probably more questions to go with it. Will you be at home?"

"All day," she said, finishing her coffee. "Feel free to

come by with as many questions as you like. You're very easy to talk to.''

"Most people would not agree with that sentiment,'' Mike told her with his own amusement as they left the booth. And to be honest, he'd just been thinking the same about her... "I'll try to call before dropping in.''

"Fine,'' she said with a smile, offering her hand. "Thanks for the coffee—and the understanding ear.''

"Understanding your situation isn't terribly difficult,'' Mike said, liking the firm way she took his hand. "Losing a brother is the hard part of life. You may not have liked your brother, but that doesn't mean you didn't love him.''

She looked as though she was about to say something else, then apparently thought better of it. After retrieving her umbrella she left the diner, unaware of the way Mike's gaze followed.

You'd better watch that, old man, he thought as he stopped to pay for the coffee. *No matter what you said, she* is *a suspect, and it won't do you any good to let gray eyes make you forget that. She isn't the first attractive woman you've met, so get a grip on yourself.*

With that firm advice ringing in his head he went back out into the rain, but it didn't do the good he'd been hoping for. He never *had* met a woman like Tanda Grail before, and it was more than the possibility of new answers that made him look forward to their next meeting. Maybe he would even find an excuse to ask her out to dinner...

TANDA GRAIL CLIMBED into her van, then sat there for a moment with her eyes closed behind the hand covering them. Events around her were growing from bad dream to nightmare, and she had already begun to feel helpless to stop them. But that didn't mean she intended to quit on the promise she'd made herself. She *would* find the one who had killed Don, and make sure he or she faced everything the law demanded.

Through the rain-soaked windshield Tanda saw Lieutenant Gerard come out of the diner and head back toward the motel. He was dark-haired and dark-eyed, handsome in a tired, overworked way. He wasn't the police officer she'd spoken to when Don's body had first been found, but he should have been. There was something about the man, something that said he knew what he was doing.

Which meant she would have to be very careful. Her resolve had caused her to make a mistake and call in an outsider, and now an innocent man was dead. She should have handled the investigation herself to begin with, which was what she intended to do from now on. The police would gather the clues, she would work on them in her own way, and then—

And then she would find the person who had caused her to be all alone in the world.

Chapter Two

Mike Gerard got back to his office in a thoughtful mood. This newest victim just might have given him a lead the death was supposed to have prevented, and it was certainly worth checking into. But not if it had already been checked, which was the first thing he had to find out.

Detective Sergeant Rena Foreman sat at her desk, leaning back in her chair while she argued desultorily with her partner, Detective Larry Othar. The two were always arguing about *something,* a clear sign that as partners they were really close. Rena was tall and slender with auburn hair and blue eyes, and Larry was tall and broad-shouldered with brown hair and blue eyes. They were also good cops, but that hadn't kept them from being replaced as team leaders of the serial-killings case when the fourth body was found.

The brass was being screamed at by the press and public alike, so they wanted action and an arrest as quickly as possible. When they hadn't gotten the arrest by the time the third body was discovered, they'd put Mike in charge instead of calling in the FBI.

"Hey, you two," Mike said, approaching Rena and Larry. "I need to ask you about your part of the serial-killings investigation. How much of a background check did you do on each of the victims?"

"The checks were routine but fairly thorough," Rena answered. "We knew where the victims came from because of their ID's, so we checked with the police in those places. Our counterparts confirmed that the victims were who we thought they were, but there was nothing in the way of records or files on the deceased parties."

"And that first victim, Don Grail, is originally from around here," Larry added. "He'd gotten into some trouble as a kid, but his old man managed to get the charges dropped. Something about getting into an argument with a girl, and starting to beat up on her. The argument was loud enough that somebody called the cops, and they got there before Grail did worse than slap her around a little. The girl and her family were the first ones we checked, but they'd all moved away years ago and never came back."

"We traced them to Colorado, and the locals checked for us," Rena continued. "Every one of them was accounted for, including the girl's present husband. She was in the hospital having her third child, the rest of the family and the husband were there with her, and none of them had left the state for at least two years."

"And this is more involved than a simple revenge killing," Mike said with a nod, showing them he knew they'd realized that. "You did exactly what I would have done—and did do—with the fourth victim, but now there's something to add to the rest. Victim number five was a private detective brought in by victim number one's sister."

Rena and Larry both exclaimed in surprise over that, and Mike gave them a quick rundown. After telling them what the dead man had said to Tanda Grail, he added, "So that means Saxon saw someone he knew, but not from the city and probably not from his work for the agency. If he's the only one who could have spotted whoever he did spot, that tells us we have to look into Saxon's past life. Private detectives are often retired cops. If Saxon happened to be one, where did he live and work? If it was another agency he'd been with, again, when and where?''

"What makes you think it was a person he saw?" Rena asked. "Maybe he spotted some *thing,* and was able to recognize it because he came from a small-town area like this one, and everyone else at the agency is city-raised."

"That's a possibility that should be checked, but I don't think it's what happened," Mike answered with a distracted head shake. "Spotting some *thing* would not have gotten the man killed unless some *body* went along with the thing, which leads us back to an individual. And there's one more job that has to be done—take the pictures and prints of all five victims, and have them sent along the network to the entire country. None of the victims have police records where they live, but how about elsewhere? And see if you can find out where they were all supposed to be before they turned up here and dead."

"According to his sister, Grail was supposed to be nowhere but here," Larry offered. "Grail came back here every year on August first, and stayed for the whole month."

"Which he'd been doing for five years," Mike agreed, remembering what Tanda had told him. "Take another look at who he associated with while he was here, where he went and what he did. Your first investigation said he kept to himself, but that doesn't feel right. People go home to show off for the people they used to know, especially if they make it as big as Grail did. If they go home to hide, they stay longer than a single month. And why hide for just one month of the year? Did August mean something special to Grail? Did his friends know about it back where he came from? If August has nothing to do with the murder, I want to know so we can forget about it."

"We'll get back to you with whatever we find," Larry

said as he reached for the phone, Rena doing the same. "Damn, but it feels good to actually have something to work on with this case."

Mike understood how the man felt, so he left Larry and Rena alone to go back to his small office, where he took care of paperwork while he waited for the preliminary report on Roger Saxon. He wasn't expecting the report to tell him anything he didn't know, not unless this was the time the killer had made his first mistake. If it was...

Well, no sense in daydreaming. Mike brought himself back to the present with a shake of his head, then buckled down to finishing that paperwork. It needed to be done before he could leave to interview Tanda Grail again, an interview he was definitely looking forward to. But not because she'd given him his first real lead, and might somehow give him another of the same. Despite knowing better than to get involved with a possible suspect, he realized it was the woman herself he wanted to see. There was just something about her...

IT WAS STILL DRIZZLING when Tanda reached home, but pulling the van into the carport meant she didn't have to use her umbrella. Not that the umbrella would have helped. Tanda was already so damp that nothing but a change of clothes would help.

For once, walking into the house didn't give Tanda the usual feeling of being safely home. The kitchen, usually so bright and cheerful in yellow and white with touches of red, looked as drab and gray as the weather. Tanda remembered when her father had redone the kitchen for her mother, adding the surprise of a brand-new gas range. He'd been trying to bring some happiness into the life of a woman who grieved endlessly for a missing son, but it hadn't worked. The heartbroken woman had still grieved herself to death, and the gift had gone unappreciated by anyone but Tanda.

Now she stood and looked around, finally understanding why a new kitchen hadn't distracted her mother. She, herself, would give that kitchen and all the rest of the house to find her brother's murderer and bring that person to justice. She still didn't know if Don had seriously changed or had been playing some kind of game, and now she'd never know the truth. The chance to find out had been stolen from her, along with the last member of her family; for that she would find the guilty person, even if she had to do it alone.

Tanda went through the kitchen into the hall, and from there to her bedroom. The large room had originally belonged to her parents, and after her father died it had taken Tanda six months to make up her mind to use it. It wasn't as if she'd really believed her parents had gone off for just a little while and would return very shortly. It was more that the realization they were gone forever had to be actively accepted, and that had hurt. She hadn't been able to ease the pain until Don took her to dinner a couple of weeks earlier, and now...

Rather than going through it all again, Tanda forced herself to drop the subject and change her clothes. Once into dry clothing she went into her old room where she'd set up an office, then sat down to do some work. People who do business with you may sympathize when tragedy strikes your life, but they still don't enjoy having their business unduly delayed.

Tanda worked for a couple of hours, paying bills, adding to her monthly supply list, answering letters from people. There were those people who wanted to buy a trained bloodhound, and those people who already had dogs and simply wanted them trained. Of course, the second group never understood that their request wasn't all that simple. Dogs, like people, don't always do what they're able to, and some are better at the doing than others. Teddy, for example, had taken to the training immediately, while one of her litter brothers had had to be sold as a pet. He'd had no interest in tracking, and hadn't even been willing to notice a fresh scent, let alone one that was days or a week old—

Suddenly Tanda sat straight, silently cursing herself for being an idiot. Her brother's body had been found in his rental car not half a mile away, but no one had known why he'd been there. He certainly hadn't come to visit her, otherwise he would have driven all the way to the house. The police were assuming that Don had gone to the spot to meet someone, and either that particular someone or somebody following one or the other of them was the murderer. But what if he'd parked there to go somewhere on foot, and knowing where he'd gone would point to who had killed him? Not once had she thought to check the possibility, but it might not be too late. That pup that had to be sold would never have been able to follow a scent better than a week old, but his sire was a dog of another color.

Once she'd made up her mind, Tanda didn't hesitate. Her first stop was her brother's old room, where she'd put the clothes the police had given to her after going through them. Their laboratory hadn't been able to find anything in the clothes, but hopefully they hadn't ruined Don's scent on his shirt.

Once Tanda had stuffed the shirt into a spare plastic bag and that into a shoulder bag, she went out to the runs which were to the right about fifteen feet from the house. Happily, it had stopped raining by then, so she didn't need to choose between fooling with an umbrella or getting wet. Only three of the five dogs she had were currently in training, and two of those, Teddy and Masher, were from the same litter. The third, Angel, belonged to someone attached to a police department in Rhode Island, and he would be going back to his owner once his training was finished. Teddy and her brother Masher were already sold, and since their training was almost complete, they would be leaving first.

Which left Robby and Merry, her first breeding pair. Merry was sweet and a top-notch tracker, but Robby was something special. His long, homely face had bright, eager eyes, and he'd never failed to follow any trail that was definitely, even if faintly, there. He might be a plain, light brown mass of furry wrinkles and drool, but to Tanda he was downright beautiful.

"All right, you bunch, settle down," she told the dogs, who had quickly come to the front of their runs at her appearance. "This time I need a professional, so it's Robby's turn. The rest of you can watch and learn."

Once Tanda had put Robby on a lead, the dog obviously expected to be taken to the van, but Tanda had already decided against driving. If someone saw her out with one of her dogs only half a mile away from home, they couldn't possibly consider it suspicious. If they saw her *drive* a dog there, though, they could only conclude she was there to snoop.

"Which is just what we *will* be there for, but we don't have to advertise it," she told Robby as she headed him away from the van. "Whoever killed Don and the detective I hired would be stupid not to keep an eye on me, and I don't think he's stupid. We'll have to look around carefully before we start."

Tanda took Robby along the tar road leading to Old Stage Road at a pace close to strolling, and once they reached the blacktop she casually headed them left. The side of the road was muddy from the rain, but it wasn't so bad that they had to leave the shoulder and walk either on the blacktop or in the grass and bushes. That area had a small number of houses like Tanda's, each of them isolated with woods all around, and from the blacktop they were hard, if not impossible, to see.

It was still overcast and very humid, especially under

all those trees, but Tanda moved along as if enjoying a simple walk. While pretending to give the neighborhood a pleased and casual inspection, she tried very hard to see if anyone was watching her. If they were it would have to be from the woods, so she kept an eye on Robby. A watcher might be able to hide from *her,* but her dog would know immediately if someone was there. He might not do anything about it, but he would certainly know.

Half a mile isn't far to walk for someone used to working with tracking dogs, and it also didn't take very long. The place where Don had been found was a small, cleared area just off the road, half again as long as a large car, wide enough for two cars to park side by side. It was a place for someone with car trouble to stop, or someone who simply wanted to sit for a while and look at the woods. It was also a place where people could meet secretly, especially at night, when the normally light traffic turned to nothing coming by at all.

Tanda stopped a few feet away and stared at the spot, searching inwardly for the strength to go nearer. That was where her brother, Don, had been killed, the place where his body had been found by the police. She hadn't come this way since the murder, and now she knew she'd been wise. It was almost possible to picture the murder, Don suspecting nothing until the knife appeared, then—what? Did he scream and try to get away? Did he beg for mercy? Try to fight?

"Stop it!" she whispered to herself, struggling against the need to shudder. "You can't change what happened, but you might be able to help keep it from happening again. You came here to do something, so go ahead and do it."

Robby stood watching her as he waited patiently, and he paid no attention to the surrounding woods. That should mean they weren't under observation, so there would hardly be a better time. It was more than possible that Don hadn't gotten out of his car to go somewhere on foot, but if he had and there was anything of a trail left...

After taking one final look around, Tanda reached into her shoulder bag. While taking out Don's shirt, she walked Robby into the center of the clearing, then bent to give her dog the scent and the command, "Find him!" Robby seemed to have no trouble taking the scent, and then he began to cast around, searching for a matching scent on the ground. *Oh, please let it be here,* Tanda prayed silently as she watched. *And if the scent is here, please let it be enough for Robby to find...*

And then, with his usual baying bark, Robby announced that her prayers had been answered. After a full week of time, through the scents of dozens of people, and even after a rain, her dog had found enough of a scent to follow. Filled with incredible pride and an ocean of relief, Tanda let him take the lead to follow the trail.

Robby immediately led the way into the woods, back in the direction from which they'd come. Tanda looked around as they went, remembering that section of woods from the time of her childhood. She'd played and explored all through it, just as Don had before her. Could he have used the woods as a shortcut to wherever he'd been going? Could he have had an idea about what would happen, and managed to leave a clue of some sort hidden in the woods?

Question after question filled Tanda's mind, but they didn't keep her from continually looking around when she wasn't watching Robby. She'd stuffed the shirt back in her purse once it had served its purpose, mostly to get it out of the way. If anyone saw her, they'd hardly need sight of the shirt to figure out that she was meddling. *Oh, hurry, Robby, please hurry...*

And Robby didn't disappoint her. At one point he lost the trail, but casting around let him pick it up again beyond the point it had been lost. With full confidence he led her on, and when Tanda knew their destination for certain, she was stunned.

"But how can that be?" she whispered aloud, staring as they approached her own house. "He didn't come to see *me* that night, I know he didn't. What's going on?"

Robby, the only one within hearing, didn't answer, but he also didn't stop. He led her directly to the house and around to the back on the right, avoiding the runs to the left. Once in the back he hesitated momentarily by a tree, then went directly for the closed wooden doors leading to the cellar. The doors were still closed, which stopped Robby and made him bay with frustration. Obviously the trail led through the doors, which were usually kept locked. When Tanda leaned closer, she saw that the lock had been ruined with metal cutters.

"And I never even noticed," she muttered, disgusted with herself for having missed something so obvious. She might have had other things on her mind during the past week, but still... "All right, Robby, calm down. I'll open the doors for you."

Once she did, the dog went unhesitatingly down the stairs. Now Tanda was busy wondering what Don could have wanted in the cellar, the possibility of his having taken something a strong one. It would have to have been something Tanda would never have parted with if she'd been asked, so what could it be? She didn't keep anything valuable in the cellar, not even things of sentimental value. So what—

Her churning mind quieted a second time, but now with a guess bordering on certainty. Robby had led her to the shelves her mother had used for preserves, still filled with the empty jars that had been there for years. The dog was casting around to find where the trail would pick up again, but Tanda knew they'd reached the end of it. After stopping here Don had retraced his steps, unknowingly reinforcing the track his sister would follow after his death.

Dropping the leash and her purse, Tanda walked slowly up to the shelves. It would be on the shelf at eye level, she knew, the place her mother had decided was safest for hidden money. Easily reached but not easily seen, at least for adults. Two children, one after the other, had had no trouble spotting the hiding place. The shelves were so well built and solid, they'd been perfect for rainy-day climbing on...

It was dark in the cellar even with the doors open, but pulling the cord of the hanging light took care of the problem. The next step was gently pushing aside the jars in front, dust-covered jars with lids protecting their insides. Behind was the one jar standing alone, this one without a lid. At first glance it looked empty, which brought stabbing disappointment to Tanda. But then she lifted the jar—

And heard the clank of metal on glass! Inside the jar was a key, and when Tanda spilled the key out onto her palm she knew it was one she'd never seen before. Don must have left it, in the spot he'd once stolen money from, but what did it mean? What was it a key to, and why hadn't he told her he was going to leave it? And, even more importantly, did his murderer know she had it?

The chill that came with that thought was immediate, and then Tanda jumped at the sudden pounding on her front door. Had the murderer seen her tracking something, and decided she was a loose end that needed eliminating? But it couldn't happen now, not when she'd just found an important clue! Robby growled while Tanda trembled and tried to decide what to do. She would first see who it was, and then—and then—

Would she still be alive to have to worry about it...?

Chapter Three

Mike Gerard knocked on the door again, seriously beginning to worry. Tanda Grail had said she would be home, and her van was parked next to the house under the carport. There wasn't anyplace around there for her to have gone on foot, and it looked as if it was going to rain again. With all that in mind, where could she possibly—

"Oh, Lieutenant Gerard," a surprised voice said, and Mike turned to see Tanda Grail. She had a bloodhound on a leash, and the two of them had apparently come around the side of the house. "That's right, you said you'd be coming by. I'm afraid I managed to forget."

Mike wondered why she sounded relieved as well as apologetic, but he was too relieved himself to waste time on the thought. He hadn't known Tanda long, but the last thing he wanted was to find her as the next victim.

"I hope I'm not interrupting something important," he said, gesturing to the dog on the lead. "As a police officer, it would be wrong of me to get in the way of someone tracking fugitives."

"Oh, we've already caught our fugitives," Tanda told him with a laugh that brightened her pretty face. "Just give me a minute to put him back in his run, and then I'll be with you."

Mike nodded without speaking, then stood and watched

her with the dog. She patted the bloodhound and told him what a good boy he was, then led him to an empty metal-mesh run. Once the dog was inside the run with the gate closed she came back, folding the leash she'd removed from his collar.

"I have to admit I'm surprised you use runs," Mike said as she rejoined him. "I was picturing at least one dog in your house, if not all of them."

"Only someone who likes slobber keeps bloodhounds in their house," she answered with a smile. "I consider my dogs wonderful people and I love them, but I don't feel the same about slobber. Come on in."

She showed the front door was unlocked by simply opening it and walking through. As he followed her, Mike was tempted to point out how dangerous a practice that was, especially with a murderer running around loose. Then he realized she might just have been out back with her dog, and decided to save the comment for another time.

"Can I offer you a cup of coffee?" she asked over her shoulder as he closed the door and followed her. The living room they passed through was plain but neat, a gold-and-brown flower pattern on the couch and chairs and drapes. The light gold carpeting and dark-wood furniture, along with the rest, gave Mike the impression that it was all a holdover from an earlier era, probably her parents'. Tanda Grail lived in that house, but hadn't yet put her own stamp on it.

"I'll have coffee if you're having some," he answered her offer as he followed her into the kitchen. "Which means yes, thank you, I'd love a cup, so I hope you *are* having some."

"I admire a man who won't drink alone," she said with a small laugh, glancing at him as she headed for her kitchen counter. "Personally, I drink alone all the time, but then I'm not a man, so it's all right. Have a seat."

"You seem to be in a really good mood," Mike said, going to one of the chairs around the heavy wooden table she'd gestured toward. "Has something happened to make you feel better than you were feeling this morning? If so, I could use some of the same myself."

"I—just enjoy working with my dogs," she answered without turning, all her attention on the mugs she filled. "It's always such a pleasure, at least once they're past the awkward-puppy stage. I'm afraid that's all it is, so there really isn't anything to share."

She turned then with a coffee mug in each hand, and the direct way she looked at him told Mike immediately that she was lying. People who had no experience with lying always seemed to do that, look straight at you to show how sincere they were being. So something *had* happened, even though he couldn't imagine what it might have been.

"Thank you," he said as she set one of the mugs down in front of him, then headed toward the refrigerator for milk or cream. "Coffee usually helps me to think, but right now my thoughts aren't cooperating. They insist on centering around how foolish Saxon was, especially for a supposedly experienced detective. If he'd had enough sense to think the thing through, he might not be dead now."

"What do you mean?" Tanda asked, coming back with a creamer and sitting in front of her own coffee. "What didn't he think through?"

"I mean, Ms. Grail, that he didn't stop to remember that four people had been killed." Mike spoke gently but stared straight at her, refusing to release that bright gray gaze. "When four people are stabbed to death by some-one, that someone isn't a person you want to fool around with. You can tell yourself they don't know what you know, or that you can handle them if they find out—and that's probably what Saxon did. He told himself those things, and ended up just as dead as the first four. If he'd gone to the police first thing, he might still be alive.''

Tanda's gray eyes had widened, and she looked as though she ought to be biting her lip. Mike hadn't enjoyed frightening her, but everything he'd said was the truth. He couldn't force her to tell him what she knew, but if she didn't speak up she had to understand and believe that she could end up like her brother. Indecision flashed in those eyes, and then she was staring at him in a totally different way.

"But if Roger had gone to the police, isn't it possible he would have just put more people in danger?'' she asked, leaning forward with the intensity of her feelings. "The police are just human beings, after all, and *they* can be killed as easily as anyone. Instead of one new body you could have had four or five, and most of them your own people."

"But don't you see that couldn't have happened?'' Mike countered just as intensely. "It's possible to kill one person to keep a secret, but when a dozen people know, it's no longer a secret. It would have been written down, put in the computer, mentioned to people on the phone… Once a secret is shared in that many ways, it's no longer a secret that can get you hurt or killed. Sharing a secret keeps everyone alive."

Mike knew he was repeating himself, but if it made Tanda Grail rethink her position, he was willing to say the same thing a hundred times. And she *was* thinking things through again. He could see that in her expression as she gazed down at the table and then she looked directly at him again.

"I hope you're right,'' she said, the words earnest. "I'd never be able to stand it if I caused the death of someone else. And I wasn't being entirely truthful with you a minute ago. I discovered something I hadn't expected, and although I'm sure it means something, I don't know what.''

"Why don't you tell me about it anyway," Mike urged with a smile. "I can put my department to work on it, and that way we ought to come up with an answer."

"I certainly hope you can," she agreed, finally letting go of the creamer. "It occurred to me that my brother's body was found only half a mile away from here. It might have been true that he was there to meet someone, but he also might have been there to go somewhere. To test the theory, I took Robby to the spot and gave him the scent from the shirt Don was wearing when he died."

"Do you mean to say the dog actually found a trail to follow?" Mike demanded. "But it's been a good week, not to mention that it's rained at least once. How could there be anything left?"

"Are you asking if Robby only pretended to find a track?" she countered with a smile, clearly amused by Mike's disbelief. "If he did, he's better at pretending than anyone you care to name. He brought me here to the house, to the cellar stairs in back, and I found that the lock on the doors had been cut open. Apparently Don did come to the house that night, but not to see me. He came to leave something."

She took a key from her jeans pocket and held it up, showing him the something she meant. Mike reached for it and she gave it to him, but looking at it more closely didn't help.

"I can't tell what this is a key to, and you don't know either, do you?" he asked, getting her head shake to confirm his guess. "Well, as I said, I'll get my people working on it. There are expert locksmiths who can tell you exactly what a particular key is for, and we'll consult one of them. After that we'll at least know what to look for."

"It doesn't seem to be a car key, a house key or a safe-deposit-box key," she said, watching as Mike put it carefully in a small evidence bag and then into his inside coat pocket. "That leaves personal safes, strongboxes, secret caches or diaries."

"Or one of ten thousand other things," Mike returned with a faint sound of amusement. "I know you're hoping it's one of the things you mentioned. For that matter *I* hope the same, but let's not set ourselves up for disappointment. This key could just be a duplicate to a lock box that has important business papers. Your brother might have simply wanted it in a safe place no one knew about."

"So he came in the dead of night, on foot, to leave it?" she countered with a sound of disbelief. "He probably used the metal cutters from the shed out back, but he still also broke in. And you want me to believe he did all that for business papers, and it was only coincidence he was murdered right after that? Really, Lieutenant Gerard, if that's what you believe, you ought to be back on foot patrol."

"You'd make a tough boss, Ms. Grail," Mike said with a smile for her indignation. "As a matter of fact, I don't believe that the key is unimportant, but that doesn't stop the matter from still being a possibility. People have been known to do stranger things at stranger times. And please call me Mike."

"Only if you call me Tanda," she conceded, not quite ready to appreciate his practical outlook, and then she smiled. "All right, Mike, you believe the key is nothing and I'll believe it's an important clue. That way at least one of us will be right, and you're here for another reason anyway. Do you have more questions, or have you learned something you think I should know?"

"I haven't learned anything myself, yet," he answered. "On the way out here I noticed a convenience store a couple of miles up the road and stopped, but the clerk doesn't remember seeing Saxon in there two days ago.

That means either he didn't stop, or he didn't do anything to bring himself to the woman's attention if he did stop. If that was where he saw whatever he saw, he didn't ask any questions about it.''

"But if he saw it then, he couldn't have understood what he was seeing," Tanda pointed out. "I mean, he didn't tell me about it when he got here, he only mentioned it last night. That should mean it's more likely he saw whatever-it-was yesterday, while he was looking around.''

"And that, in turn, means we'll have to trace his movements, but it can't be done until tomorrow," Mike agreed. "On Sunday everything closes up. The only thing I can check on right now has to do with you and your brother. Can you handle a few more personal questions?''

"I can handle all the questions in the world, if that will find the person who killed Don," she answered. "What did you want to ask?''

"Well, to begin with, are you your brother's heir?" Mike asked, very aware of how the question sounded. People who were in line to inherit big sometimes did things to hurry along that inheritance, but Tanda Grail didn't seem to realize the implication.

"As a matter of fact, I have no idea," she answered, looking surprised. "It hadn't occurred to me to think about it, not when there were so many other things... Did I mention that Don had been married, but had become a widower? For all I know, he had a child, and the child is his heir.''

"His permanent residence was outside a small town in California," Mike said, pulling out his notebook and a pen. "The police there told us he lived alone with a couple of servants. If there's a child, there should be some record of it, so we'll have to get in touch with the locals again. Do you know if he used a lawyer from around here at all? Who handled the purchase when he bought his house?''

"You're making me feel very useless," she said with a sigh. "Not only do I know too little about my brother's death, I know even less about his life. How can I possibly be of any help, when even simple questions are beyond me?"

"You do all right for someone without any answers," Mike told her quickly, meaning every word. "You didn't have to know the details of your brother's life to find that key. It's a clue that will probably turn out to be a lot more important than knowing who his lawyer is. Don't forget we have a bet going on the point."

"I didn't realize there was a bet involved," she said with a smile that warmed her soft gray eyes. "You can't have a bet without stakes, and we never discussed stakes."

"Don't you know there are certain standard stakes?" Mike asked, finding that her smile warmed more than her eyes. "In matters of this sort, the loser buys dinner for the winner. You aren't going to try to back out of the bet, are you?"

"No, I won't back out," she assured him with a gentle laugh. "Even if I lose. Do you make a habit of going to dinner with murder suspects? I know no one has said it out loud, but my being involved with two of the victims has to mean I'm a suspect."

"Eighty-five percent of all serial killings are committed by men," Mike told her. "In some ways these murders don't fit the standard pattern, but the department shrink has assured us there's a definite ritual involved that isn't being faked. She's certain all the victims were killed for essentially the same reason, and very possibly by someone they knew. Did you know any of the other three victims?"

"No, thank God," she answered with a shudder, the smile long gone. "Two in five is too many. Is it my imagination, or do you and your people expect even more murders?''

''We're hoping there won't be any more, but once people like this start, they don't stop again until the imagined job is finished.'' He grimaced and shook his head. ''They never kill just because they get a kick out of it, or because they have a grudge against someone. There's always a very special reason, one that's completely logical to them. And compelling, which is why they don't often stop by themselves. Others have to stop them, which is where I come in.''

''And let me say how glad I am that you do,'' she remarked, but this time her smile didn't make it all the way out. Mike realized immediately he'd said too much, and Tanda Grail was really shaken.

''Look, as long as you don't deliberately involve yourself in this, you should be fine,'' he said, leaning forward to touch her hand. ''Always make sure your doors and windows are locked before you go to bed, don't leave the house without doing the same, and especially don't arrange to meet anyone in a deserted place alone for any reason. All the victims but Saxon had apparently gone to meet someone, and even he might have been expecting his visitor. If anything happens to frighten you, just pick up the phone and call me. That's my home number at the bottom of my card.''

Handing her one of his cards seemed to help, and after she looked at it her smile was better.

''As an amateur detective, I'd say this tells me you aren't married,'' she ventured. ''The invitation to dinner was a clue that can't always be relied on, but handing out your home number to a strange woman usually clinches it. Am I right?''

''Absolutely,'' he confirmed with a grin. ''Men with wives do tend to keep their home numbers to themselves, even though that doesn't always apply to cops. Which is why, all too often, cops aren't men with wives or women with husbands. It takes a special kind of patience to put up with our crazy hours and spotty home life.''

"Not to mention the possibility that the person you're chasing could catch you instead,'' she added, sober again. "That must be terrible for some women, the ones who don't stop to think about it. I mean, perfectly ordinary people are killed every day, in traffic accidents, or when someone goes suddenly berserk and starts shooting everyone in sight. At least your people are armed and can defend themselves. An accountant, say, in his car and about to be run off the road by a drunk driver, isn't and can't.''

"That's a very good point,'' Mike said, surprised and pleased. "You sound as though you've had occasion to think about it. Does that mean you used to date a cop?''

"For a while,'' she answered with a nod, toying with her coffee cup. "We even started talking about marriage, but then he was accepted on a force in Vermont. He came from there and really wanted to go back, but it would have meant leaving my father here all alone if I went with him. He finally decided to go alone, and I stayed here.''

"I'm sorry,'' Mike said, reaching out to touch her hand again. "My former wife thought being married to a cop would be no problem at all, but it didn't take long before the life got to her. She grew to hate it when I was called out in the middle of the night, or wasn't home on time for a meal even when I'd promised to be. I was only a sergeant at the time, but a detective sergeant is on call twenty-four hours a day. I moved heaven and earth to be sure I'd be home for our second anniversary, but when I walked through the door with her present she wasn't there. A week earlier I'd had to miss a barbecue with some friends, and her note said that that time had been the last straw. The next time we saw each other was in divorce court.''

"That must have been horrible for you,'' Tanda said,

sympathy in those soft gray eyes. "These days not being married seems to mean being lucky enough to miss the divorce experience, but some people do it right. My parents wanted to be together, and when my mother died my father was glad the pain was his rather than hers. He missed her terribly, and wouldn't have wanted her to miss him like that. Mike...is there any chance you'll catch this murderer before he does it again?"

"All we need is a little luck," he assured her, going back to the topic now that she was ready for it. "Saxon was obviously killed to silence him, but I have the strangest feeling that the ritual used means something very specific. Once this is all over, we'll find he somehow fits in with the other victims."

"I wish it was already over," she said, running a hand through her dark blond hair. "You asked about Don's house. Does that mean you intend to go there, to look for clues? Is that why you need to find his lawyer?"

"A team has already been out there, but yes, I do intend to go again," Mike said. "We now have a key to match to a lock, and the logical place to look for it first is in your brother's house."

He didn't add that he also wanted Don Grail's lawyer in order to find out if the man had done more for his client than help buy a house. That could be considered official police business, at least until he knew whether something had been done that might upset Tanda. She was upset enough, and Mike wanted very much to keep from adding to it.

"When you go to Don's house, I'd like to go with you," she said then, not quite surprising him with the request. "I've never been there, and I'd like to see it at least once before whatever happens to it happens. If that would be against the rules, let me know once you're finished there, and I'll go alone."

"No, I think it will be all right if we go together,"

Mike decided at once. The house wasn't a crime scene, after all, so there was no legal way to keep Tanda away from it. But if she was going to be there, he wanted to be with her. "I'll call you tomorrow, and tell you what time I'll be going over. Do you know where the house is?"

"From the address, yes," she said, then gave Mike her telephone number for his notebook. "You let me know when, and I'll meet you there."

Mike agreed to that, joined her in talking about the weather until he'd finished his coffee, and then he left. Once in his car and back on the road, he found himself thinking about the next day. And about the dinner he'd owe Tanda when the key turned out to be an important clue after all. She was the most attractive and interesting woman he'd met in a long time, but he couldn't help wondering how smart he was being.

"You'd better remember that no matter what you said, she *is* still a suspect, old son," he muttered to the single-lane road he traveled. "Until you know for certain she has nothing to do with this mess, you'd better watch your step."

And until you know for certain that she isn't trying to recapture an old love, he added silently. That was the part he feared the most, the possibility that *any* cop would do as someone to replace the man who hadn't loved her enough to stay with her. Mike considered the man a fool for giving up someone like Tanda Grail just to live in a particular place. The right woman could make hell into a suburb of heaven for a man, but she did have to be the *right* woman. Maybe...

And maybe not, no matter what the question was, Mike decided with a sigh. Right now all he could do was concentrate on finding a murderer as quickly as possible.

TANDA STOOD and watched Mike Gerard's car pull away, then went back to the kitchen for another cup of coffee.

It was really strange how attractive she found the man, especially after the way she'd sworn never to get involved with another cop. Len had been good-looking and a lot of fun, at least until it became time for him to decide to go back to Vermont or stay here in Connecticut with her. It took a short while before it became clear to Tanda that Len wanted to go home because he would have a local badge to flash around, something to show people what a big man he'd become. He hadn't been homesick, he'd been desperate to prove something.

"But, obviously, not every man with a badge feels the same," she murmured to her coffee. "Some consider the job really important, but still just a job. Not something to rub other people's noses in."

Like Mike Gerard. After thinking about it, Tanda was certain he'd known she was hiding something well before the point she'd told him about the key. But he hadn't accused her of trying to withhold evidence, not before and not after. He seemed to understand that it would tear her apart if anyone else was hurt because of something she did.

Tanda looked around herself then, feeling more alone than she had after her father had died. Lock all your doors and windows, Mike had said, when you go out and before you go to bed. If the killer thought she knew something that could hurt him, he'd hardly hesitate to come after her. One more body would mean nothing…

After putting her coffee cup down, Tanda headed for the front door. Robby might be used to living in a run, but he was completely housebroken. And very protective of her when strangers were around. She would bring him into the house before checking windows and door locks, and he would also be her company.

But not quite as good company as someone else, she realized with a smile as she stepped outside. Mike Gerard was very good company, and didn't even slobber the way

Robby would. The only thing that worried Tanda about him was one very important question: was he seriously interested in her, or only concerned about someone tangled up in a murder investigation? And did he really think she was innocent? A man who'd had a bad marriage didn't usually trust women or think well of them; was he just leading her on to get what information he could, with nothing in mind beyond solving the case?

Each question she asked herself bred ten others, and the rest of the day disappeared behind a blur of uncontrolled thinking. When suppertime came around, Tanda broiled herself a steak, then shared it with Robby. The dog had no idea why he was in the house with her, but didn't mind enjoying the experience. The day had started very early, so it wasn't late when she let Robby out for the final time, checked the locks one last time, then went to bed.

The soft hum of the bedroom's air conditioner helped her to fall asleep quickly, but suddenly she found herself awake again. Had there been a noise, or was it just Robby moving around the room? Half-asleep, Tanda looked at the clock to see that it wasn't even midnight. She couldn't have been asleep long, then.

And that was when she heard it again, a low bang from somewhere outside. A wild animal, maybe, trying to get to her garbage? She twisted around and turned on the light, then sat very still as she saw Robby. The dog was on his feet by the bedroom door, standing and staring at it, a low growl sounding deep in his throat. He never did that for an animal, Tanda realized, putting a trembling hand to her mouth. Robby only growled when strange humans were around. *Humans...*

Chapter Four

For a moment or two Tanda sat motionless with fear, and then the low banging noise came again. This time it sounded like someone trying to break something at the back of the house while struggling not to make too much noise. Animals were notorious for not caring *how* much noise they made, and that, along with the barking of the other dogs, clinched it. Some *human* was out there, and at that time of night it couldn't possibly be a friend or neighbor.

But it *could* be a police patrol, sent by Mike Gerard to keep an eye on her. Poking around to be sure she was all right shouldn't sound like that, but it was still possible. Maybe she ought to go and take a look…

"But I think I'll call and ask first," she muttered, reaching for the bedside telephone. "They'll know at headquarters whether anyone is supposed to be out here."

She would have preferred calling Mike Gerard rather than some stranger at police headquarters, but there was no need to bother the man over a false alarm. And that was what Tanda hoped it was, nothing but a false alarm…

"Police headquarters, Sergeant Walters," an official voice announced from the other end of the line. "How can I help you?"

"Sergeant, this is Tanda Grail, out on Old Stage

Road," Tanda replied. "I'm involved with Lieutenant Gerard over that murder this morning, as well as my brother's murder a week ago. Can you tell me if Lieutenant Gerard left orders for officers to check my house during the night? I hear someone out there, but I'll feel silly if I charge out to confront a couple of police officers just doing their job."

"I'll check on that, Ms. Grail," the man's voice said, no longer remote and indifferent. "But please don't talk about charging out and confronting. If someone is out there... Well, we'd rather you didn't. And are you certain there's someone there? Could it be an animal, or an unlatched door swinging?"

"No to both," Tanda answered. "I might not be sure, but my dog is. It's definitely not an animal, and definitely not a door."

"Then hold on for a moment." Tanda expected to be switched to hold, but the sergeant just put a hand over the mouthpiece of his phone. She could hear the mutter of voices in brief conversation, and then the sergeant was back. "Ms. Grail, there were orders left for you to be checked on, but the unit assigned to do the checking isn't currently near your house. We have them on their way now, and they'll be there in a few minutes. Please stay inside until they knock on your door and announce themselves. Do you understand?"

"Yes, I do understand, and thank you," Tanda said automatically before hanging up. Once the connection was broken, she realized she could have stayed on the line until the patrol unit arrived, but what was the point? If whoever was out there broke in, having a cop on the other end of the line wasn't likely to keep her from being killed.

Tanda ran both hands through her hair, trying to fight off the creeping numbness of fear. If it wasn't the police out there, it had to be the murderer. The idea of it being someone else, just at this time, even an ordinary burglar,

was too far-fetched to consider. Another muffled clank
came, telling the nearby world that the person was still
out there, and the sound did something strange to Tanda.
It made her realize that her brother's murderer was in
reach, the person she wanted so badly to find. Was she
just going to sit here and tremble, forgetting about what
had been stolen from her? Wasn't there something she
could do to make sure the man didn't get away?

Tanda knew there had to be something, and reborn anger drove away enough of the fear to let her get out of
bed. Robby was still growling softly as she began to throw
on clothes, and that bolstered her courage even more. Between her and her dog the murderer would be outnumbered, and once the police got here, the nightmare would
be over. An outcome like that was worth taking a chance
for, more than worth it.

It didn't take long before she was dressed in jeans and
a T-shirt and sneakers, and Robby was beginning to be
calmly excited. The dog knew they were going out after
whoever was making that noise, and he was ready to do
his job. If the intruder tried to run away, so much the
better. Robby would be right behind him, and more than
able to run him to ground.

Tanda turned out the light in the room before easing
the door open, wishing she had Robby's serene confidence. She was determined to do whatever she could to
catch the murderer, but that didn't mean her fear was
gone. Slipping out into the dark of the hall was hard, but
turning on a light was out of the question. If the person
outside realized she was awake and coming after him…

Yes. Tanda dropped that line of thought quickly, paying
more attention to making her way toward the front door.
She'd briefly considered going down to the cellar and confronting the intruder directly, but had dismissed the idea
as impractical. The new lock on the cellar door in back
was on the outside; even if it hadn't been, she didn't care

for the idea of opening the bolt on the door in the house leading down to the cellar. Just because the sounds seemed to be coming from outside, that didn't mean the man hadn't managed to get inside. Meeting a murderer face-to-face indoors seemed fractionally worse than meeting one outdoors, and whether or not that was true, it was still the way she felt.

So she edged through the kitchen and on toward the living room, grateful for the kitchen's night-light and wishing the living room had one, too. After tonight she'd make sure it had one—assuming nothing happened to keep her from seeing to it.

"Stop that!" she whispered to herself almost soundlessly. "Of course nothing will happen. You'll just have to be very careful…"

And stick close to Robby. Tanda was aware of the dog despite her nervousness, or maybe even more because of it. He'd stopped in the living room to her left, momentarily unmoving, which made her stop as well. It was almost as though he was listening to something, and she'd never seen him do that before. A tracking dog isn't in the habit of listening…

And then he did what he *was* in the habit of doing, something that nearly made her jump out of her skin. With the sort of baying bark he used when he was almost on the quarry, Robby loped directly toward the front windows. Tanda was so startled she banged into the coffee table, bruising her legs and nearly falling. She had no idea what had made Robby do that—until she realized the banging at the back of the house seemed to have stopped.

"He's coming around to the front!" she whispered, suddenly frantic. "If I don't get out there before he reaches the door—"

Then there would be nothing to keep the man from coming in when she opened the door. And she had to open the door, or the opportunity to catch her brother's killer would be gone. Understanding that helped Tanda to ignore the pain in her legs as she stumbled around the coffee table, and by the time she reached the front door Robby was beside her. Taking courage from his presence she flipped on the porch light, flung the door open and charged outside—

Only to see nothing and no one. Her heart pounded like that drum people always talked about, and it took a moment to realize that part of the noise she heard wasn't from that. Someone was in the woods and running, definitely away from the house, and Robby stood quivering and staring in that direction. Tanda dashed back inside, got the flashlight from the table near the door, ran back out and told Robby, "Find 'em!"

The dog took off like a launched rocket, the command freeing him to do what he'd been waiting and longing to. Tanda yelped and ran after him, all the excitement having made her forget that the dog wasn't on a lead. If she didn't really move she would lose him, especially in the dark. When he reached the quarry—and he would—she fully intended to be right there.

Happily the flashlight was a powerful one, and Tanda was able to glimpse Robby as well as hear him. The woods were more than nighttime-quiet; with two people and a dog running through them, night birds and small animals were keeping silent and playing invisible. Tanda knew these woods well enough to run with confidence, which gave her real hope that in just a few minutes she would at least catch sight of the man responsible for her brother's death. And if Robby could corner him and hold him until the police arrived—

The sound of a car door slamming ended that line of thought in the worst possible way. An instant later the car's engine roared it away, showing that the vehicle had probably not been turned off. Taillights flared redly a short distance ahead, and then they, too, were gone, back to Old Stage Road. Tanda immediately whistled for Robby, and after a moment the dog trotted up.

"Poor guy," Tanda commiserated as she leaned down to gently rough him up. "I'll bet you were no more than half a jump behind when he got to that car. It's too bad it didn't stall out and leave him stuck, the way it probably would have done if I was the one being chased. We might as well go back to the house."

Robby wasn't happy about abandoning the chase, but he still followed right after Tanda. The dog seemed to understand somehow that it wasn't an exercise or a game they were involved in, or even a job for some nearby police department. It was his own house that intruder had been prowling around, and that apparently made the matter personal.

The walk back didn't take long, but Tanda wasn't given the chance to go inside. Headlights flared along the tar road, silently announcing the approach of a car, and for an instant she thought it might be the intruder coming back again. Then she saw the wide set of lights on the car's roof, and realized the police had finally made it. The way they headed right for her said they thought she might be the intruder they were there for. When they stopped about ten feet back and got out, their hands were cautiously close to their weapons.

"It's all right, Officers, I'm Tanda Grail," she called to them, patting Robby to calm away his growl. "There *was* someone out here, but he got away. If he hadn't left a car in the woods with the engine running, my dog would have had him."

"You saw the prowler, ma'am?" one of the officers asked, a young man with light brown hair and a calm expression. "Can you give us a description of him and his car?"

"Unfortunately, no," Tanda admitted. "He was doing something at the back of the house, but started around to the front just before I came out. My dog heard him and began to bay, and that must have frightened him. He was already into the woods by the time we got out here, and the head start let him reach his car before my dog reached *him.* By the time *I* got there, there was nothing to see but vanishing taillights.''

''You were probably lucky he didn't stick around,'' the second officer said, the first being busy writing. He was older than the first man, and not quite as calm or neutral. ''I'll call this in, and then we'll have a look around.''

There wasn't much Tanda could say to that, since disagreeing about being lucky would only start an argument. She waited until the incident had been called in and written up, then led the way around to the back of the house. The two officers had their own flashlights, but Tanda was first to see what the intruder had been up to.

''Look at the scrapes on that lock!'' she exclaimed, shocked in spite of herself. ''It was brand new when I put it on only a few hours ago, but look at it now!''

''Likely it was a tire iron he used,'' the second officer said after bending down to examine the lock. ''Or maybe he found something in that shed.''

He'd turned to flash his light at the shed, but Tanda shook her head.

''There's nothing left in the shed he could have used,'' she said. ''I put the bolt cutters and anything else that might be used to force a lock into the cellar. There didn't seem to be much sense in putting on a new lock if I left something to force it open with.''

''It's a good thing you thought of that, ma'am,'' the younger man said with respectful approval. ''A lot of people wouldn't have, and their house would have been broken into again.''

''Considering what you're involved in, Ms. Grail, I think we should get a forensics team out here,'' the older man said. ''At the very least they should be able to get tire-track impressions, if you can show them where the car was parked."

"If I can't find the spot again, my dog can," Tanda assured the man.

That time both men nodded, then they began to lead the way back to their car. With the most immediate excitement over, Tanda was beginning to feel just how tired she was. It would have been nice to go back to bed—with the light left on for the rest of the night—but it was fairly clear that that would not be happening for a while.

MIKE GERARD TRIED not to break any traffic laws on his way out to the Grail place, but it was a near thing. He kept wanting to do ninety to get there faster, just to be certain Tanda really was all right. He felt disappointed that she'd called headquarters rather than him, but at least she hadn't tried to handle the matter all alone. He must have made his point about the foolishness of trying to face a serial killer alone.

The turnoff to the Grail place wasn't difficult to find even in the middle-of-the-night darkness. Two police units and a forensics van were parked on the tar road leading to the house, and all three vehicles had their lights on. Mike pulled up to the left of the van, and when he got out he saw Tanda sitting on the porch steps with one of her dogs. Flashlight beams coming from the woods to the right and darting out from behind the house told him where everyone else was.

"I was asked to keep out of the way," Tanda called softly when she saw him, obviously following his thoughts. "They were all very polite about not wanting to bother me anymore, but what they meant was, stay out of the way. I'm sorry you had to be dragged out of bed after all. I should have realized they would call you once they saw there really was a prowler."

"My beauty sleep can wait," Mike told her with a

smile as he stopped a couple of feet from where she sat. "My people know I'll enjoy that sleep a lot more once this serial killer is caught. They also passed on what you told the officers. Are you sure you saw nothing of the man or his car?"

"By the time I got out here, he was already in the woods," she said, then put a hand on her dog's head. "Robby here heard him coming around to the front of the house, and let loose with one of his 'here comes the quarry I'm going to have for lunch' barks. It makes him sound really dangerous, and the prowler must have panicked. He got to his car fast, and all I saw of it was headlights in front and taillights toward me. The only thing I can tell you about the car for certain is that it didn't have its windows open."

"You were able to see that?" Mike asked, wondering how it could be possible. "That and nothing else?"

"No, no, I *couldn't* see it," she corrected with a slightly wider smile. "I keep forgetting you don't know much about trained dogs. I know the windows weren't open because Robby gave up the trail once the car pulled away. If the windows had been open, he would have bayed to show he was still on the trail. Do you understand?"

"Do you mean to say a bloodhound can follow someone in a car as long as the windows are down?" Mike demanded, then realized how the words must sound. "I'm sorry, I didn't mean to all but call you a liar, but…"

"But the idea is a hard one to believe," she finished when he didn't, amused rather than insulted. "The movies have a lot to do with it, because they'll have a fugitive escape in a car when the script calls for it. The windows on the car are usually wide open, but the script insists the fugitive escapes, so the dogs have to lose the trail. If those dogs were mine, they wouldn't."

Mike just stood there shaking his head, at the same time wondering why bloodhounds weren't used more.

"I'd better check to see what the forensics people have found so far," he said at last, then gave Tanda a grin. "After that, I won't feel so stupid, and you can tell me some more about bloodhounds."

"Not knowing about bloodhounds doesn't make you stupid, only uninformed," she assured him with a soft smile, then the smile faded. "If they've found anything important, will you be able to tell me about it?"

"I'm sure I will," he soothed her, wishing he could take her hand or put an arm around her shoulders. "I'll be right back."

He waited for her nod and then walked away, heading around the back of the house. The other dogs in their runs to the left were awake and alert, but weren't making any noise.

"Glad you made it, Gerard," one of the forensics people, Alec Ellison, said as soon as Mike appeared. "There isn't too much here, but I can tell you one thing: whoever tried the break-in was no professional. My six-year-old son would have had better luck—without it being a matter of luck."

"Your six-year-old son could probably get into a bank vault," Mike pointed out, causing Ellison to grin. "Like father, like son. What specifically makes you think it wasn't a pro?"

"All those scratches and small dents on the lock, for one thing," Ellison answered. "The perp used either a tire iron or a crowbar, or maybe just a length of pipe, but was also obviously trying to use strength instead of leverage. Slip some cold steel through the lock loop, brace the steel and lean. If the lock doesn't fly open from your body weight alone, the hasp will probably come free of the wood. Whoever was here seemed to be trying to pull the lock open, and when that didn't work he tried banging on it. Even dead drunk a pro would do better than that, and would certainly have been quieter.''

''Make that 'she' rather than 'he,''' a voice corrected, and Mike turned to see forensics expert Lora Clark approaching. ''We found more than just tire tracks out in those woods, we also found a couple of good footprints that are definitely from women's shoes. People should learn not to go sneaking across open ground after a rain.''

''Are you sure, Lora?'' Mike couldn't help asking. ''All the profiles insist it's a man, and if it isn't we're back to square one. Could you have found Ms. Grail's prints instead?''

''Not unless Ms. Grail is able to leave two different sets of footprints telling two different stories,'' Lora denied cheerfully. ''You know how I hate to ruin perfectly good theories, but unless this was done by someone just happening by, your quarry isn't a man. Ms. Grail's prints were easy to match up, and the other woman's were totally different. I'd say about five foot five or six, about a hundred twenty-five pounds, not very athletic. Even when she was running it wasn't full out, as if she didn't know how to run properly.''

''That agrees with what I found here,'' Ellison put in as Mike groaningly took out his notebook. ''A woman who isn't very athletic, and never even thought about breaking in somewhere. A desperate amateur trying a desperate gamble.''

''That doesn't fit the profile at all,'' Mike said as he noted down what both of the forensics people had told him. ''And there's been no indication that the murders were committed by more than one person. What about the tire tracks?''

''They seem to be standard tires that can be found on most midsize cars,'' Lora supplied with a sigh. ''Steel-belted radials that almost everyone sells, but we'll be able to give you the manufacturer as soon as we do a tread-pattern comparison. The tires weren't new, but there should be enough of a pattern left for identification. And we'll sift through everything again to be certain we didn't miss something useful.''

''A picture ID supplying a name and address would do nicely,'' Mike said as the two began to turn away. ''If you find one, I'll be around front with Ms. Grail.''

''If we find one, *I'll* be passed out cold in a faint,'' Lora countered over her shoulder as she headed back toward the woods.

As Mike turned back toward the front of the house, he decided he'd be better off without something like an accidentally dropped picture ID. He'd find it almost impossible to believe that the thing had been dropped accidentally, and would resist considering it a real clue unless or until he caught the pictured person in the act of committing murder.

Tanda no longer sat on the front steps where she'd been, but the inside door was open and through the screen door Mike could hear her moving around. A moment later she reappeared carrying a tray, and after holding the door for her dog to come through, she set the tray down with a smile.

''I thought everyone might want a cup of coffee as badly as I do,'' she said, gesturing to the pot and cups on the tray. ''I feel silly playing hostess at a time like this, but— Have you found out anything?''

''Nothing useful,'' Mike admitted as he walked to the tray. ''And I don't know about the others, but I find a cup of coffee at a time like this something to be grateful for. My people tell me the intruder's footprints say it was a woman, and the attempt to break in was unskilled. Either we were wrong about our murderer being a man, or he has a non-burglar female confederate we hadn't even suspected. It's highly unlikely that someone totally unconnected with the murders just happened to decide to break in."

"Could it possibly have been a man wearing women's shoes?" she asked, watching Mike fix a cup of coffee. "You know, just to throw everyone off? Most people do know they'll leave footprints in still-wet ground, so maybe it *was* the murderer trying to confuse everyone."

"That's a definite possibility, but it still doesn't feel right," Mike answered, aware that he sounded fretful. "Serial killings have a very specific relationship between the killer and his victim, the killing coming about because of who each of them is. A serial killer's identity is very important to him, I'm told, so for him to deliberately pretend to be someone else entirely—I don't know if he's capable of doing that in the context of the murders."

"I don't think I understand that," Tanda said, taking her own cup and sitting on the steps with it. "Don't serial killers always try to hide who they are?"

"Only during the times between murders," Mike answered, sitting down not far from her. "During those times they're not really themselves, since their real selves are dedicated to completing whatever ritual they've come to believe they must complete. When they're in the middle of that ritual, however, they can't be anything but their true selves or the ritual won't have meaning. Even if they're forced to tell people who they are—in the notes they leave, or the symbols they sometimes paint in blood on the walls—they can't refuse to do it. That part of it is lucky for us, because it's usually the way we catch them."

"Then that would mean if it *was* the murderer, he wasn't here in connection with the killings," Tanda said slowly after sipping her coffee. "But if that's true, then what was he here for?"

"That's as easy to answer as what a woman was doing here if it *wasn't* the murderer," Mike grumbled in response. "There are too many unexplained things happening, too many events that seem completely unrelated. I know we're missing something important, but I don't yet know what it is.''

He lapsed into a brooding silence with that, and Tanda joined him. From what she'd said, she'd been convinced the intruder was her brother's murderer, and now she seemed a lot less sure. He hadn't yet spoken to her about the way she'd gone out after the prowler instead of waiting for the police to arrive, but now didn't feel like the time to go into it. He wanted her to be safe, but once they left she would be all alone in that house. Telling her horror stories to keep her awake the rest of the night would benefit no one. Leaving one of the police units there for the night and discussing it tomorrow was a much better idea.

They sat quietly drinking their coffee for a while, and then the forensics people began to come over to join them. Most of them accepted the offer of coffee, but had nothing to add to what they'd already told him. The casts made in the woods of tire tracks and footprints were put carefully in the van, and while that was being done Mike arranged for one of the units to stay. Once everyone else had left, he walked back to the porch where Tanda still sat.

''Well, that's it,'' he said, feeling the words were totally inadequate. ''That car will be out here for the rest of the night, so there shouldn't be any more trouble. Is there anything you'd like me to do before I leave?''

''I really don't think so,'' she answered with a tired smile. ''If we're going to be doing things tomorrow, we need at least *some* sleep tonight. Or should I say, 'this morning'? Most of the night is long gone.''

''I think we'd all prefer it if criminals confined their activities to the daytime,'' he returned with his own smile. ''It's so much easier chasing them after a good night's rest. I'll call you tomorrow, and we'll set up a time to meet at your brother's house.''

"That sounds fine," she answered. "Good night, Mike.''

"'Night, Tanda," he responded, and then had no further excuse to stand there. He waved once before getting into his car, and then he was turned around and heading back to Old Stage Road. He felt tired and needed to get back to bed, but wouldn't have minded sitting on that porch with Tanda for another hour or two. If only he'd been invited...

TANDA WATCHED Mike Gerard's car out of sight, then began to take the coffee things back inside. The man had looked so rumpled and tired, she hadn't had the heart to ask him to stay another few minutes. The two police officers in their car were a reassuring presence, but Mike Gerard was a good deal more than that. She even enjoyed simply sitting next to him, with nothing of conversation going on. If *he* could have stayed rather than them...

But that was ridiculous. Tanda held the door open for Robby to go inside, then followed with the tray. She'd only met Mike that morning, which meant she didn't even know him a full day yet. Asking a virtual stranger to stay with her was something she normally would never have considered; it was just that there was something about the man...

"I trust him," Tanda realized aloud, then hurried back to close and lock the front door. If one of the officers heard her talking to herself... Well, she could always claim she was talking to her dog.

"But I *do* trust him," Tanda told Robby, smiling at the dog's long-faced, mournful expression. "I know it's ridiculous after knowing him for so short a time, but I feel safe when he's around. Not that I need to be protected, but still..."

She let the words trail off when she discovered she couldn't quite put the rest of her feelings into words, but Robby didn't seem to mind. In fact, the dog had stopped growling at Mike almost as soon as he'd first seen him, and hadn't started again. Robby was a pretty good judge of character, so if *he* approved of Mike Gerard…

Tanda laughed softly as she went around checking all the doors and windows. She really did need to get back to bed, and she was sure she would sleep in spite of the night's excitement. Tomorrow would be another day for thinking about and seeing Mike Gerard—and then her amusement abruptly disappeared. Tomorrow would also be another day for trying to find Don's murderer, no matter who he—or she—might be. That had to come first before anything else, and it would.

"Afterward, I'll have time to think about men I trust," she whispered to Robby before leading the way to her bedroom. "To find out if there's anything there besides the trust—if there *is* an afterward."

There was nothing to say about that, so she quietly closed the door on the rest of the night.

Chapter Five

Tanda deliberately reached her brother's house a little early, and parked to wait for Mike Gerard to show up. She'd thought she might have some trouble walking right into a house she'd never been invited to while its owner was alive, and from the way she felt the guess had been right. It was a beautiful house, apparently split level, and if Don hadn't been killed he would have been the one showing it to her. Instead her guide was the man investigating his murder, and the very thought of that made her close her eyes and put her hand over them.

It wasn't yet two-thirty in the afternoon, but closing her eyes made Tanda think it was almost midnight. The impression came from the heavy tiredness she'd awakened with, a result of the intruder's visit the night before. She'd spent the morning working with Angel, and after lunch she'd just reached the point of thinking about a nap when Mike called. He was running a little late, he said, but how was two-thirty for meeting at the house?

She'd assured him two-thirty was fine, and then had begun getting ready. This certainly wasn't anything like a date, but for a minute or two she'd felt that happy excitement that usually comes because of the person you're looking forward to seeing. And then she'd remembered what they were in the middle of, and the feeling had dissolved. But not entirely. It was possible her brother's house would have a clue involving his murderer, and if it was there she would find it. She owed that even more to Roger Saxon, who would still be alive if not for her.

Remembering her intentions made Tanda suddenly impatient to get on with it. Logically speaking, there had to be some reason that Don had been murdered, even if the reason turned out to be a crazy one. Roger Saxon's murder had just about proved that; he'd been looking for something connecting someone to Don, and had seen someone whose very presence suggested a connection. There was no reason for Roger to have been so pleased otherwise, and then he'd ended up dead. That meant the clue was there for anyone able to read it, and Tanda was determined to be that anyone.

Almost as though her wanting it made it happen, that was when Mike's car pulled up on the side of the street closest to the house. As she got out of her van, Tanda realized neither of them had parked in the wide double driveway. They were both obviously feeling like intruders, then, but that had to stop. Intruders would never find anything of value.

"Sorry I'm late," Mike said to her as he got out of his car. "We were having trouble getting Saxon's personnel file faxed to us from his office. Apparently he was not only good, but also very well liked. The news of his death hit them hard, and it took time for the shock to wear off."

"But now you have the file?" Tanda asked. "If so, it should help."

"Yes and no," Mike answered wryly with a sigh. "Yes, we have it now, but no, it isn't immediately helpful. Saxon worked on two major forces, one in Phoenix and one in Miami, about five years in each place. That doubles the area and time frame of our search, since he was a patrolman in Phoenix, and a detective in Miami. Whatever it was he knew about, he could have come across it in either place."

"I'd check first on anything he might have come across in both places," Tanda said with sudden inspiration. "The way he said no one but him would have spotted what he did. Isn't it more likely he meant that no one would have that particular combination of experience, rather than no one would have been on either of the two forces?"

"You could be right," Mike answered slowly, seriously considering her suggestion. "And rather than make the search harder, you might have just made it easier. We can check with his detective squad in Miami, and at the very least his lieutenant or captain should still be there after almost four years. It's a long time to remember one incident out of a five-year career, but we're due for some good luck."

Tanda smiled at the way he muttered to himself as he wrote in his notebook. It was almost as though he'd forgotten she was there, which wasn't much of a compliment. But it was also as if he felt relaxed enough around her to speak his thoughts out loud. Tanda preferred looking at it that way, and his smile when he looked up at her made her glad she had.

"I'm going to consider that great idea number one," he said after putting the notebook back in his jacket. "Let's go inside and see how many more great ideas you can come up with."

"I'm glad you find me of so much use," she answered with a laugh. "When do I get put on the payroll?"

"Oh, any time now," he assured her with a solemnity a two-year-old wouldn't have believed. "You know how paperwork always slows things up. Let's go inside now."

His grin made her laugh again, and between that and her resolve to find something of value, she was able to follow him inside with only a small twinge of upset. The front door opened on a wide landing with two small doors to either side, and Mike gestured to them.

"According to the detectives who went through here, the door on the left is a coat closet, and the one on the right a powder room," he said. "Upstairs are four bedrooms, two full baths, a kitchen, a dining room and a living room. Downstairs are another two bedrooms, another full bath and powder room, a laundry room, a playroom and a gym. Which level would you like to start on?"

"The lower level, I think," Tanda answered slowly, looking at the deep carpeting on the floors and the expensive paper on the walls. Both appeared spotless and almost brand new, as if they had only just been put in. "This place feels like a model house, where lots of people come in but no one ever stays."

"I suppose that's unavoidable when you only live in a house one month of the year," Mike reminded her. "My place usually looks like a tornado hit it, except for about half a day after my cleaner comes in. She doesn't understand why everything is upside down so often, but that's because she's never seen me trying to find what to wear in the middle of the night. Just because an emergency call wakes you up, that doesn't necessarily mean your eyes are open."

"You ought to play it safe and set things out every night before you go to bed," Tanda suggested as she followed him down the stairs. "It's just as hard waking up really early in the morning to track fugitives, so that's what I do. If I had to decide on what to wear when I got up, I'd either end up going out naked, or looking like I was going to a masquerade."

"See there, I knew you'd come up with another great idea," he said over his shoulder with a grin. "And as someone who's come too close too often to walking out naked, you have my profound thanks."

Tanda was amused even though it was unlikely he'd

never thought of the idea himself, but then she paused to reconsider her first impression. Even the most capable of men sometimes had blind spots when it came to taking care of themselves, so it was possible Mike never had thought of the idea. Too many men were raised to depend on women, at least as many as the number of women raised to depend on men.

As far as Tanda was concerned, both groups were handicapped if not downright crippled. She'd been raised to know she was fully capable of taking care of herself, and Don had been raised the same. Using people instead of associating with them had been his own idea.

"This looks like the playroom," Mike said when she stopped beside him at the bottom of the stairs. "It's certainly large enough for any kind of playing you would care to do."

Tanda nodded as she looked around at the very big room. To the left was a pool table and a wet bar, the latter stocked with what seemed to be every drink imaginable. Four stools stood in front of the bar, and four leather chairs were arranged against the wall around the pool table. A large fluorescent lamp hung above the table, and the bar had signs that probably lit up.

The center of the floor was parquet rather than carpeted, and led to double glass doors that were obviously to the backyard. To the right was a leather conversation pit surrounded by single and double leather chairs, all cozily close to a fireplace and a large-screen TV. A tall bookcase built into the wall held what looked like videotape cases, and there was even a small portable bar.

"I suppose walking across the floor to the full-size bar would have been too much of an effort," Tanda said, finding it impossible to hold the comment back. "Is that all Don thought about when he stayed here? Drinking?"

"He also watched a lot of movies," Mike offered, apparently trying to make it easier for her. "Since most of the ones in that library are ordinary rather than X-rated, I'd say his biggest problem was loneliness. When you spend too much time by yourself, you can get into the habit of considering booze your friend.''

''I suppose you're right,'' Tanda said, suddenly remembering how little Don had had to drink when they'd had dinner. An alcoholic wouldn't have been able to stick to a single glass of wine, so maybe Don *had* just been lonely.

''Those pictures on the walls,'' she said, just to change the subject. ''A couple of them look expensive, but they're all so…neutral. Now, this place feels like a hotel, and I can't help wondering—if Don disliked it so much that he refused to put any part of himself into it, why did he keep coming back here?''

''When we learn the answer to that, I think we'll also have the answers to a lot of other questions,'' Mike said. ''Through that door near the video library are the two bedrooms, the laundry room and the full bath. On the other side, near the bar, are the doors to the gym and the powder room. Let's look at them first.''

Tanda nodded, and they walked through the dimness toward the door to the gym. Daylight was coming in through the double doors in the center of the room, so Mike hadn't turned on a light. That might ordinarily have bothered Tanda, but the house felt too empty to be threatening. She knew the shadows held nothing but shadows, and oddly enough that was disappointing.

The gym was large with a separate sauna, and sliding glass doors in the same wall as the outer room led to a terrace with privacy walls, a dining porch and an Olympic-size swimming pool. Beyond the pool was rolling green lawn, thickly luxurious and almost manicured. In the distance it was possible to see another wall of some sort, and Mike came up beside her and gestured to it.

''That's probably the end of your brother's property,'' he said, also looking at the nearer sights. ''He has a couple of acres at least, which insured his privacy. His neighbors said he did occasionally have visitors, but they had no idea who the people were. All they knew was that it wasn't any of them.''

"And you aren't having any luck finding out who it was," Tanda said, turning her head to look at him. "Don't you think that means something?"

"Of course it means something," he answered. "The problem is we don't know what, but you can't say we haven't been trying. A team came out here after the third murder, hoping to find even a partial print to link the victims, but the first team to go through here hadn't been careless. The only prints found were your brother's, which led us to believe a very good housekeeper had been through the place not long before your brother was murdered."

"What about the housekeeper herself?" Tanda asked. "Surely she'd know if people had been visiting, and maybe she'd even seen one or two."

"When we found her, she did tell us there had been a party of sorts," Mike admitted. "There were used glasses all over this level, but she had no idea how many there were. She just put them into the dishwasher, then replaced them on the bar shelves. It should give you some idea of what she's like if I say even her own fingerprints weren't on those glasses. When she got here, not even your brother was at home, so we can forget about her having seen anyone."

"I'm beginning to get a better idea about why you haven't found the murderer yet," Tanda said with a sigh. "With dead ends everywhere you turn, I'm surprised any of you are still working on the case."

"We may be walking bundles of frustration, but we're not about to give up," Mike assured her with a smile. "Let's see if there's anything under this roof that's worth a closer second look."

They started with the gym and its almost brand-new equipment, then worked their way back through the bar and play room.

The two bedrooms looked as if no one had set foot in them since the day they were furnished, and the bathroom had a full roll of toilet paper. By that time they were long since turning lights on and off in order to see better, and the light in the laundry room brought a surprise. There were actually clothes in a basket between the washer and dryer, clothes that had apparently come from the chute above the basket. There wasn't much, but Mike bent and then held up an electric-blue sports shirt.

"Look at that," he said. "The breast pocket is almost completely ripped off, but it's still in with the dirty clothes. It must have ended up down the chute by accident, instead of simply thrown out."

"You think it should have been thrown out because it's obviously worn," Tanda said, coming forward to get a better look at the shirt. "You ought to be ashamed of yourself, Mike. I thought you were supposed to be a detective."

"Okay, now I know what I missed," he said as he straightened. "If the shirt is worn, that must mean it was a favorite of his. You know it was, because either blue in general or electric blue in particular was his favorite color."

"Electric blue in particular," Tanda confirmed with a smile, pleased with how quickly he'd seen that. "He loved the color from the first time he saw it, and bought everything in it he possibly could. I'd love to know who he had the fight with."

"So you see it that way, too," Mike said, gazing at her thoughtfully. "Not an accident, but something caused by a fight or struggle. It could have happened in a bar somewhere, but I'm prepared to doubt any kind of coincidence in this case."

"I wonder if that key was involved," Tanda mused. "He could have had it in that pocket, and someone ripped the pocket and almost got it. That's why he brought it to my place and hid it."

"I suppose it's possible," Mike granted, looking at the shirt again. "It's more likely someone was telling him something he didn't want to hear, and when he started to walk away, they tried to pull him back. Or there was an argument, and the person he argued with tried to make a point by grabbing him. If I had a key important enough to hide, a shirt pocket would be the last place I kept it."

"Aha, then the key *is* important," Tanda pounced. "Tell me what you found out."

"Just that the key is to a special strongbox of some kind," Mike answered while obviously trying to look innocent and virtuous. "The box is a Rensaeler, one of the fancier models, and if you're implying I held back information that proves I lost our bet, you're misjudging me. Just to prove that, how about dinner tonight, say, about six?"

"Just to prove I was misjudging you," Tanda echoed with a nod and a hidden smile. "I understand completely. A police lieutenant has a certain reputation for virtue to maintain. If I refuse, it would almost be like working against the public good."

"Exactly," he agreed with a hidden smile of his own that wasn't all that well hidden. "So are we on for tonight?"

"We're on," she answered, and the words brought both of their smiles out into the open. The moment could have been awkward, but they still had half a house to search. Mike checked quickly through the rest of the clothes in the basket, and then they got on with it.

It took them another hour to go through the rest of the house, and they might as well not have bothered. Not only wasn't there a strongbox of the kind they were looking for, there was scarcely a speck of dust. In Don's bedroom there was a bookcase filled with paperbacks, and almost all of them looked as though they'd been read.

Tanda remembered how much Don had enjoyed reading, and looked for his favorite book, which was right in the middle of the top shelf. *Trail of Gold* had been written by someone Tanda had never heard of before or since, but Don had reread the original copy of the book so many times it had fallen apart. When he went to replace it he bought two copies, and treated them like the gold he thought they were. She'd had to sneak into his room when he was out and read it in bits and snatches herself, and afterward had never understood why he liked it so much. As a poor-boy-makes-good story, it had been juvenile and completely unreal.

"If there's anything hidden in this house, it must be behind one of the walls," Mike said from the other side of the room, sounding disappointed. "Do you see anything in that bookcase?"

"Not really," Tanda answered, then reached for the copy of *Trail of Gold*. "Do you think anyone would mind if I took this book? Don's had it since before he ran away."

"I doubt that taking a single paperback will hurt anything," he replied, then came closer and reached for the book. "But first let me check it. If he's had this since he was a boy, he could have hidden something in it."

That thought had already occurred to Tanda, but there was no sense in refusing. She'd wanted to be the one to find any clue there might be, but she *had* located the book... Rather than saying anything, she simply handed the book over.

Mike held it by its covers and shook it, then riffled its pages with a thumb. No secret notes or documents came flying out, and none of the pages seemed marked in any way. It was just an old paperback with yellowed pages, and Mike handed it back with a rueful smile.

"So much for the secret message left in a place only the victim's sister would know about," he said. "I'm glad your brother didn't put you in a position like that, but I'm also a little disappointed."

"I know what you mean," Tanda said with a sigh, putting the book into her shoulder bag. "At this point I'd welcome a little personal danger, just as long as some solid information came along with it. What do we do next?"

"We check with Miami P.D. to see if we can find out what Saxon meant by his comment," Mike replied, beginning to lead the way out of the bedroom. "I thought we might have had something when we learned Saxon spent time on Saturday in the library, but that was just another dead end. There were only two librarians in that day, Janice, a young assistant, and Miss Baderlie, the head research librarian, but more than a dozen people used the facilities. Janice didn't know even half of them, but was as certain as possible that none of them approached or talked to Saxon."

"After a steady diet of dead ends, how do you make yourself believe it when a lead finally does come along?" Tanda asked as they moved up the hall. "I mean, if someone suddenly came forward and said they saw someone they knew talking to Roger on Saturday, wouldn't you automatically assume the someone was trying to sell him insurance or something? Even if the someone was holding a knife, I'd probably assume Roger was being asked if he'd dropped the weapon."

"You're talking about the this-is-too-good-to-be-true syndrome," Mike said with a soft laugh. "That's one of the dangers in an investigation like this, the view that you've found nothing until now, so that smoking gun lying on the floor over there can't be anything but a plant.

The other side of that attitude is to see everything as a clue, even the lint at the bottom of the victim's pocket. You find yourself wanting to arrest the neighborhood paperboy, simply because he happened to go collecting on the day of the murder.''

''So what do you do?'' Tanda persisted, stopping at the head of the stairs. ''How do you act rationally, when everything inside tells you rational action is a waste of time?''

''You take a deep breath, step back and stretch, then try to start over from the beginning,'' Mike said, looking down at her with an odd little smile. ''You also rely on your instincts a lot, hoping they won't take you too far off base. The main thing to keep in mind, though, is that no one is perfect. The killer you're after *did* make a mistake, and the more times he killed, the more mistakes he made. If you refuse to let yourself be overwhelmed, you *will* find those mistakes.''

''In other words, you have to keep believing in yourself,'' Tanda said, then shook her head. ''I already believe in myself, but so far it hasn't helped. If that doesn't change pretty quick, I'll have to find someone else to believe in.''

''Feel free to choose your friendly neighborhood police lieutenant,'' he said, his smile now warm with understanding. ''I won't give up on this, Tanda, and I want you to believe that.''

Tanda did believe it, along with the conviction that Mike was about to kiss her. She wouldn't have minded, but suddenly he glanced around, as though just realizing they were all alone in a place where she might feel cornered. Cornered wasn't what she felt, especially when he took half a step back and forced a smile.

''So, what did you think of the house?'' he asked, a neutral question for an awkward moment. ''That kitchen had so many gadgets, I was tempted to take my coat off and start cooking.''

"Let's just say I *wasn't* tempted," she answered, then shook her head again. "But that doesn't mean I don't consider this the most beautiful house I've ever seen. I expected to feel—odd and out of place in it, but I don't. This was my brother's house here at home, and I think he would have given it up in a minute if he could have had his old room at my place back again.''

"I think you're right," Mike said, glancing at the cabinet of crystal figurines in the living room. "He probably expected to enjoy this house, but I'll bet he never did. Well, we'd better get going.''

They were silent all the way back to Tanda's van, and once she was inside and behind the wheel, Mike put his hands on the window.

"I've got to go back to headquarters for a while, but I'll be at your place at six," he said. "Unless six is too early, and you'd rather make it later?''

"Six is fine," she assured him with a smile. "I've got a couple of things to do myself, but I'll be ready.''

"Then I'll be there," he said, and stepped back from the van. "Drive safely.''

"You, too," Tanda said, then turned on the van and pulled away. As she rode up the street she could see Mike in her side-view mirror, still standing where he'd been. "And next time you'd better follow through on some of those instincts, my friend," she whispered to his dwindling image. "If you don't, I'll start to believe you see me more as a suspect than as a woman. But that's something we'll have to find out about, won't we?''

MIKE WATCHED Tanda's van disappear up the street, and only then realized he was still standing and staring. Feeling like a fool, he went to his car and got in, but didn't turn it on immediately. He needed a moment or two to bring himself back down to earth, instead of soaring like some teenage idiot. He hadn't ever felt like this about a girl, not even the girl he'd married. He hadn't even known the feeling was possible, not until Tanda Grail walked into his life.

"Well, at least you did one thing right," he muttered to himself. "You grabbed the opportunity to invite her to dinner, and didn't make it for next week some time. What you didn't do was really make her believe you'll succeed in catching her brother's murderer. Until she does believe it, she'll continue to go poking around. Which means that if anything happens to her, it will be your fault."

Which wasn't completely true, but was close enough to the mark to bother him. Mike had watched her as they searched through the house, and if Tanda Grail hadn't been hoping to find a definite clue, no one ever had. And the reluctant way she'd handed over that paperback... If her clue was in it, she hadn't wanted to share it, not with someone she associated dead ends with. When people lost confidence in you, they sometimes started to believe you were the one causing the dead ends.

And then they began to withhold things from you. Or to go off on investigations without telling you about them. Most people would have had no idea where to start with something like that, but Tanda Grail had already proven she wasn't most people. She had imagination and she had her dogs, and if she thought of another trail she might follow and the dog found it...

Mike used one hand to rub his face and eyes, unwilling to go on painting that particular picture. Part of it was a reluctance to think about Tanda in danger, but the rest... It was a selfish viewpoint, he knew, but what if she'd agreed to go out to dinner with him only to find out whatever new information he might come up with? As much as he hated the thought, that might be the only attraction he held for her. It would hardly be the first time.

"Central to Unit A17," he heard then from his radio. "Mike, this is Rena. Are you in your car?"

"I'm here, Rena," he answered as soon as he lifted the handset. "What's up?"

"I think you'd better get back here as soon as possible," Rena's voice said, thick with excitement. "We may have just gotten our first break."

"Tell me," Mike said without preamble.

"You remember the information on the victims we put out on the cross-country police net?" she said. "Well, we just got an answer you won't believe until you see it."

"I'll be right there," Mike said, then started his car. Ten minutes, he thought as he drove up the street. I can be there in ten minutes. And that will be the beginning of the end to this nightmare.

Chapter Six

"Everything they have is right there in the fax," Rena said, gesturing to the papers Mike held. "Because of lack of solid evidence no charges were ever filed, but no one working on the case had any doubts. The cause of death might have started out as an accident, but even so, the end of it definitely had help."

Mike sat in his chair staring down at the case papers, the excitement and enthusiasm he'd walked in with considerably dimmed. Tanda Grail had told him her brother had been a widower, and it had obviously bothered her that she hadn't even known he'd been married. How much more would it bother her to learn that his wife had been wealthy, and had died under very suspicious circumstances?

"So Grail ended up with her estate, and right after getting it he moved away," Mike said at last. "He must also have covered his tracks to a certain extent, since the police in his new hometown had no idea he'd been involved in a suspected murder."

"And that means we now have his late wife's family as suspects," Rena said, obviously trying to rekindle his enthusiasm. "His covering his tracks means it took them a while to find him, but once they did they didn't let him disappear again. They could have hired a pro to kill him in a way that wouldn't likely be traced back to them, and that's the reason for the other murders. The pro set it up to look like a set of serial killings, when in fact it was just in revenge for the murder Grail committed.''

"You'll have to check that out just to be sure, but I'll bet right now it isn't our answer,'' Mike said, tossing away the papers. "It's too complicated, Rena, and much too extreme. If you hired someone to kill the murderer of your daughter or sister, say, would you stand still for having three innocent people killed right along with him? That doesn't even count Roger Saxon, of course, and also doesn't explain his murder. If he spotted a professional killer around here, he wouldn't have waited to contact us, and he certainly wouldn't have opened his door to him."

"Maybe he didn't know the pro would recognize him,'' Rena said, reluctant to abandon her theory. "And maybe the pro *didn't* recognize Saxon. Maybe the pro heard Saxon had been asking questions about Don Grail, fed him some kind of story about knowing secrets while letting Saxon think he was pumping an unexpected source, and then arranged to meet privately in Saxon's room. Saxon would think he found the lead because he was that good—better than anyone else at his agency—and that's why he made that comment to Ms. Grail."

"If Saxon thought that much of himself, why did so many people at his agency like him?'' Mike asked, keeping the question mild. "You know what I'm talking about, Rena, because we've both worked with ego types. Half of them thought they were great when they were no such thing, and the other half really were great. In both cases it grated when they constantly tooted their own horns, and it quickly got to the point where it didn't matter if they *were* telling the truth. People avoided them in droves, and no one liked them."

"Especially if they were telling the truth,'' Rena grudged, then she sighed. "All right, I'll admit my theories are stretched in places, but that doesn't mean they're wrong. Another thing we both know is that stranger things have happened. The people who hired the pro might not like the extra murders he committed, but once the first innocent life was lost they were just as guilty of the murder as the actual killer. What choice would they have but to continue to go along with him?"

"Unfortunately, that's a very good point," Mike conceded, picking up a pencil to toy with. "I still don't think it's our answer, but we can't afford not to check it out. First find out what family the dead woman had, and then see about what their reactions were to her death. Once we have answers to those questions, we can decide where to go from there."

Rena nodded and stood up, looked as though she was about to say something, then changed her mind and left the office. Mike had an idea what she'd been about to say—that if this lead dried up, they'd be back to having nothing—and he was glad she'd changed her mind. Once you begin to expect failure, nothing else ever comes to you. They would get a real break on that case, and then they would solve it.

Firmly holding to that thought, Mike read through the faxed case papers again. He wanted to be certain he had everything the police on the spot had had, and then he went out to see Larry. Rena's partner was doing paperwork while Rena was off somewhere, and he looked up when Mike stopped at his desk.

"Rena isn't as happy with her theory as she was," Larry commented, leaning back in his chair. "I had the feeling she was ready to forget about it, but you must have decided differently. Is it really worth her spending time on?"

"As she said, stranger things have happened," Mike answered with a shrug. "It could turn out to be what we're looking for, but even if it isn't it still has to be checked. What I have for you, though, is a lot more promising.''

Larry sat up immediately, and Mike knew exactly how he felt. At that point anything could prove to be the right track, and even a weak theory was better than none.

''You remember what Ms. Grail told us Saxon said to her,'' Mike went on, knowing Larry did remember. ''Well, I saw Ms. Grail today when we went through her brother's house together. I happened to mention that Saxon had worked on two police forces, and she suggested that the key to his remark would be someone he came across in both places. Our best shot at finding out who that would be is through the detectives he worked with in Miami. While working on a case, maybe Saxon said to a fellow detective something like, 'Hey, I know this suspect from Phoenix.' Hopefully it was important enough or odd enough for someone to remember.''

''If someone does remember, I'll find him,'' Larry promised, making notes. ''This *is* a lead, and I'll get right on it. Anything else?''

''Yes,'' Mike said, double-checking his own notebook. ''There's a video library in Grail's house in the playroom, and a collection of books in the master bedroom. Get a couple of people over there to fast-forward through the tapes, and then glance through the books. Grail might have been killed because he stumbled across something someone was willing to kill to keep secret. If he was probably a murderer, he wouldn't have hesitated over blackmail.''

''That's for sure,'' Larry agreed, adding to his notes. ''I'll get Rawlins and his partner over there first thing tomorrow. Are you going to be here if I get lucky in Miami?''

''No, as a matter of fact, I'm leaving right now,'' Mike answered. ''I've got something to do tonight, but I won't be out of reach. If you find someone with our answer, just beep me."

"You can bet on it," Larry answered, then looked up with a grin. "It's about time you had a date, so just relax and enjoy it. If anything happens, we'll let you know."

"What makes you think I have a date?" Mike asked, surprised and the least bit embarrassed. He also felt guilty over the thought of enjoying himself while a murderer continued to walk free, but it *had* been a long time since his last date.

"Let's just say I know the signs," Larry answered, then waved a hand as he reached for his phone. "Go on, get out of here and let a working man work."

Under other circumstances Mike might have hesitated, but with Tanda Grail waiting for him he didn't have to be told twice. Six o'clock wasn't that far away, not when he first had to shower and shave and dress. He just hoped she was looking forward to the time half as much as he was.

TANDA CHECKED herself in the mirror for the dozenth time, beyond the point of being able to laugh at herself. It was only a quarter to six, but she'd been ready for twenty minutes.

This is ridiculous, she thought as she adjusted the left spaghetti strap of her favorite summer dress. It was pink and white with little sprigs of green, its short but very full skirt doing its usual job of making her feel pretty and feminine. "I feel as if this is the first date I've ever had," she said aloud, "and that he's looking forward to it as much as I am. I have to remember he's a cop, and his job is the most important thing to a cop."

And that I'm still a suspect, she added at the back of her mind as she turned away from the mirror. Her medium-heeled white Cobby Cuddlers were comfortable, but after so much time in nothing but sneakers they felt odd on her feet. Maybe if they were uncomfortable, they would have distracted her from disturbing thoughts.

Like the thought that Mike Gerard might be interested in nothing but catching a murderer. She could hardly blame him if that were true, not when she wanted the same thing. Only, what about personal feelings? Would there be any left once the case was solved? Tanda didn't know, and the uncertainty was very disturbing. Not to mention the fact that he could turn out to be more like Len than she now believed.

But then she heard the sound of a car outside, and looking through the window showed her that Mike was also early. A short whuffling from Robby said the dog already knew who was out there, and that if *he* hadn't made a fuss, Tanda shouldn't have worried. Tanda laughed and patted the dog, taking his advice and letting all her worries go. Time enough to let them come back if something happened to bring them back.

Tanda deliberately waited a moment after Mike's knock before going to the door. She hated the thought of looking like an eager adolescent, even if that was the way she felt. Opening the door showed her a freshly shaved and completely unrumpled Mike Gerard, his pearl-gray suit and blue and gray tie making him look like a prosperous attorney rather than a hardworking cop. There was also a sheepish grin on his face, which his first words explained.

"I thought I'd make up for being late this afternoon by being early tonight," he said, gesturing vaguely with one hand. "It wasn't until I pulled into your driveway that it occurred to me you might not be ready early. Would you like me to go back to my car and wait there?"

"Don't be silly," Tanda said, pushing the screen door open. "Even if I weren't ready you could wait in here, but it so happens I am. I'll get my bag, and we can leave—unless there was something you needed to talk to me about first."

"No, there's nothing I need to talk about," he assured her with a quick smile as he stepped inside. "I'm ready to leave as soon as you are."

Tanda nodded and went to get her white shoulder bag, but a faint shadow had touched her good mood. Unless she was mistaken, there was something bothering Mike. If he didn't want to talk about it now, would he bring it up later?

"I'm glad to see your dog is still in the house," Mike said when she reappeared a moment later. "He's just been promising to take very good care of you, and insisted that I do the same."

Tanda, who had heard Robby's muttering even in the next room, laughed at Mike's interpretation of the dog's noise. He laughed with her, and then his smile softened.

"I tried to say how nice you look when I first walked in, but I find I'm out of practice in giving pretty women compliments," he said. "I'm making a complete hash of this, but you do look beautiful tonight."

"If that's making a hash of things, I'd like you to keep on making a hash," Tanda answered, her cheeks warming with faint embarrassment. "In other words, thank you for the lovely compliment, and I'd like to return it. I had no idea I'd have such a handsome escort tonight."

"Actually, I'm in disguise," he returned with a grin that made Tanda think he was as flustered as she was. "Dressing up like this guarantees that no one will recognize me. Shall we go?"

That was an idea she heartily agreed with, and five minutes later they were in his car heading out to Old Stage Road. It had been a while since anyone had driven Tanda anywhere, even when she'd had dinner with Don. She'd chosen to meet her brother at the restaurant, just in case things didn't go all that well. Tonight she didn't really know what to expect, but with Mike Gerard involved, she couldn't picture getting home being a problem.

Mike drove them to Crosswinds, not the most expensive restaurant in the area, but definitely the best. Don had chosen the Crystal Palace, which *was* the most expensive, and Tanda hadn't told him the food was better elsewhere. If her brother hadn't found that out for himself, it was only because he hadn't wanted to believe the most money couldn't buy the best to be had. A lot of people were like that, certain there wasn't anything better than what was charged the most for, and Tanda usually felt sorry for them.

Crosswinds lacked the valet parking of the other restaurant, but that turned into a good point for Tanda. Once Mike had pulled into a parking place and come around to help her out of the car, he offered his arm in the gentlemanly way with a wry grin. He seemed almost to be expecting her to refuse to do something so old-fashioned, and maybe even to consider it silly. But Tanda didn't consider it silly, not when it was something her father had never failed to do for her mother. She took Mike's arm with a smile, and kept it until they entered the restaurant.

They were seated immediately, far enough away from the other customers for cozy privacy, and a waitress came to take their drink orders. Tanda asked for coffee, and was surprised when Mike did the same. He must have noticed the reaction; as soon as the waitress moved away, he smiled at Tanda.

"When I'm on vacation and can leave my gun at home, then I feel free to drink," he explained softly. "I'll sometimes have a beer when I'm carrying, but never more than that and never when I'm tired. I'm supposed to protect the population around here, not do something that can end in an ugly accident."

"I'm glad to hear you say that," Tanda told him honestly. "All those movies that show cops getting drunk and it's considered no big deal... You can bet the ones who make those movies have never been near an armed drunk.

If they ever had been, they'd change their minds about how big a deal the situation really is. Scary is what it is, all the way to terrifying.''

"You sound like you speak from experience,'' Mike observed, leaning back as he looked at her. "You're not talking about the cop you used to date, I hope.''

"Len wasn't happy about how long I was taking to decide whether or not to go with him,'' Tanda answered with a shrug as she looked down at her unopened menu. "He picked me up for our usual Friday-night date, and if I'd known he'd been drinking I would never have gotten into his car. Once I did get in, it was too late, and I had to wait until we got where we were going. He spent the ride telling me how unhappy he was with me, and that I'd better make up my mind fast. At least that part was easily taken care of. I called him the next day, and told him I never wanted to see him again.''

"I didn't know my wife felt she couldn't trust anyone with a gun until after we were married,'' Mike said, his voice sounding like Tanda's must have. "She never mentioned the point while we were dating, but somehow had gotten the impression I left my gun at headquarters. Since I don't make a habit of waving the gun in peoples' faces—and she tended not to pay attention to a good many things in life—the argument we had about it was spectacular. It was one of the points she used against me at our divorce hearing.''

"But how could she?'' Tanda asked, trying not to show how incensed she felt. "Police officers are required to carry their weapons even when off duty. I thought everyone in the world knew that.''

"Apparently everyone but my wife,'' Mike answered with a humorless smile. "She also accused me of desertion because I wasn't home every day promptly at five-thirty, and sometimes had to work weekends as well. She'd kept her job as a receptionist in a psychologist's office, and had banked all her salary while we lived on mine. The account was in her name alone, but she still claimed I hadn't provided properly for her, and so she deserved a large amount of alimony. Her lawyer had been against saying any of that, but she'd insisted as usual until she got her way.''

"So what happened?" Tanda asked next, privately wondering how a man like Mike Gerard could have chosen so badly. The woman had probably been all sweetness and light when around him, not to mention artfully helpless. Strong men fell for that every time, no matter how intelligent they normally were.

"Luckily for me, the judge was a woman," Mike said, and now there was faint humor in his smile. "Linda was delighted when she first walked into court, certain that a woman judge would be on her side. That was another point she missed, that the judge happened to be a woman, not that it was a woman judge. My lawyer was asked only one question—was I agreeing to the divorce, or fighting it? When my lawyer answered that I was definitely not fighting the divorce, the judge nodded with grim satisfaction. Then she granted the divorce to *me,* and ordered Linda to pay me half of the money she had banked.''

"Good for that judge!" Tanda said in delight. "I love judges with a sense of poetic justice. I'll bet Linda screamed and fainted.''

"I think she was considering it," Mike said with a small laugh. "But then she realized no one would be very impressed or sympathetic, so she just stormed out. She tried to empty the bank account before the court's decision could be acted on, but the judge anticipated that with an immediate court order. I think the judge privately considered Linda's behavior a blot on the honor of all women everywhere, and made sure the blot wouldn't be made worse. When the money was sent to me by the bank, I turned it over to the Widows and Orphans Fund we have at headquarters.''

"If you'd given it back to her, I think I would have gotten up and gone home," Tanda said. "Instead, let's see what looks good tonight.''

They turned to the menu then, and the decision was made by the time the coffee came. They both ordered the teriyaki steak medium rare, with Russian dressing on their salads and baked potatoes. It was as though they'd previously agreed to order the same thing, and the nice part about it was that the agreement *wasn't* prearranged.

The food came quickly and was as delicious as always, and the conversation never faltered. Mike told Tanda with an embarrassed grin that as a kid he'd wanted to be a knight, riding around on a white charger and rescuing people—especially princesses—from evil. He'd managed to get the white charger—it was out in the parking lot—and did rescue people sometimes, but had as yet to come across a single princess.

In turn, Tanda confided that for a long time she'd wanted to be Charlie Chan or Sherlock Holmes. Her mother had pointed out that the two were men, so how about being Miss Marple instead? But Tanda hadn't liked Miss Marple as well as Hercule Poirot, so the problem hadn't been solved.

"And I ended up as Dr. Watson," she added, laughing with Mike over the silliness of childhood. "If anyone's Sherlock Holmes it's Robby, and I'm just around to admire him and take notes.''

"Being Dr. Watson isn't an easy job," Mike pointed out while his coffee cup was being refilled. "Holmes gets all the applause and attention, but how many people would know about him without Watson's stories? And how well would he really do without Watson to look after him? Not too well, I'll bet. How about dessert?''

"I don't think I have the room," Tanda answered, still

enjoying Mike's Dr. Watson comments. Most people cared only about the star, never even noticing the efforts of the supporting cast. "I happen to love desserts, but I've never yet eaten one here. After making a pig of myself over the meal, the desire is there but the capacity is lacking."

"Then let's share one," Mike suggested. "Until you've tasted their Nesselrode pie, you haven't tasted dessert."

So they shared a piece of Nesselrode pie, and Tanda discovered Mike was right. The pie was the best she'd ever tasted, and the piece was big enough so that neither of them felt shortchanged. It was just the right amount, in fact, and afterward they finished their coffee, Mike paid the check, and they left.

"After that meal, I really should walk home," Tanda said as they approached the car. "If I had sneakers on, I'd be tempted to do just that."

"Then I'm glad you don't have sneakers on," Mike replied, looking up at the darkened night sky. "If you decided to walk I'd have to walk with you, and then I'd have to walk back. That sky says it's thinking about raining again, and the roads and streets are already deserted. Even if it poured I'd have no chance of a ride, so I'm very glad you're not in sneakers."

"And that would be a terrible ending to such a lovely evening," Tanda said, stopping by the car to join him in looking up. "I'm very glad you lost the bet, Mike. I had a wonderful time."

"I never used to like the idea of losing, but tonight has changed my mind," he murmured, stepping closer. "I can't remember ever enjoying myself so much, and all we did was share a meal. Without a doubt, it had to be the company."

Not only were the streets and parking lot deserted, but they also stood in a pool of shadow. Tanda had always disapproved of public displays, but now she didn't hesitate. Mike had left the decision about kissing there to her, but as soon as she leaned up his arms were around her, his lips coming down to meet hers. It felt as though she'd been waiting all her life for that kiss, and they shared it even more happily than they'd shared dessert.

It didn't take Tanda long to decide she would ask Mike in when he took her home, but the fates had other ideas. Their kiss was suddenly interrupted by beeping, and Mike hastily reached into his jacket.

"Sorry about that," he apologized, looking embarrassed as well as sorry. "One of my people is checking on that idea you had about Saxon and the two police forces he worked on. My man said he'd beep me if he reached someone who could give us the information we want."

"Then you'd better call them back right away," Tanda said, disappointed but also excited. That horrible mess might soon be over.

Mike opened her side of the car first, and once he was behind the wheel he reached for his cell phone. It took only a moment for him to get through to the number that had been left, but when he heard the man's voice that answered, he looked surprised.

"Art?" he said. "Why are *you* calling me? I was expecting it to be Larry Othar."

"I don't know why Larry would be calling you, Mike, but you should know the reason why I'm doing it," the voice replied, loud enough for Tanda to hear the words. "It's the same reason as the last time and the time before that."

"No," Mike said, and the deadness in his voice gave Tanda the chills. "No, Art, not that."

"Sorry, Mike, but it's true," was the faint but weary and sickened answer. "We've got another body, complete with another note."

Chapter Seven

When he pulled up to the scene of the latest murder, Mike wasn't sure he'd done the right thing. Tanda had quietly asked him not to take her home first, and he hadn't had to wonder why. She'd looked pale even in the feeble light from his dashboard, probably from the thought of being home all alone while most of the force was busy with the newest victim of a murderer who hadn't yet been caught. He'd agreed to take her with him, but only after she'd agreed to stay in the car.

This time the murder site was a stretch of woods near a motel, but not the same motel Roger Saxon had been killed in. A couple of kids, shortcutting through the woods on their way home, had found the body and called the police. As Mike approached, he could see Art Renquist questioning two teenage boys, neither of whom looked particularly upset.

"Mike, this is Eric Parker and Sam Elvin," Art said as soon as he'd joined them. "Boys, this is Lieutenant Gerard, who's in charge of the investigation."

"Hey, Lieutenant," the dark-haired one pointed out as Eric Parker greeted him. "It gave us a jolt at first, but then we knew what we had to do. Sam stood watch while I found a phone, then we both stayed there until your people came."

"And we didn't touch anything, or let anyone else touch anything," the blond and blue-eyed Sam added. "When your people got here we pointed out which footprints were ours, so now they won't be misled."

"That's really impressive, boys," Mike told them, looking from one to the other. "How did you know to do all that?"

"It's hard to believe there's anyone alive these days who *doesn't* know enough to do that," Sam answered while Eric nodded. "People like to run down television, but there's all sorts of things to learn from it."

"Boys, I'd like to ask you a couple of questions," Mike said, exchanging glances with Art Renquist. "Did you come by here on your way to wherever you were going? If so, did you see anyone who made you think they didn't belong here?"

"We did pass by earlier, but I don't remember seeing anything," Eric answered with a thoughtful frown. "It was about four this afternoon, so if the man was murdered here rather than brought here and dumped, it had to have happened after that."

"There was a black rental car in the parking lot that isn't there now," Sam contributed, also sounding unsure. "I noticed it because it was a Buick, and I like Buicks. And I knew it was a rental because of the license tag, but all I noticed was the ICI part. I never looked at the numbers."

The boy Sam seemed almost ashamed to admit that, and didn't notice the second glance Mike exchanged with Art. Two sixteen-year-old boys had just given them one side of the time frame of the murder and a possible vehicle belonging to the murderer, and they were disappointed they couldn't do more! People who talked about how useless kids were these days had obviously never met Eric and Sam.

"But you did know enough to recognize the standard

letters of a rental car," Mike pointed out to the boy as he clapped him on the shoulder. "That's more than a lot of people would have been able to do, and I'm curious how you learned about it."

"Television," Sam answered with a shrug. "I watch commercials because some of them are really clever, and the ones that aren't are always good for a sneer. Two of my favorite programs are sponsored by car-rental companies, and when they show the cars you sometimes get a look at the plates. Both companies have plates with ICI, so I concluded ICI meant a rental car. Nothing came up to make me believe I was wrong, so I kept the idea as a working hypothesis."

"A working hypothesis," Art echoed in a mutter. "Hey, Mike, is there any way we can draft these kids to work with us? We can probably learn a lot from them."

"I'm afraid not," Mike answered with a grin while the boys laughed with flattered delight. "I agree it's too bad, but we'll have to settle for their unofficial help. Boys, I'm giving each of you my card. If you remember anything you haven't yet told us, call me right away. In the meantime, we'll appreciate it if you don't talk to the media at all."

"To keep from accidentally mentioning something you're deliberately keeping quiet about," Eric said with a nod as he pocketed Mike's card. "Not to mention to make sure the murderer doesn't start thinking we know more than we do. If I ever get my name in the papers, I'd prefer if it wasn't as this guy's next victim."

Sam's agreement was so clear he didn't have to nod, which was one less worry for Mike.

The boys left after that, and Mike was able to go over for a look at the body. The heavy male victim lay on his back just like all the others, the letter opener pinning the same note to the body. Mike stared at the note that said, "From your secret admirer" until a hand touched his arm.

"I have a preliminary, if you're ready to hear it," Frank Shuster, the medical examiner, said when Mike looked up. "I'll know more after I do the autopsy tomorrow, but I can give you a general idea."

"Go ahead," Mike said, pushing away the thought of that note.

"The man was Oscar Relling, forty-two years of age according to his driver's license," Frank reported. "He's from out of state and is here visiting, according to the motel manager, but who or what he was visiting is anybody's guess. Because of his weight it took two thrusts of the knife to kill him, the second one being delivered to his throat. All the rest of the wounds are in his body, just like with the first five victims. He was definitely killed here, somewhere between four-thirty and six-thirty this afternoon. I'll be able to pin that down more closely after the postmortem."

"Still no obvious mistakes?" Mike asked, already knowing the answer. If the murderer had slipped up, Frank would have mentioned it first thing.

"I can't believe how lucky this creep is," Frank grumbled. "He kills somebody outdoors in broad daylight, and not only doesn't anyone see him do it, he isn't even rushed into being sloppy. I recommend we look into bringing in a consulting witch doctor. If we wait for the creep's luck to run out by itself, half the county could end up decimated."

"A witch doctor," Mike echoed with a shake of his head. If that wasn't an indication of Frank's frustration level, it was proof that the stress had finally gotten him. Frank didn't believe in anything he couldn't touch with a forceps or scalpel.

"Okay, we'll have to go with what we have again," Mike continued. "I may take you up on that witch-doctor thing, but only if he or she will guarantee us some good luck. If you hear of one who'll do that, let me know."

Frank nodded as he walked away.

"You look terrible," Tanda said when he got back in the car. "Obviously it was just as bad as the others."

"'Just as bad' doesn't tell half the story," Mike said after taking a deep breath. "I was just thinking about the way we were all but joking around. An outsider would think we didn't care at all, but joking is the only way we can handle it."

"Because every time this monster kills, you and your people feel responsible," Tanda said with an understanding nod. "I can see that, Mike, but you have to see that it isn't so. You can only do your absolute best, not pull miracles out of the air. If anyone but the murderer himself is responsible, it has to be whoever or whatever twisted him so horribly."

"I know that, Tanda, but that particular truth is still hard to accept on an emotional level," Mike conceded with a sigh. "We know we're doing our best, but if the late Mr. Relling could be asked, he'd be certain to think that that wasn't good enough. He's dead because—"

"Wait a minute," Tanda interrupted with sudden upset. "What did you say that name was?"

"Relling," Mike repeated as he sat straighter. "Oscar Relling from somewhere out of town. He isn't from around here, so don't be afraid you know him."

"But I think I do know him," she all but whispered, her hands clenched into fists. "Not *really* know him, but was introduced to him. That name stuck in my mind because it was so German-sounding, while the man himself had this flat, nasal accent that wasn't even vaguely German. Mike, if it's the same man, he was introduced to me by Don."

She said the words and then just stared at him, obviously finding it impossible to make the next logical suggestion. She'd know whether it was the same man if she looked at the body, but she must have been remembering what identifying her brother had been like. Mike really needed to know if there was a definite connection between two of the victims, but rather than pressing the point he simply went on with the conversation.

"All right, tell me everything you remember about Relling," he said, trying to sound as soothing as possible. "Take your time, and don't leave out even the smallest detail."

"There aren't many details altogether," she said after taking a deliberately deep breath. "I met Don at the Crystal Palace the night he took me out to dinner. He waited for me in the parking lot, and then we went inside together. Just as we were going in, someone else was coming out, and the man and Don almost collided. The man started to snarl something nasty, and then he looked up and exclaimed, 'Grail! What are you doing here? Are you following me?'

"'Why would I be following you, Relling?' Don countered in the same annoyed tone. 'I'm here to have dinner with my sister, if that's perfectly all right with you.'

"At that point they both seemed to remember I was standing there, so Don made very reluctant introductions. Relling was just as reluctant about acknowledging them, and as soon as he'd nodded he left. Don said something about the man being a very unpleasant salesman he'd had to brush off, and then he changed the subject. After that, Oscar Relling was never mentioned again."

"Even though you couldn't possibly have believed that bit about Relling being a salesman," Mike mused. "It sounds like they hadn't expected to run into each other, so there was no easy story ready. I wonder what sort of connection they really had."

"Whatever it was, they weren't friends and they certainly didn't trust one another," Tanda said, beginning to pull herself together. "There was something close to fear in Relling's accusation, and a definite worry in Don's denial. If whatever they were involved in didn't cause them to be killed, I don't know what did.''

''Since Oscar Relling isn't exactly a common name, I'm going to assume that the victim is the same man you met,'' Mike said as he started the car. ''Forensics is just about finished here and the body is about to be taken away, so I'm free to drive you home. Tomorrow I'll come by with one of the Polaroids the morgue people will take, so you can confirm that the man is the same one you met. Will it be too hard for you to look at one of those pictures?''

''No, a picture is fine,'' Tanda said, finally relaxing all the way. ''Sometimes pictures aren't real, like on television, so I'll be able to tell myself he isn't really dead. I know I should go over there and look at him right now, but—''

''But that's more Holmes's job than Watson's,'' Mike interrupted before she decided it was her duty to go. ''He's the one who takes all the bows, so let him be the one to get sick looking at horror. Watson has more important things to do with her time.''

''Like what?'' she asked, an unsteady smile trying to soften her expression.

''Like going home and getting a good night's sleep, so tomorrow she'll be in shape to track fugitives,'' he answered with his own smile. ''And to think about everything that's happened. The great Holmes is going to need a lot of help from her on this one, otherwise he'll end up falling flat on his face.''

''I see you've promoted yourself,'' she said as he began to back his car out of the press of official vehicles. ''First you were a lowly lieutenant, and now you're Holmes. Well, I don't mind. If you want to feel equal to Robby, I can't blame you.''

Mike chuckled at that, and the ride back to her place was filled with a close, easy quiet. Their disturbance over

the latest murder was still there, but they'd worked together to keep the despair away. Mike didn't even try to
picture Linda doing the same. His ex-wife simply wasn't
in Tanda's league.

When they reached the Grail house, Mike went inside
with her to check each room while she let out the dog.
Robby was back before Mike finished the last room,
though, so he had no excuse to hang around a little longer.
He gave her cheek a quick kiss before leaving, and she
touched his hand in gratitude before closing and locking
the door behind him.

Mike called in to have a unit assigned to the Grail
house for the night, then parked across Old Stage Road
until they got there. He spent the waiting time trying to
think about that kiss they'd shared in the dark, but worry
refused to step aside for pleasure. Every time something
else happened, Tanda Grail became more deeply en-
meshed in the problem. She already had ties of some sort
to three of the victims. How long would it be before the
murderer decided she would be safest as a victim herself?
And, more to the point, how long could *he* keep it from
happening?

TANDA WATCHED Mike's car disappear up the road, regret
so heavy in her that she felt like crying. It had been a
wonderful, magical evening, going as well as anyone's
best daydream. She'd actually been ready to invite a man
she hardly knew to spend the night with her, and then
he'd gotten that call.

And the whole beautiful bubble had exploded in both
their faces. Mike would have stayed the night if she'd
asked him to, but anything that happened between them
then would have been desperation rather than attraction.
It would have been unfair to both of them, and he seemed
to have felt that even more strongly than she. That kiss

on the cheek he'd given her before leaving was full of concern and empty of passion. Not that *she* had much in the way of passion left.

"We'd better catch this guy fast," she said to Robby as she turned away from the window. "He may be killing others, but he's ruining my life in pieces."

Robby whuffled his agreement, so she patted him and went to the kitchen to check the mail she'd brought in with her. During the day she'd forgotten to check the box, but Mike had stopped to let her do it on the way in. There was something of a stack, with four inquiries about the training fees she charged, three inquiring about buying puppies, and only one bill. That made her feel the least bit better—until she reached the small white envelope on the bottom. It was sealed and had her name on it, but there was no address, stamp or postmark. It had been hand-delivered, then, and hidden under the rest of the mail.

Tanda stared at the envelope for a long moment, trying to get up the nerve to open it. It wasn't going to be a flyer advertising used cars or a new pizza place, that was certain right now. It would have something to do with her brother's death, and might even be from his murderer. *That* was what frightened her, that it would be an offer of information she couldn't refuse, and it would turn out to have been sent by Don's killer. It would be a lure to bring her to a place where she, too, might be killed.

"But if you don't look at it, you'll never know," she growled, hating the weak-kneed reaction she couldn't seem to control. Anger helped the way she'd hoped it would, and despite a pounding heart she was able to tear the envelope open. Too late she remembered about fingerprints, but right now that was another issue. Most important was the letter itself, which was short and in a tight, choppy handwriting.

We know who killed your brother. If you want to know, meet us tomorrow at noon at your brother's house. Don't tell the cops, or we just won't be there.

It was unsigned, just as there was no salutation or date. It could be from anyone, even as a sick joke, but somehow Tanda didn't believe that. And that "we." Was there really more than one person involved, or had that been done to confuse things? They claimed to know who the murderer was, but if so, why hadn't they gone to the police themselves?

Tanda let the letter fall to the table as she leaned back and closed her eyes. She'd known she would have to make a hard decision, but now she was faced with two. The first was the easier one, and it was simply whether or not she should go. It could be a trap, but it could also be a legitimate offer. If she didn't go she would never find out, and would probably always regret being a coward.

But the last of it, *that* was the hardest to decide about. If she did decide to go, could she do it without telling Mike? Telling him could ruin everything, and they needed all the help they could get, but—

Should she tell him? Should she?

Chapter Eight

Mike made it to his office early this time, but not because he had anything special to follow up on. His main hope was pinned to new information that might come in, just as some had come in the day before. He felt faintly guilty about not having told Tanda about her brother, but in that particular situation being a coward was also a relief. He'd wait until he also had something good to tell her, and then he'd break the news about her brother's probable complicity in a murder.

"Hey, Mike," he heard, and then looked up to see Rena Foreman just inside his office door.

"You got something!" Mike pounced at once, knowing it from her grin. "What is it, and how helpful is it on a scale from one to two?"

"It's a definite one and a half," Rena laughed, coming forward with a stack of papers. "Or maybe I should say, *they* are. As in more than one."

Mike took the papers fast and started to go through them. There were two separate files, apparently, and each file had an introductory fax above the rest of the stack.

"Two more of our victims were identified by other states," Rena said, obviously too excited to wait for Mike to read it for himself. "The big difference between them and Grail, though, is that they changed their names when they changed localities. Olivia Warren was originally Olga Weeks, and Jeffrey Styles was John Sorliss. Note the originality in the new names they chose.''

''Come on, Rena, you know most people do that,'' Mike reminded her. ''They use the same initials to comfort their sense of identity, or to make sure any overlooked monograms match. So Olivia Warren was suspected in the death of her frail and wealthy aunt. But that was when she was still Olga Weeks, and the police couldn't prove the suspicion. Plenty of publicity, but no charges filed.''

''And Jeffrey Styles—as John Sorliss—was involved in the collapse of a parochial school that killed five children and crippled three more plus a couple of adults,'' Rena said. ''A very large amount of money was collected to renovate the school building, which was cheaper than building or buying another place of the same size. Sorliss was in charge of getting the work done, and he supposedly paid out every penny in his keeping. He took a vacation when the work was 'finished,' and never came back. A month later the building collapsed.''

''And by then the man could have been anywhere,'' Mike said, skimming through the second file. ''He'd covered his tracks with a great deal of care, and no one was ever able to trace him. The story got a lot of publicity, but nothing ever came of it. Nice people, these two.''

''Nice people all three,'' Rena corrected, reminding him about Grail. ''There was publicity galore in all three cases, but they were still able to disappear. You'd think somebody would have spotted at least one of them.''

''Speaking of spotting people, how are you doing with Grail's late wife's family?'' Mike asked. ''Anything to show your theory might be true after all?''

''Not exactly,'' Rena answered with a sigh. ''She was an only child whose mother died when she was very young, but her father *had* been a self-made millionaire. I thought he was it—until I discovered his entire fortune—

except for a measly few hundred thousand—was transferred to his daughter less than two years before she was married. He'd been diagnosed with Parkinson's, you see, and right now he doesn't even know how nice a nursing home he's lying in. The only other relative is a cousin on her mother's side, a woman with seven kids who hadn't seen her since they were both small children. The local cops got all that when they were first investigating, on the off chance someone was setting Grail up. Back then there was no one but the father, and he kept forgetting he had a daughter, not to mention that she was dead.''

"So that theory is down the drain, but now we have the chance at another," Mike said, leaning back to study her. "Three of our victims were involved in crimes they were never punished for. That suggests some self-appointed avenger, but Saxon doesn't fit the pattern. He was one of the good guys, or at least was supposed to be. Unless or until we find out differently, he becomes the fly in the ointment.''

"And there are more flies," Rena said, returning his stare. "How did our avenger know about these people? We won't even ask how he knew they were all here, since that's a question of another color. Part of it is, did he somehow bring them here, or simply find out they were coming? We know Saxon was here because he was hired through his agency, and Grail came here every year. Did the others come on business or to visit a mutual friend, and what about the last two? Would it be stealing to bet they'll turn out to have similar backgrounds?''

"At this point, I refuse to bet on any of it," Mike said with a head shake. "I may be getting superstitious in my old age, but I don't want to turn a sure thing into a sure miss. We'll get last night's victim on the wire as fast as possible, and simply keep our fingers crossed. And we may have a link between last night's man and Don Grail.

Tanda Grail thinks her brother introduced her to the man once.''

Rena raised her eyebrows questioningly, so Mike gave her the story as he'd gotten it from Tanda. When he was through, Rena nodded.

"So it looks like it's finally starting to come together," she said. "The victims do have a common link—or at least some of them do—and at least two of them knew each other. But something still doesn't make sense. If they all turn out to know each other, why are we still finding bodies? After the third murder at the very most, the rest should have disappeared like your well-known dust in the wind.''

"But since they didn't, there's a reason why they didn't,'' Mike said with a nod. "Something held them here that was stronger than a possible threat to their lives. But that goes only if they did know each other. If not, they might not have known they were next on the list.''

"Which would then change the picture entirely,'' Rena agreed with a sigh. "But whichever way it goes, we're definitely on the right track now. I'm going to take these three case files and feed them into the computer. If there's some one person or situation all three have in common, the computer might find it.''

Mike nodded as she hurried out of his office, satisfied that she really was back on track.

"Excuse me, Lieutenant, but you have a visitor,'' a uniformed cop said after knocking and stepping halfway in. "His name is Arthur Weddoes, and he said you were trying to get in touch with him.''

Mike had to think for a moment, but then he remembered that Weddoes was Don Grail's lawyer.

"Bring him in, Ralph,'' Mike directed. "And on your way back to the desk, let Larry Othar know he's here. I think Larry meant to go see him personally today.''

Ralph nodded and stepped outside to gesture, and a

moment later Arthur Weddoes was being ushered into Mike's office. The lawyer was somewhere in his mid to late forties, tall and husky with light brown hair and very light blue eyes. His smile was professionally cool when he stepped forward to offer his hand, and Mike matched it when he rose to accept the handshake.

"Thank you for coming in, Mr. Weddoes," he said, then gestured to a chair. "Please make yourself comfortable. We were going to come by to see you later today, so this is something of a surprise."

"To me it was more of a shock," Weddoes said after taking the offered seat. "I've been out of town for two weeks, and had no idea what was going on. I still can't believe Don Grail is dead."

"We were wondering why you didn't come forward when Mr. Grail was first killed," Mike said, settling himself in his chair again. "What can you tell me about the man? We're particularly interested in who he associated with."

"There's a problem with part of that question," Weddoes said, again looking professional rather than bothered. "I can tell you that I didn't know the man all that well, only that I handled the purchase of his house and the drawing up of his will. I also represented him on another matter, but I'm constrained by law not to discuss it."

"But the man's dead," Mike pointed out, trying to ignore a flash of frustrated annoyance. "And not only dead, but murdered. Any information you hold back could be the key to finding his murderer."

"I'm aware of that, but I have no choice," Weddoes said in a strangely emotionless way. "Under the circumstances, a court order could breach the confidentiality of the situation, but nothing less. Do you understand what I mean?"

For an instant Mike felt the heat of insult. Weddoes seemed to be suggesting that Mike needed the law explained to him in words of one syllable, but then he took a closer look at the man. The cool and professional lawyer was sweating, and a faint edge of desperation could be seen in his eyes. He'd come here this morning because he *wanted* to tell Mike what he knew, but professional ethics kept him from speaking. When he'd asked if Mike understood what he was saying—

"Yes, Mr. Weddoes, I do understand you," Mike finally answered with a smile. "I need a court order to get my information, so please excuse me for a moment."

As Mike reached for the phone, he was certain he could see relief in the slump of Weddoes's shoulders. Whatever the man knew must be something that put him in danger, but he couldn't simply speak up. Mike admired that in the man, and made a mental note of who to call if *he* ever needed a lawyer.

Mike got through to the commissioner, and told him about the court order he needed. As expected, the commissioner asked only if the matter related to the murders. When Mike said it did, the commissioner replied, "You'll get it," and hung up. That would cut out a lot of red tape, and get the ponderous political machine working on his side.

"The court order should be here as soon as they can reach a judge," Mike told Weddoes. "While we're waiting for it, I have a couple of other questions. You said you drew up Grail's will. Can you tell me who the heir or heirs are?"

"Yes, that I can tell you," Weddoes said with another cool smile. "Until almost a year ago there were two heirs, Don's father and sister. When his father died, Don named his sister as sole heir."

"Then there were no children from his marriage?" Mike asked, feeling a twinge at hearing that. Tanda was in line to inherit, which would probably make her very uncomfortable.

"I had no idea he'd been married," Weddoes said with faint surprise. "He never mentioned an ex-wife when I asked about anyone else who might have a claim on his estate. Where large sums of money are involved, it's best to take care of problems before they become problems."

"Grail wasn't divorced, he was widowed," Mike supplied. "As far as we can tell, his late wife had almost no other family, so that might explain why he failed to mention it. And you can't tell me yet whether Grail had any friends or associates in this area?"

"Not yet," Weddoes agreed almost heavily. "Any comment at all would be improper, so I'm best off saying nothing at all."

"Then how about mentioning where you were for the last two weeks," Mike suggested instead. "It seems odd that you were so far out of touch you heard nothing about what was going on here."

"The West Coast is more than just three thousand miles away," Weddoes answered, his smile faint and on the wry side. "My sister and her family live in Sacramento, and my parents and I went there to attend my oldest nephew's high-school graduation. The ceremony had been delayed because of the large number of forest fires in the area. We also took the opportunity to visit for a while, and since the entire family was there, we had no reason to make any calls back here. We got back to Bridgeport and my parents' home late Sunday night, so I left a message for my assistant on the office answering machine, and came back early this morning. That's when I found out about all—this."

The man waved a well-manicured hand vaguely, but his meaning was perfectly clear. If he'd gotten back sooner, he probably would have been to the station sooner.

"If you like, you can go back to your office until the court order comes through," Mike offered. "I'm certain

I don't have to worry about you leaving town again suddenly.''

"Considering how good the idea sounds, you shouldn't be too sure of that,'' Weddoes returned dryly. "You'll understand what I mean when I'm able to talk to you, but for now I'll simply thank you for the offer and respectfully decline. I'd rather wait right here and get this whole thing behind me.''

"Then it might be best if we found someplace more comfortable for you to wait,'' Mike said, working to hide his surprise. Was the man *that* afraid? "There are conference rooms on this floor where you can relax in privacy, and please feel free to help yourself to the coffee. With the commissioner hurrying things up, it shouldn't be too long a wait.''

Weddoes nodded and stood. It only took a couple of minutes to get the lawyer settled with a cup of coffee by his hand, and then Mike headed to his office. On the way, Larry joined him, and gestured back toward the conference room with his head.

"Do we now have our own private lawyer?'' he asked. "If so, do those of us who have made detective grade get to use his services for free? If so again, I have two or three little matters I'd like to discuss with him.''

"I don't think he handles breach of promise or paternity suits,'' Mike couldn't help remarking. "Besides, that's one worried man right now. I may be wrong, but I think he's afraid he'll be next on the murderer's list if he doesn't tell us what he knows as fast as possible.''

"Then what's he waiting for?'' Larry demanded, letting Mike walk into the office first before following. "If it's all that dangerous to know what he knows, why doesn't he just get it off his chest?''

"Because he's the kind of man you find so rarely these days,'' Mike said, sitting behind his desk again. "He knows the difference between right and wrong, and refuses to knowingly do wrong even if he has a good excuse for it. I wish I could say the same about me.''

''You and me both,'' Larry muttered, then sat in the chair Weddoes had used. ''You like to think you'd always do the right thing, but it never turns out to be as easy as that. One of the men Roger Saxon worked with on the Miami force is now a lieutenant, and he said there's definitely a case Saxon had there and in Phoenix as well. He remembers Saxon and his partner talking about it.''

''But?'' Mike prompted, knowing they didn't have the brass ring in their hand yet.

''But this lieutenant doesn't know which case it was, and Saxon's ex-partner isn't available,'' Larry said with a sigh. ''The man was shot two years ago on a drug raid with the DEA, and died shortly thereafter. It was particularly hard for everyone down there to take, because Saxon's wound four years ago, the one that forced him to retire for medical reasons, was sustained saving his partner's life. The lieutenant said he remembers the approximate time that case happened, so he'll have someone go through the files and fax every case Saxon worked on at the time to Phoenix. Then Phoenix can pull their files and compare the two.''

''And they'll let us know the results in whatever retirement home we end up in,'' Mike said disgustedly. ''Or maybe just in time to celebrate our murderer's ninetieth birthday. Unless a miracle happens and they get the answer right away, we're still on our own. Do we have the autopsy results on last night's victim yet?''

''I think it's on its way over to us,'' Larry said, rubbing his face with one hand. ''So if we're still on our own, what do we do next?''

''My next move will be to take one of the morgue shots of Relling and bring it to Ms. Grail for identification,'' Mike said, glancing at his watch. It was after eleven, and maybe Tanda would be available for lunch. ''Your job is more important, since I want you to baby-sit Arthur Weddoes. Make a visual check on him every ten or fifteen minutes, and as soon as that court order gets here I want to know about it. And have a stenographer standing by to take a formal statement from Weddoes."

Larry nodded as he walked out, but Mike was too distracted to notice. He was already in the middle of punching in Tanda's telephone number, and looking forward to hearing her voice. The phone rang, and rang again. Mike frowned, wondering if Tanda was out with one or more of the dogs. She'd known he meant to come by with the snapshot of Relling today. Why hadn't she called to tell him she was going out, or at least when she'd be back. Didn't she know that with a murderer still at large, he'd worry?

"Excuse me, Lieutenant, but you have a call on line three." The words were from Ralph, who had put just his head through the door again. Mike nodded to show he'd heard, but didn't immediately switch to line three. Just a couple more rings, and maybe she would answer. She couldn't possibly have gone anywhere dangerous, could she?

Chapter Nine

Tanda pulled up across the street from her brother's house, in the same place she'd parked the day before. There was no one to be seen for a good distance up and down the street, not with how far apart those houses were. But there was something very deliberate about the privacy in that area, more so than where she lived. In her neighborhood the distance between houses was comfortable elbow room; here it was a fortification against intrusion.

There were two cars parked across the street, not terribly close to one another, sedate late-model sedans that didn't look out of place. Her van must look out of place, though, unless someone decided she was here to fix something. Then it would be perfectly acceptable, since certain trades and repair people were one of life's necessary evils.

You're stalling, she told herself silently but sternly. *They're in there waiting for you, and you're afraid to go in. Are you going to sit here for the rest of the day, or turn around and go home?*

Tanda knew she wasn't about to do either of those things, so she took her keys from the ignition and dropped them into her shoulder bag. The fact that she refused to leave didn't mean she didn't want to, but at least she wasn't here alone.

"You stay in the car and be a good boy, Robby," she

said, turning to pat the dog in the back of the van. "I don't know if you'll need to work today, but if you do you're here and ready."

Robby wurfled at the word *work*, but since his leash wasn't being taken he knew the time for it hadn't come. Tanda sometimes thought tracking was a delightful game to the dog, which made the word *work* mean something entirely different for him.

And she was stalling again. Taking a final deep breath, Tanda got out of the van, then walked purposefully toward the wide driveway. She felt she was being watched, and probably was. They'd demanded that she come alone, and were certainly watching to make sure she had.

Tanda was practically to the front door when it began to open, something that made her heart pound harder. She had no idea who would be waiting, and first sight of the person in the doorway was anticlimactic. A short man in his fifties stood there, wispy light hair covering his head in neat patches. His body was round with too much good living, something his very expensive suit couldn't hide. His face was also round and tinged with red, looking as though it should be wreathed in smiles. But there was no smile visible, especially not in his voice.

"It's about time," he said very flatly, watching her approach with dark and narrowed eyes. "You were told to be here at noon, not four or five minutes after."

"Well, I can always turn around and leave again," Tanda said with sudden annoyance, stopping just at the steps. The man was withholding information in a multiple-murder investigation, and he had the nerve to try to scold *her?* "The choice is yours, of course, so just tell me how you want it."

"If you leave, you won't find out what you came to about your brother," he pointed out, but with considerably less absolute authority. He'd backed down so fast, in fact, that Tanda was sure he was pure bully. Ready to run over anyone in his path—unless that anyone showed they were prepared to fight back. Then *he* was the one who stepped aside, with typical bully cowardice.

"I've already decided there's only a small chance I'll find out anything useful at all," Tanda told him, deciding to let him know exactly where she stood. "The reason you asked me here was to get information, not to give it. I don't know what it is you're after, but it must be important if you took the chance to get me here."

The man's face flushed redder, proving Tanda's guess was very close to the mark. He'd obviously been expecting a frightened, bewildered innocent, not Dr. Watson behaving in the way Holmes most approved of.

"If you think you're wasting your time, why are you here?" the man blustered, trying to regain control of the situation. "If it were me, I would have stayed home."

"Yes, I'm sure you would have," Tanda returned dryly, for some reason needing to push the man. "But the reason I'm here should be obvious. A very small chance of learning something isn't the same as no chance, especially since you need something from me. If you want what you need, you'll have to trade for it."

"I see," he answered, not at all happy. "Well, if we're going to trade, you'd better come inside and meet the others you'll be trading with."

He opened the door wider and stepped aside, the spider inviting the fly into his parlor. Despite the bravado Tanda had been showing, she wasn't terribly happy as she began to mount the steps. That "we" in the letter hadn't been camouflage, then. There really were others.

Once Tanda was inside, the man closed the door quietly behind her, then led the way upstairs. There were five other people sitting in or standing around the living room, and even at that hour of the day one of them held a glass of something that was almost certainly alcoholic. The short man left Tanda to more or less put himself with the others, then turned to face her again.

"Everyone, this is Don Grail's sister," he said with a faint smirk supported by the presence of his friends. "Not everyone wanted to do this, Ms. Grail, and one of us even went so far as to walk out before you got here, but the rest of us have grown determined. We believe your brother gave you something before he died, and that's what we want. It will let us find out who's doing these murders, one of which was your brother's. With such a noble end in view, we're sure you won't refuse us."

"So you want me to believe you don't know anything," Tanda said, looking around at all of them. She'd become the center of very intense interest, a position she didn't care for. "But you haven't yet introduced me to your friends, or to yourself, for that matter. Why don't you do that, and then you can tell me what your interest is in all this."

"Don't play with us, girl," another man growled, the one holding the drink. The only woman in the group stood to the back of the others, thin lips pressed into a narrow line. "We had very little patience to begin with, and the last week or so has long since used it up. Give us the key."

The man was quite a bit taller and thinner than the one who had met her at the door, with a face of rugged handsomeness. In age he was anywhere between mid-thirties to mid-forties, worry lines and the slackness of skin caused by heavy drinking making it impossible to tell for sure. He had very light eyes, green, Tanda thought, and once they must have been his biggest asset. Right now they were bleak and bloodshot, matching longish dark hair that looked pulled apart rather than combed. His clothes were casual slacks and shirt but very expensive, something that didn't help *him* any more than it did the short man.

"So the bunch of you think you're next on the murderer's list," Tanda said after a moment, the simple and obvious conclusion still drawing a couple of gasps and paling some faces. "If you haven't run or gone to the police by now, there must be a reason. What is it?"

"My dear child, you must be reasonable," a third man said before the others could speak, his voice as beautiful as golden sunshine on a pond. "If we were able to tell you anything, would we not have done so already? We are desperate strangers begging for your assistance. Surely the goodness so clearly inside you won't allow you to refuse us?"

The sadness and note of pleading in the man's voice were very effective, so strongly felt by everyone there that they stood staring at her again. The man who had spoken was of middle height and weight and indeterminate age, average brown hair and eyes, wearing a conservatively dark suit. He was so unremarkable that Tanda had barely noticed him at first, but that had ended when he spoke. His voice and delivery would have had him stand out in any crowd, and it was almost impossible to disbelieve or ignore him.

Almost impossible. Tanda felt resentment growing inside her, the same sort the short man had bred. He'd tried to bully her to get the upper hand, but this one was twisting at her emotions instead. They both considered her an idiot female who could be forced one way or another into doing what they wanted, but she wasn't about to oblige them.

"I think we'd better get something straight," Tanda said, once again trying to see herself as a coolly competent Watson. "Whatever goodness may be inside me did not bring me here to help a bunch of people who selfishly refuse to tell the police what they know. It doesn't bother any of you that the next victim could be entirely innocent, as long as it isn't one of you. With that in mind I'll tell you yes, Don did leave a key with me before he died. If you want to know where that key is, you'll tell me what I want to know. If you're not in the mood to trade, say so and I'll go home.''

"You silly little bitch!" the woman exploded, coming forward to stand beside the second man. They were all on their feet now, and the two men who hadn't yet spoken were muttering malevolently with nasty expressions on their faces. "Do you think we have to tell *you* anything?" the woman demanded with an ugly sneer. "You aren't anyone we have to worry about, and you'll go home when we say you can. *If* we say you can. Right now you'll tell us where that key is, and you'd better be damn quick about it. If I have to ask again, it won't be until after some of my associates here have had private—conversations—with you. They'll like that, but I guarantee you won't.''

The woman's sudden smile chilled Tanda, a smile that said the woman hoped she would refuse. The sole female member of the group wasn't beautiful or even pretty, but she seemed to think she was. Her too-red hair was intricately curled and arranged, and her unlined face suggested cosmetic surgery. Her pants outfit was silk and in a green that should have looked sleek and fashionable, but the way it clashed with her hair made it seem cheap instead. Her green high-heeled shoes were too high and totally wrong for the outfit, and although the long dangle earrings and bracelet and rings she wore were probably diamonds, matched to the rest they looked like low-grade rhinestones. *No class pretending to be high class,* Tanda thought with distaste. *And vicious on top of it.*

"I'm glad you all have such a high opinion of me," Tanda said at last, fighting to keep her voice from trembling. "Did you really think I'd come here without telling anyone where I was going? Am I supposed to have forgotten there's a murderer running around loose?"

"You didn't tell anyone," the short man scoffed, looking absolutely certain. "You're the kind of female I despise, thinking she's as good as a man and always trying to prove it—at the expense of her betters, I might add. You should have known we chose this house because of the privacy it offered, something we learned about the few times we were your brother's guests. I'll admit I deplore violence, so this is your very last chance. Tell us where that key is."

Tanda looked around at the six faces again, seeing the same thing on every one of them. They were determined to have the key Don had left, and would do anything to get it. They weren't going to tell her anything at all, not when none of them believed she hadn't kept her appointment a secret. There was only one thing she could do, but first she took a deep breath.

"All right, I'll tell you," she said, and the faces of her audience turned avid. "Don didn't leave the key with me, he hid it in my house. When I found it I knew it must be important, so I turned it over to the police. If you want it, you'll have to talk to them about it."

"Ridiculous!" the tall, handsome man shouted, and "I don't believe that!" came from the woman, all of it mixed in with disappointed or furious exclamations from the others. The truth was they didn't want to believe it, and Tanda felt the definite urge to turn and run.

"You'll regret lying to us!" the short man snarled, the red in his round face having deepened. "You didn't give the key to anyone, not when you must have had some hint about how valuable it was. Do you want us to pay you, is that it? Don't you understand we don't have to pay you?"

"And we won't pay," the woman added, her expression even more vicious than earlier. "You'll be the one to pay, for thinking you can lie to us. You—"

"I'm not lying!" Tanda interrupted as forcefully as

possible, her heart thudding again. "I gave the key to the same man I told I was coming here. His name is Mike Gerard, and he's a police lieutenant."

"And that's why you showed up alone?" one of the men who hadn't spoken before scoffed. "How stupid do you think we are? We watched carefully before you arrived, and if we'd seen any cops we would have been gone. Give it up, lady, there's no one here who believes you."

"Yes there is," another voice said, one that made the six people freeze in sudden fear. "*I* believe her, because I'm the one she told."

And then Mike was coming up the stairs the rest of the way, three uniformed officers behind him. Tanda was so relieved she wanted to throw herself at him, but considering the circumstances she only smiled.

"It certainly took you long enough," she said, trying to sound cool and Watson-like. "For a minute there, I thought you'd show up too late to do any good. There wasn't a single sign of any of you when I got here."

"That's because I knew they'd be watching," Mike answered, stopping beside her while his men spread out around the six conspirators. "We saw *you,* though, and as soon as you were inside we came in downstairs through the back. That means we didn't miss much of the conversation."

He turned his head with that to look at the six people, and the way most of them wilted said they saw his expression clearly. His arm had also circled Tanda protectively, making her feel safer than she ever had in her life.

"This won't work, you know," the last of the five men who hadn't spoken said, coming forward to stand in front of the others. "We can make an excellent case for entrapment, and probably even have a basis for a lawsuit against your department. You'll let us all go right now, or you'll have six of the best lawyers in this area all over you in an hour.''

"I don't think so," Mike said as the rest of them began to smirk or get ready to leave. The man who had spoken was the only one of the six who looked as though he belonged in expensive clothes, his neat haircut, clean-shaven face and Italian shoes telling the same story. If he wasn't a lawyer himself then Tanda had never seen one, but Mike wasn't in the least impressed.

"I don't think you'll be going anywhere at all at the moment," he said, ruining the resurgent good mood of the group. "You'd have to go some to prove you were entrapped into a meeting with someone who had no idea you existed before *you* contacted *her*. But aside from that, I can also charge you with illegal entry. None of you has the right to be here, even if you happened to use a key to get in."

"But then you'd have to charge that girl with the same thing," the man said immediately, refusing to be brow-beaten. "If we're here illegally, her joining us makes her just as guilty. Do you expect me to believe you'll arrest *her?*"

"I wish you would stop thinking I know nothing about the law," Mike answered the man's smirk with a sigh. "Ms. Grail told us about your note, and she came here today with both our knowledge and consent. Or was I supposed to forget about that part of it?"

The man no longer had anything to smile about, and the rest of those behind him looked, at the very least, extremely uncomfortable. Tanda thought Mike was doing a great job, but he wasn't through yet.

"And just to make your position perfectly clear, I'm also going to be naming you as material witnesses in six murders," he added, recapturing their attention immediately. "The court won't like it when it hears you have information you refuse to pass on, and will probably find you in contempt and hold you without bail. Six dead bodies tend to affect a court like that, so I suggest you rethink your decision about keeping silent.''

Silent wasn't what they were once they heard that; everyone began speaking or shouting at once, but the apparent lawyer shouted them down.

''We'll want a moment to discuss the matter privately,'' he snarled to Mike, glaring at his associates. ''We'll just step into one of the bedrooms—''

''You'll just step over to the far side of *this* room,'' Mike interrupted to correct, his tone inflexible. ''If I have to arrest you, I don't want to need to chase all over the landscape first. If that doesn't suit you, we may be able to find you a room to talk in at headquarters, after you're booked.''

The man snarled wordlessly this time, then stomped across to the far side of the large living room. The others were furious as they followed, but the only way out available to them was telling Mike what he wanted to know.

''You have no idea how glad I am that you called me before coming to this place,'' Mike murmured while the six people began a low-voiced but bitter wrangling. ''That bunch has to be the worst I've ever seen, and even Attila the Hun would probably need protection from them. If you'd come here alone and somehow managed to survive, I would have strangled you myself.''

''If I'd come here alone, I would have deserved to be strangled,'' Tanda returned quietly with a soft smile. ''It took about ten minutes of thinking last night to decide that, but I was afraid to call you from home. For all I knew, they'd tapped my phone or something, and doing the wrong thing would have thrown away the opportunity.''

''So you called me from a pay phone this morning,'' he said, his dark eyes filled with approval. ''And early enough that we had the time to sneak into position before you got here. That was great work, Watson, far from elementary and definitely capital.''

''I'm delighted you approve,'' Tanda said with a grin that matched his, but then she remembered something she'd wanted to ask him. ''Mike, did you get here soon enough to see someone leave? That man who met me at the door said something about one of them leaving before I got here. That means one of them is still running around loose.''

''We didn't see anyone, so it's a good thing you mentioned it,'' he answered, no longer amused. ''I also didn't hear it being spoken about, so you get a double pat on the back. Do you have any idea who the missing one is?''

''None,'' Tanda answered with a head shake. ''You'll have to ask them about it, but don't worry if they refuse to tell you. I brought Robby with me, so we've got a good chance to find out on our own.''

Mike looked startled, but before he could ask any questions the conference broke up. The six people came forward in a bunch, with the lawyer again as their spokesman, and Tanda realized that that was it. Now maybe they would find out what they needed to know.

Chapter Ten

"We've decided to cooperate with you as far as we can without putting ourselves in jeopardy," the group's spokesman announced, and this time his attitude was close to being grim. "We do, however, refuse to give up our rights against self-incrimination, which full disclosure would certainly accomplish. We'll tell you what we can and you may ask questions, but don't expect an unacceptable question to be answered."

"That's very generous of you," Mike responded dryly. "I'm overwhelmed by your desire to cooperate. Just to test how well you'll do, tell me first about the one of you who left before Ms. Grail arrived. Name and address, please, plus an adequate description."

"I think my answer to that question will be, 'I have no idea what you're talking about'," the man responded at once with a faint but nasty smile. "If there were such a person and you observed the departure, you'd have had someone follow and would therefore need none of those questions answered. Again, if there were such a person and you'd personally heard reference being made to them, you would have asked your question a good deal sooner. I'm sorry, Lieutenant, but if Ms. Grail believes she heard reference to such a person, I'm afraid she's mistaken."

"So you've decided to keep your last member as an

ace in the hole," Mike said as he put away the notebook he'd taken out. Tanda was bristling with anger, but he sounded no more than faintly annoyed. "You think the unknown will get you fast legal help if I decide to arrest you after all, if for no other reason than to make sure he stays anonymous. Personally, I think you're all kidding yourselves, but we'll let that pass for now. Tell me about what's been going on here, and how the bunch of you are involved with the murders."

"It isn't quite accurate to say we're *involved* with the murders," the spokesman corrected immediately. "It's true they've been happening around us and almost in our laps, but they're certainly not *our* doing. Or at least not the doing of most of us. We have our suspicions in the matter, but—"

The easy flow of words broke off, and real fear shadowed across the man's face. An obvious battle was going on inside him, and Tanda noticed that Mike made no effort to hurry the man.

"All right," the spokesman said at last, still looking faintly frightened. "It won't help to keep our privacy if we all end up dead, but if we survive, that privacy is essential. Suppose I tell you a story that could possibly be true elsewhere, but doesn't apply to any of us here. There will be suppositions included that should be helpful to you, as long as you agree there won't be any attempt on your part to dig for greater detail on the extraneous parts of the story. Do you agree?"

"Go ahead," Mike told him with a nod. "Unless I know for certain that your details will give me the murderer I'm after, I'll make no attempt to dig them out. But let's get to it now."

"All right," the man said again, this time taking a deep breath. "Let's assume for the sake of the story that there's a group of people who were—foolish in their youth. They committed minor transgressions they regretted immediately, but it was too late to undo what they'd done. Instead, they tried to put their mistakes behind them, while building honest and worthwhile lives.''

The man had begun to pace, but that didn't distract Tanda from noticing the others. Every single one of them wore the sort of neutral expression that meant they were listening to someone lie on their behalf, and therefore had no intention of interrupting. Tanda wondered briefly just how far those lies went, but the man was continuing, so she put the question aside.

''One day,'' the man said, ''each of those people who had built new, happy lives for themselves, received a terrible shock. Someone had learned about their minor transgressions, and was now threatening to remind people all about them. Now, none of the acts was all that terrible, but no one wants to be reminded about the mistakes they made as a child. It's embarrassing and potentially painful to loved ones, and who is there alive today who doesn't have enemies who would make the incident worse than it was?

''So the people, in order to protect the innocents in their lives, agreed to pay a certain amount each year to the person who threatened their peace. It was, after all, the path of least resistance, and also harmed no one. Two of the people in the group came from the same area, so it was decided that the once-yearly meetings to make the payments would take place in *that* area. With two natives to give advice, the rest of the group would find it easier to blend into their surroundings.''

''Why did there have to be physical meetings?'' Mike interrupted to ask. ''In most—unpleasant—situations of this sort, the payments would be sent to an anonymous post-office box, or left under a bench in a nearby local park. And usually the people involved would be kept as far as possible from one another.''

''The group in our story considered that question themselves,'' the man answered with a nod. ''At first they decided the person threatening them enjoyed exercising power over them, at the same time guaranteeing that no one would be able to set a trap or trace the guilty party. At the very first meeting, part of that theory seemed to be proven. The people were told they must stay in the area an entire month, even though their payments were made shortly after they arrived.

''Two of their number, far worse than the others, were outraged by the order and refused to obey. They made their payments and then left, but they might as well have kept their money. Two days after they returned home, details of what they'd done were made completely public. The two were ruined, and no one ever tried to leave early again. Especially after they were warned that the same would happen to the rest of them without fail, no matter what the reason for their leaving. The group thought it might be some automatic setup keyed to the place each of them stayed. Show up every day, and you're all right. Disappear, and the automatic backup kicks in.''

''And those two never tried to tell anyone they were being blackmailed, or that there were others in the same position?'' Mike asked. ''If for no other reason, you'd think they'd want to ruin the blackmailer's neat little setup.''

''They might have done just that, but they weren't given the opportunity,'' the man answered after clearing his throat. ''As I said, those two were much worse than the rest of the group. They were wanted by the police for terrible crimes, and neither of them lived to be arrested. One was foolish enough to try shooting it out with the officers who came for him, and the other saved everyone the trouble by committing suicide.

''In later years a female member left early, hoping to prevent her lover from running off with another woman, but even that wasn't an adequate excuse. She failed to keep her lover, but when her secret came out he returned—to strangle her to death. There was something about what she'd done, and that she'd done it to get the man to begin with. The details were very sordid, not to mention beyond the point.''

''You said the people in your story believed 'at first' that the arrangement was a power trip,'' Tanda observed, refusing to let herself think of it as anything but a story. ''Does that mean they eventually changed their minds?''

''Very observant, Ms. Grail,'' the man said with a small, ironic bow. ''It does mean exactly that. After the incident with the woman, several years went by. Then, one year, one of the people showed up at the yearly meeting with a different idea. Once everyone was together, the man told the others he believed there was a very good reason for their yearly meetings, and it had nothing to do with power.

''He'd apparently decided everyone was together so that the blackmailer could join them, pretending he or she was a victim just like everyone else. That way he or she could spy on the real victims, in order to judge if any of them was getting to the point of wanting to do something foolish. All plots to uncover the blackmailer's identity would be known on the spot, and once known could be countered. He also believed the blackmailer was using the opportunity to laugh at them.''

''*That* must have caused a small stir,'' Mike observed, too much of an understatement in Tanda's opinion. ''How could they possibly have separated the one sheep from all those goats?''

''The same man, who had obviously been thinking about it, had a suggestion,'' the spokesman answered. ''He said they couldn't discover the blackmailer on the spot, but there was a way to make sure they would know by the following year. All of them would, right there on the spot, write a short description of what they were being blackmailed with. Once that was done, they would immediately go to an attorney, and have all the slips of paper sealed away in a strongbox.

"There would be three keys to open the three locks on the box, and everyone would get a copy of one of the keys, distributing them evenly."

"Just a moment," Mike interrupted. "That arrangement sounds a bit confusing. Are you saying that there were twelve people involved, so each of the people got a copy of one of the keys? If the distribution was even, then there were four people in the group who had the same key."

"That's correct," the man acknowledged. "Three groups of four people, each group having a copy of a different key. That way no one person would be able to open the box alone. The following year, when everyone gathered again, they would bring along the keys and some kind of proof supporting what they'd written on their slip of paper."

"And the one without the proof would be *it*," Mike said, interrupting the narrative. "But wouldn't that be the same as cutting their own throats? I mean, if the blackmailer knew he or she would be exposed the following year, there would be nothing to lose by exposing everyone else first."

"He'd thought of that, too," the man replied, rubbing the back of his neck with one hand. "They would make an arrangement with the lawyer, so that if any of them failed to check in with him once a week during the following year, the lawyer would tell the others. If all but one failed to check in, the box and that one's name would be given to the police.

"The box would also contain a full letter of explanation, along with detailed descriptions of everyone involved, and if no one checked in, again the box would go to the police. If everyone had been exposed, the process of elimination would name the blackmailer, and then those who had been ruined would return the favor by pressing charges.''

"The person who thought up the idea must have decided it wouldn't be possible to disappear completely in a week," Mike observed. "You know, send all the appropriate letters and such, and then take off before check-in time. I don't know if I agree with that."

"That's because you would have nothing really worth taking with you," the spokesman said, all but sneering. "If *you* ran, some clothes and cash would be all you had to worry about. Considering the amounts the blackmailer had taken in over the years, it would be a fortune plus expensive bought-items that he would have to move. And you may not be completely aware of it, but thanks to drug-dealer transactions, transferring large sums of money is almost impossible to do without some government agency being aware of it. No, the blackmailer could not have disappeared in a week, not unless he or she left almost everything behind."

"Or used the year to move things elsewhere a little bit at a time," Mike said. "But what if that disappearance was accomplished sooner? Wouldn't everyone be in danger of exposure then?"

"We—I mean, they were constantly in danger of exposure, not to mention being bled like victims of a vampire," the man disagreed with a shake of his head. "After years of that, most of them were willing to take the chance. And besides, everyone was given the impression that arrangements had been made for all of them to be watched. It's even harder to disappear completely if you're being watched, so exposing the legitimate victims would only be exposing yourself. And it was pointed out that anyone who disagreed with the plan could reasonably be considered the guilty party."

"Ouch!" Mike said with a wry expression. "That's one

way of making sure everyone does what you want. And the blackmailer had to go along, or else be exposed on the spot. Assuming, that is, that he was actually one of the group."

"There are incidents I haven't mentioned that almost guaranteed the fact," the spokesman assured him. "The man used those incidents to convince the others, and soon everyone was in agreement. The object of the game was to discover the identity of the blackmailer, and make some sort of arrangement to guarantee that he never black-mailed the people again. There are ways of doing that that don't include murder, so kindly remove that expression from your face."

"Now we're up to hearing what happened when the people arrived at the meeting place *this* year," Mike said, ignoring the comment about his expression. "Logically they should have gone directly to the attorney involved, and found out what they wanted to know."

"Logically they tried to do just that," the spokesman agreed. "It was necessary to have the attorney present when the box was opened—no, in fact it was vital. They needed someone with an unblemished reputation for honesty as a witness, to offset the—colorful—pasts of the rest of them. The presence of an honest man who could be counted on not to speak out unless they were betrayed, in other words. The box couldn't be opened without him, not and have it accomplish what they wanted it to.

"Unfortunately, it hadn't been possible to arrange a prior appointment with the attorney, an appointment that couldn't be made by just one of them. If just one tried it alone, the others would have been immediately informed. All of them had to be together to do it, and when all of them tried they discovered that the attorney was away taking personal time. He was from a place a couple of towns away from their meeting place, and they wasted half a day and more finding he wasn't available."

That last was said so blandly and in so offhand a way, it made Tanda suspicious. She glanced at Mike to see if he'd noticed the same thing, but Mike was all but ignoring the comment.

"So the group discovered they'd have to wait," he said instead. "And then the murders started happening."

"And then the murders started happening," the spokesman confirmed with a grim nod. "The first one killed was the person who had thought up the idea about identifying the blackmailer, and then others quickly followed. The remaining members of the group were terrified, but they didn't dare go home or anywhere else. One of their number reminded them that releasing information on them could be an automatic procedure, and if so it would happen no matter why they left. The choice was between certain ruin and possible death, which meant there was no choice at all. They had to stay and take their chances.

"And then someone finally came up with a conclusion that should have been obvious sooner." His expression was really grim now, and he'd begun to run a nervous hand through his hair. "The blackmailer had become unhinged from a year of constant worry, and had decided to murder them one by one. There would be no more money coming from any of them, so why would they have to be kept alive? After a lot of—animated—discussion, the majority agreed they would be best off getting the attorney back at once by explaining the emergency, and immediately opening the strongbox. They would then know who the blackmailer-murderer was, and could take whatever action they deemed necessary. That, of course, was when they made a most unsettling discovery."

"That among them, they only had two of the three keys," Tanda said, knowing it for a fact. "There weren't any keys found on any of the victims, otherwise the police would have asked me about the point once other bodies began to show up. What I don't understand is, how did you know I had Don's key?''

"I'm sure I don't know what you're talking about," the man responded stiffly. "It's possible, however, that in my fictional story the man who's idea the whole thing was, warned everyone to hide their keys. If the blackmailer used the delay to steal enough keys, it would take a court order to break the box open. The people would have to identify themselves and prove their right to the contents of the box, and maybe even describe the contents before the court agreed to act.

"All of that was completely out of the question, of course, so hiding the keys was the most practical solution. And since the fictional man in my fictional story had a fictional sister in the area and the people knew he'd been seeing her, what more natural conclusion was there to come to than that she'd been given the key to hold?''

"All very logical," Mike said with a nod. "There were four chances out of five that the key was the very one you needed. It was definitely worth taking the risk to get it, but the risk didn't pay off in quite the way you'd hoped."

The spokesman began some sort of protest, probably to insist again that it was fiction they were discussing, but Mike cut him off.

"Let's not go through that nonsense again," he said, sounding very official and very impatient. "Six people are dead, and one of them wasn't a member of your group but was involved tangentially with it. There's nothing to say there aren't more murders being planned, there's every reason to believe there are, and you've already admitted you think the murderer is one of you. I happen to agree with that opinion, which is why we'll stop playing games right now. The first thing I want is the name and address of the person who left earlier, and then we'll get on to the rest."

"I thought we had your word about not getting us personally involved,'' the spokesman replied, very stiff and pale. ''Under the terms of the agreement—''

''I agreed not to dig for details about your past lives unless those details would give me the murderer,'' Mike interrupted. ''I'm not asking about the past, only the present, and your refusing to name your last member could be viewed as shielding a murderer. If it's possible that any of you could be the one doing this, then—''

''Sorry, but it doesn't work like that,'' the spokesman interrupted in turn. ''We still don't know to whom you're referring, but if there were such a person, it would be someone we all agreed would be incapable of committing the murders. Despite your opinion to the contrary, we aren't stupid, nor are we suicidal. If we ever did shield someone as our 'ace in the hole,' as you put it, it could only be someone like that.''

''And you'd like me to believe you aren't stupid?'' Mike said with a snort of disdain. ''Given the proper circumstance, just about everyone is capable of murder, whether you think they are or not. But I don't have the time to debate philosophy with you. Are you going to tell me what I want to know or not?''

The spokesman, obviously insulted, simply compressed his lips and stayed silent. Tanda saw Mike also looking over the others, but when they stayed just as silent he turned to her.

''Okay, Ms. Grail, it looks like we get to try it your way,'' he said. ''Would you like us to clear the room, or what?''

''No, no, just let everyone stay right where they are,'' Tanda answered, unexpectedly excited over the idea that she and Robby were being given their chance to show what they could do. ''I'll go get Sherlock and be right back.''

Mike grinned at that, but Tanda was already hurrying toward the front door. *Oh, let them have kept their car window down,* she prayed silently. *It's not so hot out that air-conditioning is absolutely necessary, so please...*

Chapter Eleven

Mike heard the low, angry muttering going on among the six people behind him, but made no effort to listen or even to turn around. He hadn't yet asked them to identify themselves, but that was only because he'd been trying to encourage them to talk. They might believe they would walk out of here still as anonymous as they'd been when they'd arrived, but it wasn't going to happen. Now that he'd narrowed down his suspect list to under ten thousand, he had no intention of being sloppy.

But he still wished he'd had the time to ask Tanda what she and the dog were going to do. He *had* to know who the person who had left was, and if necessary he would grill these six until one of them broke down. Even with what their backgrounds had to be, they should be rattled enough now to be easier to handle.

Their backgrounds... Mike took a silent but very deep breath, understanding that Tanda didn't yet realize her brother had truly been one of them. Things were happening too fast and the situation was too personal for her to make the connection, but once she did... Mike decided he'd just have to see to it that he was there when the inevitable happened. No one should have to face something like that alone.

"Okay, we're back," Mike heard, and looking up

showed him Tanda and her dog coming in. Even in jeans and a T-shirt there was something vital and wonderful about her, even more so than the night before. He could spend hours just standing there and watching her.

"Okay, in here we won't have a problem, but once we get outside we'll hopefully need someone in a vehicle to follow us," she told Mike briskly, all business and confidence. "I don't know how far the trail will lead, but Sherlock and I have to follow it on foot. Coming back, though, we'll want to ride."

"You expect to get somewhere using a bloodhound?" the lawyer-type who'd done all the talking asked with a lot of amusement. "You backwoods types are really too funny. What sort of telltale piece of clothing do you think your imagined quarry left, for a *dog* to be of use?"

Most of the others joined in his snide laughter, and that made Mike furious. He was about to tell them exactly what he thought of them, but Tanda did it faster—and better.

"And you ignorant city-types never know just how ignorant you are," she countered with an amused laugh of her own, which banished theirs. "My dog doesn't need a piece of 'telltale' clothing, all he needs is to know that someone was here who isn't here now. He's trained to follow the 'missing' scent, so to speak, to pick it out from all the other scents in the room and follow it alone."

"That isn't possible," the lawyer-type said flatly, a furious look in his cold, dark eyes. "This is some kind of trick, but I'm telling you now it isn't going to work."

"It's no trick, and it *will* work," Tanda returned with such serene confidence that the man clamped his mouth shut again. "Are you ready, Lieutenant Gerard?"

"As soon as I make the arrangements we need," Mike said, wishing he could hug her. Instead, he used the radio he held to call Larry and Rena, who waited outside with more uniforms. Larry would take Mike's place here in the house once he and Tanda and the dog left, and Rena would follow them in an unmarked unit while they followed the trail. When everything was settled, he nodded to Tanda.

"Okay, here we go," she said, then bent to pat the dog. "Okay, Robby, find 'em! Find 'em, boy!"

The dog, who had been standing quietly until then, suddenly became a different animal. His long face went down to the carpeting as though looking for a visible trail, his big brown body all but quivering with sudden excitement. He cast around for what seemed like no time at all, and then he bayed once, briefly, and headed for the door.

"He's got it," Tanda said with a grin over her shoulder, letting the dog pull her along by the leash. "Let's go."

The six people stood staring with frowns on their faces, still obviously convinced they were having a trick played on them. Mike wasn't too sure himself about what was happening, but that didn't keep him from immediately following Tanda.

As soon as Mike stepped outside, Larry and two more uniforms went in. Larry could be trusted to handle the group without letting himself be pushed around, and Rena would be invaluable backup if it turned out they needed backup. Rena Foreman had more sense than most people, and could be counted on to stay cool and in control no matter what happened. Besides, she'd earned being in on what might be the first and only arrest.

Tanda and her dog were hurrying down the wide driveway, and when they reached the end of it they turned right. Mike hurried to catch up, and when he did he saw the dog stop in the empty space between two parked cars. Tanda watched the dog closely, but Robby didn't even take as much time as he had in the house. One baying bark and he was heading up the street, and Tanda turned a radiant face toward Mike.

"They left the car window open!" she called back glee-fully. "Don't just stand there, come on!"

Mike turned to gesture Rena, in her car, after them, and then he did come on. He caught up to Tanda after a minute, then concentrated on keeping up.

"It's a lucky thing I'm in decent shape," Mike said after they'd settled down to a steady pace. "I'd feel silly if you or Sherlock ended up having to carry me."

"Oh, I'd be the one who had to do the carrying," Tanda assured him with a grin. "Sherlock won't let him-self be interrupted while he's working, not even by the person he's working for."

"Well, the person he's working for is too impressed to mind that," Mike returned with a laugh. "I can't believe he actually found a trail to follow in the midst of all those people."

"Oh, that wasn't a lot of people," Tanda told him, and her expression said she was serious. "There could have been twice that number, and he still would have been able to do it. He found the scent that didn't match to anyone in the room, and that's how he knew which one to follow. It's really quite simple."

"'Simple for you, difficult for me,'" Mike paraphrased wryly. "I'm just glad you're on my side."

"I'd be happier that Robby is on your side," she re-torted with a pleased smile. "He's the one with all the talent."

"That doesn't happen to be true, but we can argue about it later," Mike said. "Specifically, when I have the breath to spare for it."

Tanda smiled again, but made no effort to keep the conversation going. It was clear she was used to trotting along behind the dog, but Mike wasn't. If he expected to keep up, he'd be wise to save his breath.

Robby led them to the end of the street, then unhesi-tatingly turned right. They were now on a county road, and although there wasn't a lot of traffic, there was still some. Mike glanced over his shoulder from time to time, and gestured any cars coming up behind Rena into going around them. Their procession moved directly up the center of the road, and Mike felt safer having Rena's car blocking for them.

The county road kept going, but after what seemed like a couple of miles Robby left it for a side road. This neighborhood wasn't far from the center of town, and the street was quiet with the serenity of a dignified older age. Tall and stately trees lines both sides, and the houses were far from new but beautifully kept up. There wasn't as much distance between the houses as there had been in Don Grail's neighborhood, but somehow the lack wasn't a lack. The other neighborhood might have represented more money; this one represented breeding and class.

"I think we're almost there," Tanda told him suddenly, the first words they'd exchanged since they'd started. "If memory serves, this street dead-ends in another block or two. You can't use it to go anywhere else, only to one of these houses."

"You're right," Mike confirmed, happily having gotten his second wind. He *was* in good shape, regular visits to the gym having made sure of that. "Once we know for certain we've reached the right place, you and Robby get to step aside. With the hard part done, Rena and I will hog the easy part."

"The easy part, right," she muttered in answer, momentarily looking disturbed. Their quarry could well be the serial killer, and Tanda's expression said she knew it. But it also said she would stay back out of harm's way, and that was all Mike was concerned about.

They kept going for two-thirds of the length of the block, and then Robby veered left. The house he headed toward was a very neat tan and cream, with a wide front porch and recently mowed lawn. In the driveway stood a midsize Toyota, also in tan. The driver's window was open, and the dog paused for an instant to sniff the ground beside the car before heading directly toward the house's front door.

"Hold on," Mike called softly to Tanda. "We'll take it from here."

"We'll be ready in case there's more than one person in the house," Tanda whispered back, taking the dog with her to one side of the house. Calling him off seemed to disappoint Robby, but he also knew he'd done well and didn't refuse to obey.

Mike waited until Rena came up, then gestured her around toward the back of the house. There was almost certain to be a back or side door, and Mike didn't want to have to follow behind Robby again. He waited until he was sure Rena was in position, and then he climbed the steps, crossed the porch and knocked.

For a moment there was no answer, and then Mike heard, in a sharp female voice, "Who is it?"

"It's the police, ma'am," Mike answered from his place to one side of the door. "We need to speak to you for a minute."

"Of all the foolishness," the woman responded, obviously short-tempered and annoyed. "Very well, I'll be right there."

Mike immediately wondered why there would be a delay before the woman could open the door, but the answer to that might be anything. There could be food cooking that might burn if the heat wasn't turned off, or she might not be fully dressed, or—

Or she might be using the time to sneak out the back door. Mike heard Rena's shouted, "Halt!" just an instant before Robby began to bay, and then they were all racing around to the back. The dog got there first, of course, but the two humans tied for second place.

The backyard was enclosed by a short white wooden

fence and gate, and Rena stood beside a large shade tree with her weapon drawn. The person she covered looked furious rather than frightened, and Mike quickly stepped through the gate to head off trouble.

"You didn't mention you'd be stepping outside before coming to the door, ma'am," he commented as he moved closer to the woman, pulling out his badge and ID. "I'm Lieutenant Gerard, and that's Sergeant Foreman. Please identify yourself."

"You're the one coming to *my* house, young man!" the woman snapped, drawing herself up straighter. She was of average height but on the thin side and not particularly young, with hands clasped rigidly in front of her. Not to mention the fact that she looked tougher than nails. "Suppose you tell me who you're looking for, and I'll tell you if they're here."

"I'm looking for the person who came to this house in that car," Mike answered, gesturing behind him to the car in the driveway. "Was that by any chance you?"

"Whether it was or was not is none of your business," the woman said, her tone and stare as cold as winter seas. "I know my rights under the law, and if a car like mine was seen somewhere, you first have to prove it was mine, and then that I was in it. You can't—"

"That's enough," Mike interrupted, fighting to keep his temper. "I'm getting really tired of having the law explained to me by every second person I talk to. A car like yours wasn't *seen* anywhere, it was followed here from another location. As for the driver of the vehicle— Ms. Grail, if you turn your dog loose, will he go after the driver of that car again?"

"He certainly will," Tanda said, holding Robby tight as she came up to join Mike. "He hates to end a hunt without actually reaching the fugitive."

The dog was now whining and trying to work himself free, his full attention on the woman they all stared at.

The woman herself, although still looking furious, now looked pale as well.

"If you dare to release that animal anywhere near me, I'll sue," she said, faint trembling in her voice. "You have no right to do this or be here, especially not with an animal dangerous to innocent people. The courts support me in that, and—"

"No, they don't, Miss Baderlie," Rena interrupted the woman, her weapon still out and her grin strong. "The courts know the value of a well-trained bloodhound, and allow their following of a trail into evidence against an accused. I'm surprised at you for making that mistake— or were you just trying to bluff?"

"You know her, Rena?" Mike asked as the older woman drew herself up even farther in outrage and insult. "If so, I'd like to be introduced."

"Certainly, Mike," Rena answered with a small, evil smile. "This is Miss A. Baderlie, head research librarian at the town library, one of the rudest, most intolerantly nasty people it's ever been my displeasure to meet. I had some research to do a couple of years ago, and she made my life miserable because I wasn't doing it for what she considered a worthwhile purpose. Just because she's worked at the library forever, she thinks she owns it. I've always hoped that someday I might return the courtesy, and I think I can do that by pointing out some of the woman's vital statistics—she's about five-five or five-six, about a hundred twenty-five pounds, is obviously not athletic and owns a midsize car with worn steel-belted radials that might match certain casts taken out at Ms. Grail's place."

"The intruder trying to break into my house!" Tanda exclaimed while Mike silently patted Rena on the back. That thought had already occurred to him, but he'd been on the scene and taken the report. Rena had only read

about the incident, but obviously she did well with remembering details.

"I want a lawyer," Miss Baderlie announced, even
more pale now and her voice trembling noticeably. "I
demand that you let me call a lawyer."

"All in good time, Miss Baderlie," Mike answered.
"There are certain procedures to be taken care of first,
and then we'll be charging you. Right after that you can
call a lawyer."

The woman clamped her lips together and glared, still
trying to intimidate him as though he were a child subject
to her whims and discipline. Mike, never having found
that sort of tyrant particularly impressive, ignored her and
went about his business. The additional units and forensics teams he called would be there as quickly as the
search warrant was issued, and while he waited for the
teams he let Robby complete his hunt.

Rena went inside and unlocked the front door, and then
the dog took Tanda through the house and directly up to
the sullen Miss Baderlie. There was no doubt in anyone's
mind that the librarian was the one who had been in Don
Grail's house, and even she was no longer bothering to
deny it.

Mike placed Miss Baderlie under arrest and read the
woman her rights, then let Rena and one of the uniforms
take her to headquarters. A private word with Rena made
sure the booking procedure would be as long and drawn-
out as possible, and while the team began to go through
the librarian's house, Mike drew Tanda aside for a private
word. She'd been keeping herself and her dog out of the
way, but her earlier excitement and elation seemed to have
disappeared completely.

"Are you all right?" Mike asked, wishing he could
hold her in his arms. "Is it the end of the chase that's the
letdown, or is it something else?"

"I believe I've had just a little too much time to think,"

she answered with a wan smile, sitting down on a stone bench in front of some flowers. "When those people back at Don's house started talking about blackmail, you weren't surprised. It also finally and really came through that Don was one of them. He was also being blackmailed about something, and I think you already know what it was."

"Only in general," Mike admitted, sitting down beside her. "I had no idea how to tell you, though, not without hurting you. I can tell you now, if you like, or not if you don't. There *is* something you do have to know, though. You're your brother's heir, and there's a very large estate involved."

"Which means I'd better hear what you have to say even if I don't want to," she responded with a sigh. "How did you find out I was his heir?"

"We located your brother's attorney," Mike said, and then explained what he'd learned and what he'd been involved with when her call came that morning. "So I left Mr. Weddoes in my captain's charge until the court order came through, and tore out to meet you at your brother's house."

"No wonder you didn't blink when that man told you the lawyer handling the matter for them was from out of town," she said, obviously trying to shake off depression. "You didn't have to ask who he was because you already knew. And that expression the spokesman showed when he mentioned an out-of-town lawyer probably meant he thought you'd never find the man. But it looks like my brother was a man who killed his own wife for her money. I wonder if he took me out to dinner just to make everyone *think* he'd given me his copy of the key."

"That I doubt," Mike said at once, giving in to the urge to cover one of her hands with his. "Your brother would have done that only if he meant to leave the key elsewhere than in your house, which he obviously didn't.

If I had to bet on it, I'd say he was looking forward to not being blackmailed anymore so that you and he could get reacquainted. I'm sure he stayed away from you until then because he didn't want to get you involved in his troubles.''

Her hand was resting on her jeans-covered knee with his on top of hers, but she didn't seem aware of the touch. Her lovely gray eyes searched his face as though looking for answers to questions she couldn't put into words, and then she smiled faintly but very, very warmly.

"You really are the most wonderful man," she murmured, turning her hand so that she might touch him as well. "You have no idea whether that's true or not, but you said it just to make me feel better. I should scold you for fibbing, Mr. Holmes, but instead I'd rather thank you."

"It was my pleasure, Ms. Watson," Mike answered with what had to be the most ridiculous smile. "I always enjoy doing a service for invaluable assistants who think I'm wonderful. There aren't too many of those around, you know, so they're very precious to me."

Mike had never been very good with words in personal situations, but the softly amused look in those beautiful gray eyes said he hadn't done all that badly. They might have sat there smiling at each other for the rest of the day, if one of the uniforms hadn't come over and cleared her throat.

"Excuse me, Lieutenant, but they want you back at headquarters," she said, looking around at the garden rather than at him and Tanda. "They want you to hurry."

"I can probably guess why," Mike muttered, getting to his feet. "Seven people yelling about their rights and demanding to be released. Tell them I'll be right there."

The cop nodded and headed back to the house, and Mike turned toward Tanda again.

"I think you'd better be in on this," he said to her.

"You're the one who almost had her house broken into, the one who tracked the missing group member from your brother's house, and finally are his legally named heir. If we have a problem with any of that, you may have to play outraged private citizen."

"Don't forget that those six at the house threatened me," she said, also getting to her feet. "If you do need an outraged citizen, you'll get one in spades."

"Good," Mike said with amusement. "It's about time somebody ganged up on *them*. I had your van brought over from the house, so you can follow me to headquarters as soon as I check to see what the forensics team has found."

Lora Clark, standing outside the back door near the driveway, dangled a plastic bag filled with shoes at him. She also pointed to the two people taking tire impressions from the librarian's car, and her smile said she'd just eaten two or three canaries rather than just one. Lora wasn't the sort to say anything until she confirmed her guesswork in the lab, but if there had been any doubt she wouldn't have been smiling. Mike had definitely found the woman who had tried to break into Tanda's house.

Now all he had to do was narrow a group of seven down to a single serial killer.

Chapter Twelve

Tanda was glad she'd left Robby in the van when she followed Mike into headquarters. The place was like a quiet madhouse, with people rushing wordlessly from place to place. They all looked as if they didn't dare simply walk, not when there were so many important things to do. When a phone rang, someone answered it quickly, almost with a sense of relief. If they were on the phone, they could stop rushing around for a while.

"I'll bet any amount you name that the commissioner's been here, maybe even with the mayor," Mike told her very softly. "His visits always have this sort of effect, especially if he's unhappy."

"Why would he be unhappy?" Tanda whispered back. "You've just about got this case solved."

"Not quite," he answered, once again sounding frustrated. "I have the list of suspects narrowed down to seven, which isn't the same as having it solved. You have to remember that six of those seven people are, at least as far as the murders are concerned, innocent."

"And the commissioner is worried about suits for false arrest," Tanda said, the revelation finally hitting her. "You know, there are times I feel really sorry for professional politicians. They always have to worry about doing the politically expedient thing rather than the right thing."

"The biggest problem is that everyone defines 'right' differently," Mike told her. "I consider it right to inconvenience six people in order to catch a murderer, but too many judges consider the six's comfort to be more important than preventing a theoretical next murder. They—Hey, Larry, what's happening? As if I didn't know."

"We're getting a lot of static, Mike," the detective who had just come over said. He was the one who had taken over at Don's house for Mike, and he looked furious as well as worried.

"List the static in order of importance," Mike said, leading the two of them toward a small office in the far right-hand wall. "Ms. Grail is here to consult with us, as well as to give as much help as she can."

"Good," the detective named Larry said with a brief but warmly real smile for Tanda. "Then I have first dibs on standing behind her when the commissioner comes back looking for more blood to spill. The first thing that didn't work right was that court order you asked him to get. The judge he meant to use is away on vacation, and the one he had to go to refused to do more than direct Weddoes to talk to us if what he knows is directly related to one or more of the six murders. If it isn't, then Weddoes isn't released from being bound by privilege."

"I should have expected that, but I think we have it beat," Mike told him with a clap on the shoulder. "I learned from those six at the house that there's a strongbox containing pertinent statements to this case, and Weddoes could be the only one, besides Don Grail, who was allowed to know where it was. Eleven of the statements are true and one is a lie, that last being the statement of the person who was blackmailing the other eleven. Five of those twelve people are dead, and if we don't get them sorted out fast, the other six victims will be next. Find Weddoes and tell him—"

"Uh-uh, no good, Mike," Larry interrupted with one

hand raised. "As soon as the commissioner came by with the sad news about the court order, Weddoes left. He said he couldn't possibly state in truth that he knew something that related directly to the murders, he only suspected it was so. What he did know, though, was that he wasn't going to let his sense of ethics get him killed. I had a hunch, so I called his office to check a little while ago. Mr. Weddoes has left town again, and his assistant doesn't know where he's gone, or when he'll be back. Personally, I don't think he *will* be back, not until we have the murderer behind bars."

"Well, they do say timing is everything," Mike remarked as he stopped to rub his eyes with one hand. "So far our timing has stunk to high heaven, and if we don't want any more bodies we'd better do something about it fast. Larry, put out a material witness APB on Mr. Weddoes. DMV can tell you what he drives and what his plate number is."

"Assuming he took his own car," Larry said with a nod. "No, *hoping* he took his own car. The next major static is coming from the six we brought in. If they're not going to be charged, they demand to be released, and so forth and so on. You'd better take care of it before the captain has to be charged with *your* murder."

"I'll talk to the captain," Mike said with a weary sigh. "You take care of the APB, and then come back to help me with the interviews. We *will* be charging those six, but not with anything that will keep them from getting bail. Before that happens, I have to try to get through to at least one of them."

Larry nodded again and left, and Mike led Tanda into the small office they'd been heading toward. Once they were inside, he gestured toward a chair.

"You might as well make yourself comfortable there," he told her with a smile. "Larry should be back by the time I'm finished with the captain, and then I'll put you in a room where you can watch the interviews. I'm hoping you'll pick up something I don't.''

"What is it you want to get through to those people?" Tanda asked, looking up at him. "And why won't you be charging them with anything serious enough for them to be held on?"

"The only charge I had where they might have been refused bail was withholding evidence in a murder investigation," Mike explained. "But that related to the identity of their last member, and we found her without their help. Now all we have is unlawful trespass, conspiracy to commit burglary and the threat to commit serious bodily harm. Even with all of that together the court will have to grant bail, and they're all rich enough to pay it."

"And what do you want to get through to them about?" Tanda prompted, wishing she could sit down and pull his head into her lap. If ever a man needed brow-stroking desperately, Mike Gerard was it.

"I have to make one of them understand that cooperating with us is the only way they're guaranteed to stay alive," he answered with a sigh. "In order to separate out the blackmailer among them, we have to confirm the crimes of the ones *being* blackmailed. That means they have to talk about what they're guilty of, and I don't think I can get them to do that. I do have to try, but I doubt if I'll get anywhere."

"I think it's just about guaranteed that you won't," Tanda said, hating to say that to him. "If any of them was more afraid of dying than being exposed, they would have left when the bodies began to turn up. Since they're all still here…''

"Yes, unfortunately I see it the same way," Mike agreed heavily. "And that in itself is really strange. If it were me, I'd rather have to change my name and move again. You'd think if they'd already done it once… Well, I'd better get in to see the captain."

She nodded and watched him leave, then sat down in the chair he'd shown her to. She'd thought it was almost over, but after everything that had happened, they were only a little better off than they'd been earlier. Seven people, and one of them was a sickly twisted murderer...

Tanda had some time to think, more, actually, than she either wanted or needed. When Mike finally came back, Larry was with him, but so was an older man with graying blond hair, a mustache to match, very cold blue eyes and the sort of square jaw normally seen only on Dick Tracy. That meant there would be a delay in telling Mike what had occurred to her, but maybe it wouldn't be much of a delay.

"Ms. Grail, this is Captain Daniel Rich," Mike said once the three men were in the office. "Captain, Ms. Grail has been cooperating with us in an effort to find her brother's murderer. I'm not exaggerating when I say that if not for her, we'd still be completely in the dark."

"That's quite a compliment, Ms. Grail," Captain Rich said in a voice that could only be described as grave, nodding rather than offering his hand. "Most civilians don't get that deeply involved in official police matters, even if the lieutenant in charge thinks they should be. I'm sure you'll understand if I say I regret the need, but—"

"But you think I'm intruding," Tanda interrupted, having already gotten the message. "You're of the opinion that I can't possibly be of help, so you'd like me to run along home and play with my dolls."

"Now, Ms. Grail, I certainly wouldn't put it quite that way," the captain began, watching her get to her feet. "It isn't that your efforts aren't appreciated—"

"It's just that you don't appreciate them as much as the other police departments I've worked with," Tanda interrupted again. "My dogs are rather well known in some police circles, but not only because of *their* ability. In order to train a bloodhound to be really useful, you have to know what a police department will require in the way of skills. Helping them out yourself means being able to train a more useful dog.''

''You've helped other departments?'' Captain Rich asked, picking up on the point Tanda had been shoving at him. ''Well, I'm sure you were very valuable, but—''

''But not as valuable as I was to your people today,'' Tanda finished for him again. ''If not for me and my dog, you'd still be missing the last member of that loathsome club. And on top of that, I now know why none of them will help you find the blackmailer. No matter how frightened they are, they can't afford to help you.''

''What have you come up with, Tanda?'' Mike asked at once, taking his turn at cutting off the captain by stepping out in front of him. ''What did you see that I missed?''

''But you didn't miss it, Mike,'' Tanda told him with a smile. ''You were the one who saw it first, but you didn't have the time to think about it. You said that if it were you, you would move and change your name again rather than sit around waiting to die. After all, they'd already done it once. But Mike—what if this time you wouldn't be *allowed* to simply move and change your name? What if being exposed meant more than just a little bad publicity? What if this time the police would be actively looking for you—''

''Because they now have proof that you did do what they only suspected you of before!'' Mike finished triumphantly, coming forward to hug her. ''Tanda, you're wonderful. You just saved me a ton of wasted effort.''

''You mean *that's* what they were being blackmailed with?'' Larry asked with a whistle. ''Proof that they were guilty of what they were originally suspected of? No wonder they don't know which way to turn. Like the old saying goes, 'Damned if you do and damned if you don't.' ''

''That's something all of us should have seen,'' Captain

Rich said with a frown, but not for those around him. "It would be easy to say we missed it because it was too obvious, but I'm not going to. Instead I'll say, 'Thank you for agreeing to consult with us on this, Ms. Grail,' and just get out of the way."

This time his nod was accompanied by a smile, and then he left the office. Mike still had one arm around Tanda, but she wasn't about to ruin things by mentioning it.

"And thank you for handling that so well," Mike murmured as soon as the captain was gone. "Rich has no imagination at all, but what makes him a good captain is the ability to recognize the trait in others. And to understand that somebody who won't be stepped on is somebody you don't push. I'm sure you noticed he'd decided he didn't want any civilians around."

"As long as I was able to change his mind," Tanda said comfortably. "So what happens now?"

"Now we interview the—victims," Mike said, unfortunately while stepping away from her. "What we need from them is a slip, either telling us they know more than they're admitting, or giving us an indication that we're talking to the blackmailer. Larry, you'll be in the interview room with me, and Tanda, you'll be watching from the next room with Rena. That makes four on our side, which should be pretty good odds."

Mike led the way out of his office, and it didn't take long before Tanda and the detective named Rena Foreman were tucked away in the small observation room. They were recording what was being said in the interview room, but Rena was also prepared to take notes. Tanda liked both Rena and her partner, Larry, who brought in the first interviewee.

"This one has identified himself as Richard Draper," Rena supplied for Tanda's sake, speaking softly but not in a whisper. "He looks and talks like a prosperous, high-powered lawyer, but hasn't claimed to be one."

"Probably because he isn't one any longer," Tanda murmured back, staring at the man who had been the spokesman in Don's house. "Whatever he did must have brought him more money than a successful law practice had."

"Which would be a hell of a lot of money," Rena agreed, then turned her full attention to the scene through the one-way glass. Richard Draper took the chair opposite the one Mike already sat in, a plain wooden table between them. Larry stayed on his feet, leaning against a wall behind Draper, but the man paid no attention to him.

"It certainly took you long enough, Lieutenant," Draper said angrily to the top of Mike's head. "And you will do me the courtesy of looking at *me* rather than at that file, no matter how absorbing it happens to be."

"As a matter of fact, it's not absorbing at all," Mike said, then raised his head to look directly at the man. "What I'm trying to do is think of something to say beyond telling you what you'll be charged with. We found your seventh, by the way. You know, the one you claimed didn't exist?"

"Why, how talented of you, Lieutenant," Draper drawled as he leaned back. "Finding someone who doesn't exist. It's a wonder you can do that, and yet still have no idea who a multiple murderer is."

"But I do have an idea, Draper," Mike countered with a very faint smile. "The murderer is one of your group of seven. And after meeting Miss Baderlie, I can't imagine why you and your group consider her beyond suspicion."

Draper's mocking smile disappeared, proving he'd thought Mike was bluffing about having found the woman. The truth put the man off balance, which was just the way Tanda knew Mike wanted him.

"I said, I want to know why the rest of you consider

her beyond suspicion," Mike repeated, the words mild but remorseless. "If you find the question too intrusively personal, I'll probably start to think you have a reason for not cooperating."

"A reason like that I'm the murderer?" Draper asked, but the scornful tone he'd been trying for wasn't there. "Now you're taking lessons from one of our late members. But you're right, there's no reason why I shouldn't answer. We eliminated Miss Baderlie as a suspect because she can't stand the sight of blood. Some years ago, when we were all together, one of us cut himself on a piece of broken glass. The wound was small, but as soon as it began welling blood, Miss Baderlie fainted. That's squeamishness to the point of incapacitation."

"Considering how the murderer kills, I see your point," Mike said. "And you don't believe it's possible she faked the reaction? It would be a good way to throw everyone off the track."

"When it happened years before this started?" Draper countered, and this time there was ridicule in his voice. "I know some people plan well in advance, but that's ludicrous. Besides, it wasn't the first or only time it happened to her. She was still groggy when she came to, and complained bitterly about being shamed so often by her only weakness."

"Okay, so all of you remembered that and eliminated her as a suspect," Mike said. "What reason did she give for not staying around with the rest of you to speak with Ms. Grail?"

"Is this absolutely necessary?" Draper complained, back to impatience. "I know you're not going to charge us, so—"

"But I *am* going to charge you," Mike interrupted evenly. "Ms. Grail has signed a complaint against all of you for threatening her with bodily harm, and I'm right now trying to decide whether or not to add the charge of conspiracy to commit burglary. The more you refuse to answer my questions, the more convinced I become that I should.''

"What burglary?" Draper asked with a snort. "You said yourself that being in Grail's house was no more than illegal entry and trespass, if that. Since we took nothing and intended to take nothing, you can't possibly call it burglary."

"I was talking about Miss Baderlie's attempted burglary at Ms. Grail's house," Mike returned, obviously watching the man closely. "The—*lady*—left shoe prints and tire tracks behind, which will let us prove conclusively that it was her. Since she's also been proven to be a member of your group, a charge of conspiracy against the rest of you isn't beyond reason."

"Since I knew nothing about that, I won't have any trouble getting such a charge dismissed," Draper told him stiffly, fingers gently tapping the table. The man denied things with every other breath, but this time Tanda believed him. Unless she was very much mistaken, he hadn't known about Miss Baderlie's nighttime excursion.

"How much trouble you'll have getting the charge dismissed isn't the point," Mike said, still looking straight at him. "Since multiple murders are involved here, the judge will want to know how cooperative you've been before he sets bail. Less cooperation will mean a higher bail, and although you'll probably have no trouble paying it, making the arrangements will undoubtedly take longer. Do you really want to be turned loose even as little as an hour after everyone else?"

This time Draper went pale, and Tanda didn't blame him. If one of the others was the murderer and was released first, Draper could find the killer waiting for him when *he* got out. No one could have found that picture pleasing or attractive, and the former lawyer was no exception.

"Miss Baderlie, as a resident of this area, feared Ms. Grail would recognize her," Draper said at last, his voice nearly lifeless. "The point was a valid one, so after a brief discussion we agreed she could leave. She was also against the rest of us revealing ourselves, but *that* we didn't agree with. The situation was serious enough to justify the risk."

"Now tell me about the others," Mike said with an encouraging nod. "Nothing personal or secret, just your opinion of them. You must have thought about who the murderer could be, or someone else it couldn't possibly be."

"Of course I've thought about it," Draper growled, running a hand through his hair as he tried to glare at Mike. "I've thought of very little else, and it's almost impossible. Any of them could be guilty, even the cowardly ones. How much strength or effort does it take to shove a knife into someone? All it takes is the desire, and one of them certainly has that. I wouldn't meet one of them alone for any amount you could name, and as far as I know, everyone else feels the same."

"Is there anything else you can think of to tell me?" Mike asked, casually looking through the file in front of him. "Do any of you have real, provable alibis for any of the murders? Do any of you have no alibi for all of them? Were all of you told where the strongbox was being kept, or only a small number of you?"

"Only the lawyer and Grail knew where the strongbox was being kept," Draper answered without thinking. "What good would the plan be, if anyone could walk off with the box containing our evidence? And the attorney was constrained not to reveal the location of the box unless one of each key was presented to him, with all living members of the agreement there before him. That's why we needed Grail's key, which had to be a copy of the one we were missing.

"As far as alibis are concerned, none of us has anything worth mentioning. When we were all in this area we got together occasionally, but the rest of the time avoided each other. We don't like each other, you see, so we spent as little time in each other's company as possible. We also had no interest in making friends in this dismal little backwater, so that leaves each of us on his or her own."

"Which now makes for a real problem," Mike said, closing the file and leaning back. "I'm returning you to your holding cell, Mr. Draper, where you'll wait until I've finished interviewing the rest of your group. You'll all be charged together and allowed to call attorneys together— unless someone proves uncooperative. That sort will face a very short delay in being released—but there *will* be a delay. I trust I can count on you not to speak to the others about what we discussed?"

"You know you can, damn you," Draper growled, getting stiffly to his feet. "I intend to survive this, Gerard, and once it's all over—"

"Let's go, Draper," Larry interrupted in a voice like stone. "You can daydream on your own time."

Draper switched his poisonous glare to Larry, but gave it up after a moment when he saw how unimpressed the detective was. He stomped out of the room with Larry right behind him, and once the door was closed Mike looked at what was a mirror on his side of the wall.

"And that should help to soften up the others," he said to Tanda and Rena despite not being able to see them. "They'll be able to tell he didn't come out a winner, and his refusal to comment will make it worse. Did either of you notice anything we in here might have missed?"

"What you couldn't have missed was the answer we hoped we wouldn't get," Rena said after pressing a switch. "The lawyer Weddoes *is* the only one left who knows where the strongbox is, and the man has disappeared. If we don't find him, we could be stopped dead again."

"Excuse me, but I've thought of something," Tanda put in before Mike could speak again. "About that strong-box, and how sure everyone is that the blackmailer can be found because he or she is the only one who didn't commit any crime. I know that the idea was Don's and everyone thought it was a good one, but how do we know it's true? Is there some natural law demanding that a blackmailer can't also be guilty of another crime as well?"

Rena stared at her and Mike tried to, both of them all but openmouthed. Dead silence stretched for a long moment, and then Mike put his head back and groaned.

"I don't believe we assumed it was true because *they* assumed it," he complained, self-disgust very clear. "With a case like this, you're not supposed to make any assumptions, and here we sit—Rena, I'm considering resigning."

"Not before me, you don't," she denied, no less disgusted with herself. "We can do it together, and then make sure they give the job to Tanda."

"If you threaten me like that again, I won't help anymore," Tanda said with a self-conscious grin. "I wouldn't have the job of running this investigation for anything, and as I said before, you're missing these things because you aren't being given time to think. And speaking about missing things, did you notice that Draper really didn't know Miss Baderlie had tried to break into my house?"

"Yes, it did look that way," Mike agreed, Rena simply nodding. "He may just be a very good liar, but it's worth trying to see if any of them knew. Rena, I'd like you to do something for me. Put someone on finding out if Miss Baderlie's doctor knows about her habit of passing out at the sight of blood."

"Two will get you five her doctor is on Mars, hunting

aliens from Jupiter," Rena commented, showing how fitting it was for her to be partners with Larry. Despite the wisecrack, though, she closed the speaker switch on their side and left the room. A moment later the door opened again in Mike's room, and this time it was the short man who had met Tanda at the door in Don's house. He came in looking very nervous, with Larry just behind him, and sat down so carefully he must have thought the chair was gimmicked.

"Mr. Miles Rayburn," Mike said, looking up from the file to give the frightened man a cold stare. "You're going to be charged, Mr. Rayburn, and the details are as follows."

Then Mike went through the same routine he had with Draper, but found fewer threats to counter. Miles Rayburn had nothing in the way of an openly hostile attitude, and shrank even more with every accusation leveled at him. Learning they knew about Miss Baderlie frightened and shocked him, and he babbled out answers to all questions. Rena had returned about halfway through the interview, so once Rayburn was gone and Mike turned his head toward them, Rena clicked on the intercom.

"That one has to be really dangerous," Rena said, and Tanda could see the disturbance in her eyes. "From what you said about the way he acted with Tanda in her brother's house, his current reaction is pathological. He throws his weight around against anyone he considers helpless, but crawls in the presence of those he knows to be stronger. That sort boils with resentment and hatred on the inside, and is very unstable. If he comes across someone he can safely take his frustrations out on, he'll do it."

"Which means he's capable of murder, but maybe not blackmail," Mike said with a nod of agreement. "Even an unknown blackmailer has to have enough guts to start the thing, and Rayburn might not qualify. Unless he was able to pump himself up in private, and then took encouragement from success.''

"And it was impossible to tell whether or not he knew about Miss Baderlie's burglary attempt,'' Tanda put in, impressed by Rena's profiling abilities. "Flooding people with all that shock and fear sets up a barrier in front of your real feelings and reactions, and I'm sure he knows it. He didn't tell us a thing we didn't already know.''

"But he did confirm what Draper said,'' Mike agreed again, and then he smiled. "I wonder how Draper would enjoy hearing that he's easier to get information out of than Rayburn. After he got over his outrage, I'll bet he'd decide not to believe it.''

"Draper's sort never believes in anything but themselves,'' Rena said. "Whatever they do is justified in their own mind, as long as they know it's to their own benefit. That would include blackmail and murder, and the fear he showed would come from the possibility of being caught and deprived of his just due. I hate to say it, but we're two for two.''

"Well, maybe we can eliminate some of the others,'' Mike told her with a sigh. "I don't really expect it, but maybe we'll get lucky.''

The next man to be brought in was the tall, handsome one, and if he'd looked bad in Don's house, now he looked worse. He wasn't likely to have been given anything to drink in his holding cell, not in the way of alcohol, at least, and Tanda could see his hands trembling as he sat down.

"Mr. Lawrence Ransom,'' Mike said, in what Tanda was beginning to believe was for her and Rena's benefit. "You and the others are going to be charged, Mr. Ransom, and you're here to have the matter explained.''

"Why would I need an explanation?'' the man demanded, more sullen than aggressive. "The silly little bitch signed a complaint against us, so we get it stuck to us. Isn't that the way it usually goes?''

"You consider yourself unjustly accused?" Mike said with eyebrows high. "Are you forgetting there are four police witnesses to the threats you and the others made against Ms. Grail?"

"She had something we needed!" the man answered, leaning forward to emphasize the argument. "If we needed it and she wouldn't give it to us, what else were we supposed to do? It wasn't our fault, it was hers!"

"I see," Mike commented, then went on with what was becoming a formula. Ransom remained sullen and shaky, turning furtive when it was necessary for him to answer questions. The threat of being held an extra hour turned him resentful as well as nervous, but he responded to it just as the others had. When he was gone, Mike looked questioningly toward Rena and Tanda.

"Typical spoiled brat," Rena supplied after turning on the speaker. "Undoubtedly raised by a very indulgent mother, aunt or sister, who *knew* he could never do wrong because he was so marvelous. He grew up expecting the world to be handed to him on a platter, and those who didn't oblige were the ones who were wrong. He probably gets furious when he's balked in anything, and would consider the killing of someone who crossed him as something they really deserved."

"And I'll bet he lived off rich women," Tanda put in, agreeing with Rena. "He'd consider being kept the perfect way of life, but would resent having to occasionally do as he was told. And he never does *anything* wrong. It's other people who do wrong, and he's the innocent who gets into trouble because of it."

"In other words, three for three," Mike said with a heavy nod.

The fourth one in was the woman, which led Tanda to guess that Mike was interviewing them in the order of how much they'd had to say in Don's house. Jocelyn Geroux strolled in as though making an entrance, and stopped to check her appearance in the mirror before sitting down in the chair.

Mike went through the routine, and the woman was as uncooperative as she could be without actually refusing to answer questions, but she still did as the others had. She hated the other members of the group, thought any of them could be guilty, was glad the police had found Miss Baderlie and knew nothing about the librarian's attempted burglary. The only difference from the other interviews was the way she got around to trying to...*vamp* Mike, was the only way to put it. When she was finally gone, Mike looked indecently relieved.

"So what did you think?" Mike asked Rena.

"She's one of the lost ones," Rena answered with a sigh. "She was probably sexually abused as a child, as well as physically abused and rejected in all other ways. She thinks money and sex are the answers to every problem, and if one doesn't work, the other will. She'll have learned to care about no one but herself, and value physical appearance above character. Could she kill? Picture someone rejecting her on all levels, and then try to imagine how she would react to having the constants of her world threatened. Yes, I'd say she would kill without hesitation."

"She also enjoys seeing other people hurt," Tanda put in. "She must have had so much hurt herself, that in her mind seeing other people done the same is only fair. But that's only a reason for the way she acts, not an excuse. I still don't like her even a little."

"And I don't blame you even a little," Mike said gently. "What she said to you in your brother's house... Well, it was all I could do not to go after her. At first I thought it strange that these people rarely socialized as a group, but I don't consider it strange any longer. Strange would be if they did socialize."

Once again Tanda and Rena agreed with him, and there was nothing to add to the observation. They waited in silence until the next person was brought, and that turned out to be the one man who'd tried to manipulate rather than threaten. He looked so quiet and average that he seemed like an outsider in the group, but that impression didn't last long.

"Mr. Howard Ullman," Mike said as the man brushed at his black suit. "Do you always spend your time among such an—unusual—group of people?"

"People are people, Lieutenant Gerard, as you should know," the man answered in his golden voice, gazing benevolently at Mike. "We may deplore what others do, but how can we denounce them without denouncing ourselves? Those poor souls have been through the fires of hell, as have I, myself. I'm sure we've all agreed to do what we can to help the police in this matter, and so a measure of kindness on your part would not go unappreciated by us."

"Kindness," Mike echoed, his expression very neutral. "Do you always expect kindness from those who would normally be accusing you, Mr. Ullman? Most people would expect the opposite."

"In my experience, Lieutenant, people offer kindness more often than you would think," the man answered with a warm smile that matched his voice perfectly. "We're none of us perfect, and once someone understands and accepts that, they become more willing to forgive their brothers and sisters in imperfection. They remember that those who forgive are themselves more easily forgiven, and so they evince a most commendable compassion."

"And in my experience, some people come a lot closer to perfection than others," Mike said, apparently having no trouble resisting the smoothly practiced and persuasive voice. "That, of course, refers to how hard they try, not to how hard they work to get people to *believe* they're trying. You and the others are going to be charged, Mr. Ullman, but there are certain things that need to be discussed first."

He then went on with the usual speech, but Ullman barely changed expression. He kept whatever he really felt deep on the inside, just the way the short man, Miles Rayburn, did with fearful cringing. Ullman, though, used patient benevolence, except when he was told about the possibility of being kept a little longer than the others. The disturbance in his eyes was as close to fear as Richard Draper's had been, and certainly for the same reason. When Larry took the man away, Mike turned immediately to his unseen listeners.

"What did you think of *that* one?" he challenged. "He was sadly disappointed that Miss Baderlie might have tried a burglary, but *he* certainly had nothing to do with it. Did either of you believe him?"

"It isn't possible to decide with certainty one way or the other," Rena said after glancing at Tanda. "The man has himself under perfect control, and uses that ability to control others."

"Not perfect control," Tanda disagreed wryly. "Don't forget that none of us is perfect, even though he probably thinks *he* is. He didn't like the idea of being kept longer any more than the others did, and even showed the same kind of fear. It would be easy to consider him different from and therefore better than the others, but I think he really is just the same."

"He might even be worse," Rena mused while Mike nodded thoughtfully. "He would be used to conning people into doing what he wanted, and then talking them out of pressing charges if he happened to get caught. He could be so used to it, in fact, that failure could well drive him into rage and murder. Mild on the outside doesn't necessarily mean sweet and gentle on the inside.''

''But professional con men don't usually get involved with killing,'' Mike pointed out. ''There are exceptions to every rule, of course, so there's no guarantee about Ullman, but that's the part that bothers me. He acts like a pro, and doesn't let himself get stampeded into saying the wrong thing. For my money, he'd fit really well into the picture of a blackmailer.''

''Maybe even better than the others,'' Rena agreed slowly. ''If this last one is like the first four, we'll have to consider that seriously.''

Mike nodded, and then the two of them lapsed into a thoughtful silence. Tanda wondered if they were thinking about getting the blackmail evidence from the blackmailer, and decided they were. It would mean not having to let the rest of those nasty people go, of being able to make them pay for whatever terrible crime they'd committed. And their crimes *would* be terrible, there wasn't the least doubt about that.

The last man, the one who hadn't said anything at all at Don's house, was finally brought in. He was as average-looking as Howard Ullman, and although the man was faintly nervous, it was only to be expected under the circumstances. He took the chair opposite Mike at the table, then sat and waited.

''Mr. Mark King,'' Mike said at last when it was clear the man was not going to speak first. ''Do you always spend your time among such an—unusual—group of people, Mr. King?''

''I think you know the choice wasn't mine, Lieutenant,'' the man responded evenly. ''I wasn't even particularly happy about being in that house, but there was no other choice. I would love to say I was forced into it by the others, but the truth is I was there voluntarily. We're going to be charged because of that stupidity, aren't we?''

"Yes, as a matter of fact, you are," Mike answered, once again refusing to respond to someone's manner. Ullman had a beautiful voice and used it to manipulate, but King's quiet, open manner seemed to have the same purpose. Tanda noticed that his expensive sports clothes were worn as naturally as Richard Draper's, with the same air of being used to fine things.

"Well, they say if you're made to pay for your mistakes, you do learn from them," King responded with a sigh. "Just how bad is it going to be?"

Mike told him, and then went on to the other points he wanted to cover. King was disturbed to hear that Miss Baderlie had attempted a burglary, but didn't seem overly surprised. His denial about being involved was quiet and sincere, which meant there was no possible way to tell if it was the truth. There was no opportunity to discuss what might happen if King failed to cooperate, not with him being the last of the six and also being so very willing to talk about anything. Once Larry had him out of the room, Rena activated the intercom.

"It's my fault," she said at once. "I should have waited before deciding Ullman was the only possible blackmailer, or at least I should have kept quiet about the decision. Very frankly, that one scares me worse than any of the others."

"Because he's so good," Mike agreed with a nod and a sigh. "I had to keep reminding myself that he isn't really on our side no matter what he said. He volunteered nothing at all, even when he discussed the others. His comments boil down to a confirmation of what anyone could get from five minutes of conversation with them, plus the reluctant admission that he doesn't know any of them well enough to guess about the murderer. Is there any way we can see him doing the killings?"

"Only if he's completely insane," Tanda ventured when Rena kept silent. "And that's possible, even if we're having trouble making ourselves believe it. There's no doubt he could be the blackmailer, which means he could have gone insane from worry.''

''And that also means we're still guessing,'' Mike added, the frustration back in his voice. ''Let's take a short coffee break, and then we'll get to the last of the bunch.''

Tanda stood up when Rena did, but not because she was eager for a break. She was more eager to get around to Miss Baderlie, the woman who had frightened her so badly by trying to break into her house. It was time someone frightened Baderlie, made her know what it was like to feel helpless. She would talk to Mike while they got their coffee, and see if it was possible for her to be in his room during the interview. Tanda knew it would somehow turn out to be necessary that she be there, or they would never learn anything of value.

Chapter Thirteen

Mike watched Miss Alicia Baderlie and her attorney being shown into the room, wondering if he'd done the right thing. Tanda now sat to his right on his side of the table, and he still wasn't sure why he'd agreed to let her be there. She'd insisted she would be of help, and his decision had felt more professional than personal. Somehow she *would* be of help during that interview.

Baderlie's attorney was a large, bulky man wearing an obviously expensive suit and Italian shoes. The man reminded Mike of Richard Draper, who had chosen to represent himself and his five companions. Alicia Baderlie was local and therefore had an attorney on retainer; the others were using Draper to get them bail, and would hire attorneys only if they really had to.

"Lester Arnold, representing Miss Baderlie," the lawyer said almost at once, putting a heavy briefcase on the table. "If this is someone from the district attorney's office, I'm afraid I don't know her."

He was talking about Tanda, of course, which was to be expected. He also probably knew who she was, but Mike decided to play the game.

"This is Ms. Tanda Grail, both the victim of your client and the one who tracked her down," Mike said quietly.

"Ms. Grail is consulting with us on the multiple-murder case, so I asked her to sit in."

"I consider that highly irregular, but I'll allow it," Arnold pronounced, holding the chair for his client before taking his own seat. "With the young lady here, I'll find it easier to prove you have no case at all against my client."

"Even the presence of a thousand young ladies won't help you do that, Counselor," Mike told him dryly, refusing to fall for the bluff. "We can prove Miss Baderlie is one of a group of seven people who are directly involved with the murders I mentioned a moment ago, and also that she tried to break into Ms. Grail's house a couple of nights ago. We have the shoes Miss Baderlie wore that night—still bearing faint traces of mud—and we've matched the tread on her car tires. Solid evidence that can't possibly be called circumstantial."

"But often, solid evidence can be declared tainted," Arnold returned with the same vicious little smile his client wore. "Alicia here—Miss Baderlie, that is—tells me your tracking procedure was interrupted. The dog doing the tracking was not taken immediately through her front door, but was first led around to her back yard where she happened to be. In fact, you and the only other officer with you were both around back, as was Ms. Grail and her dog. Is that true?"

"What of it?" Mike asked, fighting not to show how sick he suddenly felt. He *couldn't* lose Baderlie on a technicality, he just couldn't!

"You ask what of it?" Arnold all but purred. "Let me explain how it would go in court, assuming the district attorney was foolish enough to pursue this. You were tracing someone who was supposedly a member of this group you mentioned, which was the only probable cause you had for searching Miss Baderlie's house. Without that link the search was illegal, even with a warrant. Anything

found during the search would have to be considered
tainted evidence, and therefore not admissible in court.
Ms. Grail.''

The lawyer switched so quickly to Tanda that Mike was
almost startled, even though he should have expected it.

''Ms. Grail, you and everyone else went around to the
back of Miss Baderlie's house,'' Arnold pursued coldly.
''With no one left to watch the front door, we contend
that the person whose trail your dog was following went
out that way and took the opportunity to disappear. Miss
Baderlie had no idea they were in her house, of course,
and was shocked when your dog confused the scent he
was following with hers. Your having brought the dog
around to the back before taking him inside caused that
error, and when I get you on the stand you'll have to
admit the idea is possible. Not probable or even likely,
but as long as it's possible you have no case at all.''

His smug satisfaction was so thick it made Mike want
to hit him, if for no other reason than for his lack of
humanity. Six people were already dead, but Lester Arnold cared about nothing but showing how clever an attorney he was.

''Really, Mr. Arnold, you're dreaming,'' Tanda said
suddenly with such superior amusement that Arnold's
smugness disappeared as if he *had* been hit. ''I won't
testify to any such thing because it *isn't* possible, and if
necessary the point can be proven.''

''I don't believe that!'' Arnold snapped, his hand to his
client's arm keeping her from adding her own furious
comment. ''With everyone around at the back of the
house, no one can say positively that some stranger didn't
go out the front! It isn't humanly possible to be certain!''

''No, but it *is* 'doggily' possible,'' Tanda countered,
still looking calmly amused. ''You'd better remember,
Mr. Arnold, that my dog found your client's scent by
picking it up in the midst of the scents of eleven other

people, and then he followed it for miles. If, after that, anyone alive could believe he'd then become confused between two scents, there are at least a dozen demonstrations we can use to show how impossible that is. With my dog around, no one *had* to be watching the front door.''

Mike would have paid to see the appalled expression now on Lester Arnold's face, not to mention the dawning worry on his client's. Tanda had handled the situation perfectly, better than he could have possibly done alone, and then Larry showed how good a cop he was.

''There's something else Miss Baderlie forgot to mention to her attorney,'' Larry commented from where he stood by the door. ''Sergeant Foreman, my partner, was the one who opened Miss Baderlie's front door from the inside to let the dog complete his tracking. In her report, Sergeant Foreman states there was a chain lock on the front door that first had to be opened before the door could be opened. With every window in the house also locked from the inside, your suggested stranger would have had to ooze out under the front door.''

''So I think, Counselor, you'll have to agree that we have a solid case against your client,'' Mike drawled, enjoying himself more than a cop really should. ''The only chance of a break she has is if she talks to us, and you'd better make her understand that. At the moment we're opposing bail for her, but by tomorrow that could change. And by tomorrow, her six—associates—will have been long since freed.''

Mike watched the librarian open her mouth as if to say something, but the words never came out. She'd probably been about to demand that they not oppose bail; after all, the thought of staying in jail would be abhorrent to someone like Miss Baderlie. But then she must have realized there would be a delay in her release even if bail was granted, and that all the others would be freed first. And like the others had, she knew just what that meant.

"What sort of thing do you want my client to talk about, and what kind of deal are you prepared to make in trade?" Arnold asked after glancing at the librarian's pale face. "We'll certainly expect all charges to be dropped, and will also require full immunity for her in the event that anything she says proves to be actionable. We—"

"Mr. Arnold," Mike interrupted, using the coldest tone he was capable of. "Your client knows exactly what sort of thing we want her to talk about, and there won't be any deals. Telling us everything she knows is probably the only thing that will guarantee that she stays alive, and I don't mean the sort of information we got from the others. We're convinced she knows a good deal more than they do, and that's what we want to hear about."

Mike was really bluffing with that last, but he had to play his one break for all it was worth. All seven of those people knew more than they were admitting, and all he needed was for one of them to talk. It was the secrecy in all directions that made this case so hard to crack, but with a little luck it would soon be the secrecy that cracked.

"I—have to think about this," the woman said when her lawyer finally turned to her with raised eyebrows. "No, Lester, I don't want to discuss this with you yet, not until I've had a chance to think. But I must do it away from here, so they'll just have to let me go."

"Not a chance," Mike denied flatly, seeing the woman was serious and finding it hard to believe. "I don't know what sort of grade-B movies you watch, Miss Baderlie, but I'd belong in the worst of them if I considered that even for a moment. I can't make you talk to me, but I certainly can insist on your company until you do. You can add a material-witness charge to the rest, Arnold, and don't expect the court to be sympathetic. With six people already dead, I'm betting you'll find the court fresh out of sympathy for someone withholding vital information.''

"You'd first have to prove my client *does* have that sort of information, Lieutenant,'' Arnold said, but the smug condescension he'd been showing earlier was completely gone. "I'm leaving now to try to secure her immediate release, so you can expect to hear from me. Alicia, if you should happen to need me, just have one of them call.''

"Don't leave me alone here, Lester,'' the librarian said, but rather than a plea, the words came out as a harsh command. "I'm telling you, I forbid you to leave me here.''

"Try to keep control of yourself, Alicia,'' the lawyer responded, already on his feet and heading for the door. "I'll do everything I can for you, but my advice would be to think over your position and then cooperate fully. It was a pleasure to meet you, Ms. Grail.''

And then he was gone. The woman had turned to glare after him, but Tanda's voice caused her to turn back.

"Getting out while the getting is good,'' Tanda commented in a very neutral tone. "And yes, it was definitely a pleasure to meet him, too. Speaking of getting, it isn't as easy to *get* away with things as you thought, is it, Miss Baderlie?''

"I have nothing at all to say to you,'' the librarian returned in frigid tones, but not without a tremor in her voice. She had been all but abandoned by the lawyer she'd been counting on, and now didn't know what to do.

"Miss Baderlie isn't in the mood for conversation right now, Larry,'' Mike said after a moment. "Take her back to her holding cell until she changes her mind—or until her bail hearing. We'll see what happens then.''

The woman tried to glare at him, but she was really too shaken to be in top form. She made no effort to look at Larry when he stood himself beside her, but simply rose from the chair, turned and left. Once the door closed behind them, Mike felt Tanda's hand on his arm.

"I'm sorry I wasn't of more help," she said when Mike looked at her. "What I told him about Robby would have been of more use if you didn't also have Rena's solid evidence about the door chain."

"Let's not go into too much detail about Rena's solid evidence," Mike said with a grin. "Larry happens to be a good cop with excellent timing, even if his sense of *time* is occasionally off. Rena hasn't yet had the *time* to write her report about the episode in and at Baderlie's house, so we can't yet be sure what will be in it. If the chain was on, Rena will say so. If it wasn't, she won't. Larry was taking a chance that nerves had made Baderlie keep the chain on most of the time, so she might not remember whether or not it was on right then."

"And it worked!" Tanda exclaimed with delight. "She didn't even try to deny it, and that threw her lawyer completely off stride. He expected a quick and easy win when he walked in here, and when he didn't get it he took the fast way out. I wonder how much longer he'll still be representing her."

"At least through the bail hearing, but probably not beyond that," Mike said, loving the way Tanda looked when she smiled. "Lester Arnold pretends he wins all his cases, when the truth is he doesn't handle anything he *can't* win. Once he's sure 'dear Alicia' falls into that category, he'll drop her as fast as he possibly can. Will you have dinner with me again tonight? I was almost afraid to ask after the way last night ended, and if you'd rather not, I'll understand, but—"

"I'd love to have dinner with you tonight," she interrupted firmly, putting her hand on his arm again. "The way last night ended wasn't your fault, so why should you be blamed? Six o'clock?"

"Six o'clock," he agreed with that idiotic smile he

could feel. "And I'll try to leave orders about no problems turning up tonight."

"I hope everyone listens," she answered with a laugh, then stood up. "If I'm going to be ready for six, I'd better head home now. Unless you need me for something else?"

"No, we're just about finished here for the moment," he said as he also stood. "There are a few odds and ends I have to take care of, and then I'll be heading home myself. But first I'll walk you to the door."

Her smile of agreement made him feel as if he could even walk Tanda through fire, a reaction he hadn't experienced since he was a boy. Once she was gone and he turned back toward his office, he couldn't help grinning. Another day in her company, and he'd be walking the tops of wooden fences just to impress her.

"Well, I don't have to ask why *you're* in such a good mood," Rena commented softly with hidden amusement as she came up to walk beside him. "You may have forgotten, but I was on the other side of the mirror in the interview room. If *she's* what you were waiting for, you were right to wait."

"You like her, then," Mike said, and it wasn't a question. Truthfully, he couldn't imagine anyone not liking Tanda, but some people did happen to be peculiar.

"Not only like her," Rena answered with satisfaction. "I loved the way she handled that pompous oaf Arnold, deflating his oh-so-clever defense and all but laughing at him. And by the way, don't worry about that report I haven't written yet. Larry *was* guessing, but it so happens he was right. The chain was on, and the team that went through the house found that all the windows were not only closed, but locked. Miss High-and-Mighty was scared, all right, just like the rest of them. Do you think she'll talk?"

"Unless she decides for some reason that she's better

off not talking,'' Mike said, stopping short of his office to consider the idea. ''And since she might do exactly that, I'd better do something to shake up the rest of them. Have all their pictures and fingerprints been put out on the net?''

''As soon as we had them all,'' Rena agreed with a nod. ''We marked the inquiry urgent, so some of the other departments might not put the packet at the bottom of a pile. What do you have in mind for shaking them up?''

''Well, think about the one thing that group agrees about completely,'' Mike said, reexamining the idea even as he explained it. ''They all want to find the blackmailer together, to keep themselves from being the next individual victim. They don't trust each other to share anything learned, so they all faced Tanda together in Grail's house. What do you think they would do if they thought *I* knew who the blackmailer was?''

''Immediately try to make individual deals?'' Rena said, her eyebrows high. ''Throwing everyone else to the wolves would be perfectly in keeping with their natures, not to mention wanting to save their own skins. But how do you expect to get them to believe you? And even more to the point, what if the murderer believes you at once? You could be setting yourself up for something nasty as soon as they're all released.''

''Your last objection is the one most easily taken care of,'' Mike reassured her with a smile. ''I'm a cop, remember, and cops keep things secret from everyone else only in the movies. I'll have shared my suspicions with my superiors, so I won't be the only one who knows the truth. We haven't made any arrests yet because we don't have solid proof, but that's what we're working on right now. After that, the biggest danger I'll face is getting caught in the stampede of everyone wanting to make a deal.''

''You may be right,'' Rena grudged, considering it.

"And I think I know a way to pass on the word that they'll believe. All of them but Miss Baderlie are in one block of holding cells. If someone—Larry, for instance, goes down to tell the block guard that the group will be released soon, but one of them will be back again as soon as we can manage it... Your story gets passed on, and they believe they're overhearing something they weren't meant to know. A couple of them will be skeptical, but the rest will remember you weren't bluffing about having found Miss Baderlie. It should work, and I only hope they have something worth dealing for."

"There's a lot they still haven't told us, and things they certainly don't know they know," Mike said. "It's the little things that build up to a full picture, and you can be sure they haven't exchanged confidences even if they have tried to work together. One of them coming forward could even be the murderer, trying to avert suspicion by acting like the others. This should be what breaks the case, Rena, so we can't blow it. Let's not do anything to make them think we're bluffing."

"I hate to do it, but we'll have to pull everybody back from the surveillance we set up," Rena fretted. "I wanted to keep an eye on that bunch now that we know who they are, but you're right about not blowing this chance. If one of them decides to talk to us, we don't want them changing their mind because they spotted a tail. If we really know who the blackmailer is, we don't need to keep watch on everybody else as well."

"That's exactly the way we have to think," Mike encouraged her. "As if we know who we're after, and are just gathering enough evidence to prove it. Tell Larry what's going on, and then see about arranging that conversation to be overheard. I'll be in my office doing paperwork if you need me."

"I'll try not to need you," Rena said with a grin after nodding. "You'll want to get finished with that paperwork fast, so you can go home and get ready for your date. And I'll also pass along that order about no trouble tonight.''

"See if you can include the murderer in those you pass it to," Mike suggested as she began to move off. "I think everyone else can be trusted to follow the order even if they don't happen to know about it."

"I'll do my best," she promised over her shoulder with a laugh, and then she was moving purposefully toward Larry's desk. Rena was a good cop and a great human being, and for a moment Mike wondered why he'd never asked her out. The thought held him until he was behind his desk and in his chair, and then the obvious answer came. He'd never consciously realized it before, but subconsciously he knew that Rena and Larry were more than just partners. Although it was unlikely either one of them had mentioned their feelings to the other, not when they still talked about dating other people.

"They don't want to complicate their professional lives, so they pretend there's nothing personal between them," Mike muttered to the blank report form he'd pulled out. "It's their decision and their lives, but I'm glad it's not me. If I had to see Tanda every day, but couldn't tell her how I felt—"

And then Mike realized he *hadn't* told Tanda how he felt, not really. They'd known each other for all of three days, but to him it seemed like half a lifetime. If it felt that way to her, too, they'd have to do something about it. Half a lifetime is long enough to be alone, especially when you've just found someone you want to spend the other half with. Tonight, he'd mention it tonight. And please, God, let her feel the same way...

Mike called up the report form on his computer, and then began to type as fast as he could.

Chapter Fourteen

Yen Po's was the best Chinese restaurant in a thirty-mile radius, and Tanda wasn't surprised that it was Mike's favorite as well as hers. They enjoyed so many of the same things, it was almost as if they'd lived their lives side by side. But it had taken tragedy for them to meet, which was the only shadow on their relationship. All the rest was delight, the longer it went on, the more delight.

By unspoken but mutual consent, they spent the meal talking about everything but the murders. They both used chopsticks—again, to be expected—and before the meal was over they were feeding each other tastes of their favorite dishes. The night was beautiful when they went back outside, and this time Mike was able to start to drive her home without getting beeped. Tanda lowered her window and stared out into the peaceful, silent dark, and after a moment Mike stirred.

"Is anything wrong?" he asked. "You've suddenly become so quiet."

"I was just thinking something awful," Tanda said without turning to look at him. "Don caused a lot of trouble and hard feelings for me and our parents, but in the end you could say he made it up to me. If not for his death I would never have met you, and that makes me feel horribly guilty. What kind of person thinks even for an instant that her brother's death might have been a good thing?''

"You don't think any such thing," Mike said firmly, reaching over to take her hand. "And we didn't meet because of your brother's death, or even because of Roger Saxon's death. We met because we were meant to meet, and if it hadn't been over this case it would have been over a case of frozen vegetables some Saturday in the supermarket. You can't feel guilty about finding personal happiness in the middle of tragedy unless you're directly responsible for causing that tragedy, which you aren't.''

"Do you really think we were meant to meet?" she asked, not having considered the possibility. She'd been all but singing when she got home that afternoon, already counting the minutes until Mike would be there, and then she'd realized what she was doing. Her brother was lying dead in the morgue, murdered by a maniac, and she was in the middle of falling in love. By the time Mike had picked her up she'd managed to push away the thought, but now it had come back to haunt her.

"I *know* we were meant to meet," Mike answered, and then he was slowing to pull off the road onto one of the small shoulder rest areas. As soon as the car had stopped he put it in park, then turned to take her by both arms. "Tanda, you have to believe me," he urged, his fingers gentle but firm on her arms. "We've only known each other for three days and I meant to say this differently and at a better time, but—I can't believe I would be this crazy about you after so short a time if we *hadn't* been meant to meet. The only thing that can ruin my theory is the possibility that you don't feel the same about me. So, do you?''

His usually strong dark eyes looked faintly frightened in the light of the dashboard as he waited for her answer, but she didn't make him wait long. He'd asked a question she'd been ready to answer three lifetimes ago.

"I guess that makes two of us who are crazy," she said, trying to smile for him. "I thought only teenagers were supposed to feel like this, but they've lost their monopoly. The only problem is I *am* responsible for the tragedy, or at least a part of it. I'm the one who brought Roger Saxon out here, and if not for that he'd still be alive. My happiness started only because his life ended."

Mike sighed, but didn't answer immediately. Instead, he gathered her into his arms and held her so close it was like heaven. The faint masculine smell of his aftershave, the hardness of his body, the strength of his arms; they were all there, to comfort and support her, right along with his hand stroking her hair.

"We spoke about this once before, but obviously it's time to discuss it again," he said gently after a moment. "I'm not surprised you feel like this, you're too wonderful a person not to, but you're seeing things from the wrong perspective. I'll play cop and ask you some questions, and you'll answer them as honestly as you can. All right?"

Tanda nodded her head against his chest, willing to do anything if it would just erase that shadow over them. If it wasn't banished, it could ruin things between them forever.

"Good," Mike said to her nod. "Now, there are three parts to this, so we'll take them one at a time. To begin with, there's Roger Saxon. I happen to know you didn't ask for him by name, and it was his agency's choice that he be the one who was sent. If they'd sent someone else, would that someone else still be alive?"

"Probably," Tanda muttered into his jacket, having agreed to tell the truth. "He said himself that no one else would have recognized what he did, and whatever he saw has to be the reason he was murdered. With someone else, there wouldn't have been that reason."

"Okay, so circumstance brought him here rather than you," Mike went on. "Now, when you got that note from the group and knew it was important to the case, you got in touch with me as soon as you could. Saxon came across something important, but rather than contacting the police immediately he decided to use it first to impress his client. Was that what anyone would consider a smart move?''

Tanda shook her head, forced to admit that in truth it was incredibly dumb. If she hadn't called Mike with her clue...

''So there he was, knowing something vital in a multiple-murder case. He hasn't told anyone about it yet, which *can't* be what he learned working on two major city police forces, and then comes the crowning touch. He opens his door to the person he recognized, even though that person almost certainly had to be the murderer he was there investigating! Unless you gave him orders to act like that, his death can't possibly be considered your fault.''

''You know, that's a very interesting point,'' Tanda said as she sat up, the partial fading of guilt finally letting her think about it. ''Roger Saxon was a pleasant, outgoing man, but he didn't strike me as arrogant. And he was methodical rather than sloppy and stupid, so why didn't he call you? And why would he let a murderer into his room without at least having a gun in his hand? It really doesn't make any sense.''

Mike had seemed ready to go on with his arguments, but her questions stopped him and brought a frown to his face. It really didn't make sense, unless—

''Mike, what if he didn't call the police or hesitate to let the person into his room because he knew the person he'd recognized couldn't be the murderer?'' Tanda felt briefly excited, but then the feeling faded. ''Except that the person *was* the murderer, so that leaves us with nothing again.''

''Not quite,'' Mike disagreed, having caught her excitement. ''It had to be someone who had never killed before, even though he or she had been involved in illegalities. Saxon might have decided to use the person as a snitch, and invited him or her to his motel room to pump them. Snitches might lie to you but they never attack, so Saxon felt safe. That should mean we're looking for someone who hasn't killed before. Tanda, you're wonderful!''

"You'd better stop saying that, or I'll think it's only my mind you're interested in," she told him with a laugh. .''And how do we find out if someone has never killed before? People don't usually take out ads in the paper saying, 'This is to inform everyone that I lie, cheat and steal, but don't kill.'''

"Ah, but in a way they do take out that kind of ad," Mike retorted with a grin. "It's called a 'sensational' story, and contains a list of police suspects in a usually lurid crime. There may not be enough evidence for people to be charged, but they *are* named as suspects. We've already gotten that on some of the victims, and we're waiting for more of it on the group you uncovered. Now we'll know what to look for when the information starts to come in—and you have my word that your mind is *not* the only thing I'm interested in.''

His grin softened to a smile, and Tanda simply couldn't help herself. She leaned forward to brush his lips with hers, and his response was immediate. He had her in his arms and was kissing her back so quickly it took her breath away, but that didn't stop her from joining in. Mike Gerard always made her feel better, and his taking seriously the things that disturbed her was only a part of it. Being with him made her feel complete, somehow, in a way she'd never experienced before. If falling in love with him was wrong, nothing in the entire world could be right.

"Finally," he murmured after the kiss ended, still briefly touching her lips with his. "I've been wanting to do that for days, but the one time I actually got the nerve up to try, we were interrupted almost as soon as it began. There are certain times I don't much like being a cop."

"Being a cop is part of who you are," Tanda said, stroking his face with a gentle hand. "Len wanted the job so he could rub people's noses in it, but you—you took the job because it needs to be done. I thought I'd never want to get involved with a cop again—until I realized I hadn't *been* involved with a cop. I'd been involved with someone in a uniform who carried a badge and a gun—not with a true police officer."

"You have no idea how glad I am to hear you say that," he said, but Tanda thought he looked more relieved. "Why don't we give them another chance to interrupt us."

The smile Tanda began with was lost in that second kiss, but not entirely. Sweetness as well as desire ran all through it, right along with a delicious sense of teenage naughtiness. They were parked on the side of the road and necking; if anyone found them doing it, she felt as though she'd be taken home to have her father told.

"I think that had better be it for now," Mike said abruptly, ending the kiss rather suddenly. "I'm supposed to be taking you home, but any more of that and we won't make it. I may be ruining my image as young and daring, but side-of-the-road exhibitions are a lot of years behind me."

After what she'd just been thinking, Tanda found that really funny. She'd never been into putting on shows, and Mike hadn't embarrassed her by suggesting she might be. He'd simply made the refusal himself, although Tanda suspected he wasn't quite as shy as he claimed.

"Well, in that case, you'd better hurry up and finish taking me home," she said, putting both her arms around his right one. He'd reached forward to shift the car into drive, and her taking his arm surprised him into looking at her again. "I don't have any side-of-the-road there, so we shouldn't have a problem. And I also don't have any more doubts, so let's forget about those other two points you were going to make.''

''Are you sure?'' he asked quietly, dark eyes searching her lighter ones. ''This is too important for me to want to rush you into anything. I don't ever want you to regret anything you do with me.''

''The one thing I'll always regret is that we didn't meet over the frozen food in the supermarket,'' she answered, serious but not morbidly so. ''But if we had met that way, I might have refused to try to get to know you because of my experience with Len. I'm going to stretch a point and tell myself Don helped me to meet you, that my brother's last act was to insure his sister's happiness. I'd like to remember him like that, no matter what else he might have done. I'm not going to keep his money, so that's all I'll ever have to remember him by.''

''I don't have a right to an opinion in this, but if I were asked, I'd say you were keeping something more important than money.'' Everything about him told Tanda he really felt that way, and for the twentieth time she wasn't surprised. He'd given away the money awarded to him from his ex-wife, which meant he knew why she couldn't keep Don's money. They saw things the same, and hopefully always would.

It didn't take long for them to drive the rest of the way to her house. Once inside she let Robby out for the last time, and rather than simply stand around or try to kiss her again, Mike helped her check the windows and doors. It was incredibly exciting having him there, neither of them saying anything as they moved from room to room and window to window. But they smiled at each other every time their paths crossed: sweet, quiet smiles that were almost like a caress. Tanda knew he was there for her without his saying a word, something she'd never imagined because she hadn't known it was possible.

"I think that's Robby I hear," Tanda said at last, recognizing the scratching he'd taken to doing at the door. "If I don't let him in, he might decide to break in."

"Not him," Mike denied as she crossed the floor. "He's as much of a cop as I am, and we cops don't believe in breaking the law. If you don't believe me, ask him."

"All right, I will," Tanda said with a laugh, more than ready to join the game. She let Robby in, locked the door behind him, then turned to look down at her dog. "Okay, Robby, I want the truth. Would you ever consider breaking into a house?"

As if on cue, Robby sneezed and shook his head, then grinned his long-faced grin when Tanda joined Mike in laughing out loud.

"See, I told you," Mike said, coming over to put his arm around Tanda. "And we cops also back each other up."

She looked up at him then, and the laughter softened in both of them as they both got the same idea. This time they each brought half of a kiss, then turned it whole between them. It was wonderful being held like that in Mike's arms, but in the name of not rushing her, he was beginning to drive her crazy.

"Come on," she whispered after pulling away just a little. "If I remember correctly, we'll find this a lot more pleasant if we slip into something more comfortable."

"But I didn't bring any—" he began to protest, then saw the amusement in her eyes. What she wanted them to slip into was her bed, but it had taken him a moment to catch up. It wasn't that he was slow, she knew. He was just working so hard at trying not to rush her. Tanda sighed and took his hand, then closed the lights as they went from living room to kitchen to hall. She hadn't expected to ever be the aggressor, but if that's what it took...

Her bedroom was the farthest from the kitchen, down at the other end of the hall. She drew Mike in behind her, expecting to have to chase Robby out before being able to close the door, but the dog was nowhere to be seen.

"He's still out in the living room, lying comfortably on the carpeting," Mike murmured, obviously knowing what she was looking for. "I told you we cops back each other up. Close the door and then we can get comfortable ourselves."

"It looks like I'm going to be allowed to keep you," Tanda laughed as she did close the door. "And if Robby likes you, that's good enough for me."

"Higher praise no man can ask for," Mike said with a grin, and then he was taking off his jacket and his gun. When he turned back to her the grin was gone, but in its place was one of those smiles she liked so much.

"I really love you, Tanda Grail," he whispered, coming close to look down at her. "I hope you believe me, because I've never said anything I meant as much."

"And I love you, Mike Gerard," she answered in the same way, then noticed something for the first time. "You know, you may be right about our being meant for each other. Even our last initials are the same."

"That's interesting, but I'll like it even better when our names are the same," he murmured, beginning to slowly move his hands up her bare arms. "I expect to put that more formally as a question, but you might think about what your answer will be."

And then his arms were around her, drawing her close for a kiss that gave her no chance to think about anything. Passion flared wildly between them, as though her fire fed his, and his hers. It was incredible, electric beyond all dreams and fantasies.

Tanda had once thought mutual undressing would be awkward, but it was over and done with so quickly it was almost like magic. Mike picked her up and put her down on the bed, then followed without once pausing in the way he kissed her body. Her breasts tingled, and her ribs and her throat and her ears; she, in turn, kissed him, loving the hard muscle and dark hair her lips and hands touched.

Every now and then her lips captured his mouth, and it was hers without argument or regret. They tasted each other then for an age or two, but soon other parts of him called. When that happened, he willingly let her mouth go, and returned to kissing her everywhere else.

Finally Tanda couldn't stand it any longer, but once again Mike was right with her. Simply thinking how much she wanted him brought him to her, and then they danced together as though they'd rehearsed for years. Incredible, magical, a dream come true. Tanda held to Mike with all her strength, beyond thinking of descriptives, only able to experience and feel. They thrust and merged, kissed and touched, two halves of a complete whole.

After it was over, Tanda lay exhausted and unmoving in Mike's arms. Before that night she'd experienced sex, and had had no idea of the difference between that and making love. Now she knew the first was a shower and the second a thunderstorm, and also that she never wanted the shower again. With Mike she'd never have it again, only the sharing of the love they felt for each other.

Tanda was so comfortable, she must have dozed off. The next thing she knew, Mike was no longer holding her, but was just about dressed. She could see his shadow form moving around the room silently, and realized he must have turned off the light. The last she remembered, it had still been on.

For a moment she very much wanted to call him back to bed, but then she realized how selfish that would be. He had no change of clothes here in her house, and if he stayed the night he would have to get up extra early in the morning to stop back at his own place. His sleep had already been interrupted too many times because of her;

the next time he came over, she would suggest that he bring his necessaries with him.

"You're awake now, aren't you," Mike said rather than asked, speaking softly as he came over to her side of the bed. "I'm glad, because I didn't want to leave without saying goodbye, but I also didn't want to wake you. Do you have any idea how marvelous you are?"

"You should have said, 'how marvelous *we* are together,'" Tanda corrected with a smile as he sat down beside her. "I've never experienced anything like what happened between us, and I have a feeling I know what my answer will be when you get around to asking that question you mentioned earlier."

"Then I'll have to get around to asking the question as soon as my schedule allows for it," Mike answered, his hand stroking her arm. "I'm kind of busy these days, so I don't think it can be any sooner than...tonight at dinner?"

Tanda laughed softly as he leaned down to kiss her, but after the kiss she agreed to the date, joined him in another quick peck, and then watched him head for the door out of her bedroom. It was obvious that Mike didn't want to leave any more than Tanda wanted him gone, but neither of them had a choice at the moment.

Once Mike was gone, Tanda waited a moment before getting up and following. Once she heard his car start she would look out the window, and then watch him drive away. She would also wish him a safe journey and a safe return to her as quickly as possible.

MIKE WASN'T QUITE floating as he stepped outside, but only because he was too filled with the most incredible sense of rightness and happiness. If he'd had any doubts earlier about a relationship with Tanda, they couldn't possibly have survived what the two of them had just shared. His ex-wife wasn't the only woman he'd ever had sex with, but that's all it had been with any of them—just sex. He and Tanda had shared love, and the difference was beyond description.

He thought briefly about going back to turn on the porch light to relieve the darkness, then remembered he'd locked the door behind him. His car was a dark blob standing where he'd parked it, and he'd just have to make his way over to it without the help of more than starlight. And it was a damn good thing the door was locked. If he went back for any reason, he'd be tempted to stay the rest of the night, and Tanda didn't need the embarrassment if one of the patrol units came by and saw his car.

Mike went carefully down the front steps, surprised and delighted—but mostly surprised—that the station hadn't tried to reach him before now. It was hard to understand how married cops ever had children, but maybe they occasionally left the seriously married ones alone. Serious in the way his marriage hadn't been, with his former wife having no interest in getting to know the people he worked with. Tanda, though—

Mike had just reached the front fender of his car where the tree branches overhead cast really dark shadows, when the arm came around his throat from behind. For the merest instant he thought it might be Tanda playing a joke, but the sudden stab of a knifepoint in his back low on the right side quickly killed that idea. It also killed the idea of throwing an elbow into his attacker's left ribs; one move, and that knife would find his insides through his kidneys.

"The blackmailer," a harsh voice whispered in his ear, distorted and totally unrecognizable. "Tell me who the blackmailer is, or I'll kill you like the rest."

The arm around Mike's throat made it hard for him to breathe, but he was almost too stunned to notice. The owner of the harsh and whispering voice was the serial killer he'd been looking for, and the man had just asked a question Mike couldn't answer even to literally save his life!

Chapter Fifteen

The situation made absolutely no sense, but Mike didn't have the time to think about that. The man behind him—and it *was* a man—had demanded that he answer a question, one he didn't happen to have the answer to. And even if he had, giving it wouldn't be likely to save his life.

"How do I know you won't kill me even if I tell you?" Mike husked, just to stall for time. In the next minute or so he'd have to do something, but something that would leave him alive and able to function. If he were killed or disabled, the very next victim would be Tanda.

"God demands that you answer my question without regard to your own unimportant concerns," the voice responded in the same harsh whisper. "His Messenger in this world is being threatened, the good work His Messenger performs is in danger of being stopped. This must not happen, therefore are you commanded to speak."

And that told Mike exactly what he'd wanted to know. People with the twisted belief that they served God let no one stand in their way. He would be killed no matter what he said or did, so he might as well gamble on his luck. Knowing it would take a lot of luck he started to gather himself—and then his luck got a helping hand.

Without warning the door flew open on the house, and

the dog Robby was baying and charging at them. The knife in Mike's back wavered with the attacker's startlement, and that was all Mike needed. He brought his left elbow back hard an instant before he tried to twist away, and it almost worked. The blow to his attacker's ribs made the man gasp, but it wasn't enough to keep the knife from slicing across Mike's ribs.

Mike went down to one knee with the shock of the pain, but still groped for his gun. He had to stop that maniac before he went for Tanda—and then Robby was there. Mike heard the dog hit with a growl, there was a moment of thrashing around, and then the dog howled. That knife, that damn knife—

Dizzy with pain and loss of blood, Mike nevertheless had managed to draw his weapon. He could just make out a dark form looming over the fallen dog, knife raised high in a shadow fist, all ready to plunge down into the bloodhound again. Mike had no idea whether Robby was still alive or already dead, but either way, that knife wasn't going to touch him again. Still struggling with dizziness, he raised his gun and fired—and then blacked out.

COMING OUT of unconsciousness was a fight, but Mike gritted his teeth and clawed his way free. That maniac—and Tanda—he *had* to wake up!

"It's okay, Mike, I'm right here," Tanda's voice came, and relief flooded through him even as he forced his eyes open. She was right there, beside him and holding his hand, but she wasn't alone. Lights blazed everywhere, along with the sound of police radios crackling, and he was lying on an ambulance stretcher.

"He got away," Tanda said before Mike could ask the question. "He was about to stab Robby again, but when you fired he just turned and ran. I heard the slam of a car door and then the car drove away with a screech, but I still took your gun and held it until everyone got here."

The hand holding his was trembling, and he quickly tightened his grip around it. He could almost see her sitting in the dark, guarding his unconscious body to make sure that maniac didn't come back to finish the job.

"I told you that you were wonderful," he croaked, trying to get the rustiness out of his voice. "What about Robby?"

"My vet, Dr. Singh, got here almost as fast as your people," she answered, wiping her eyes with the back of one hand. "He took Robby back to his hospital with him, to operate on the wound. He said Robby would live if *he* had anything to say about it, but—oh, Mike! I almost lost the two of you!"

"Because of my stupidity," Mike said, reaching up with his left hand to pull her down to him. "But don't you worry about Robby. He saved my life, so he has to be all right. I believe that good deeds are rewarded rather than punished, don't you?"

She nodded against his chest without saying anything, but a small amount of tension left the body under his hand. His side was throbbing like hell under the bandage he could feel against the wound, and he still felt as weak as a limp noodle. Still, as long as he was alive and Tanda was unhurt, he definitely felt he was ahead of the game.

"If I ever listen to you again, I'll need my head examined," a very offended voice said, and then Rena was crouching down to the left of the stretcher. "There's no danger at all, he tells me. A stampede is all I'll have to worry about, he tells me. And like an idiot I believed him, and didn't even have him covered."

"Which makes all this my fault," Mike agreed as Tanda sat straight again. "That's what I said just a minute ago, so why are you giving me a hard time?"

"Because you could have ended up beyond all hard times forever," she pronounced, and Mike could see how frightened and angry she was. "I don't like losing friends for stupid reasons, Mike, so tell me—what the hell happened?''

''An assumption turned around and bit us,'' he answered, aware of how closely both women were listening. ''The Sweet Bunch told us they thought the blackmailer had freaked out from pressure and was trying to kill them all, and we accepted that. There was no real reason not to, of course, but now there is. The guy with the knife wanted to know who the blackmailer is.''

They accepted that with momentary silence, both of them obviously thinking hard. Before either one could comment, though, an ambulance attendant came over.

''Okay, Lieutenant, they're ready for you at the hospital now,'' he said, sounding delighted about that. ''We're taking you to Mercy rather than to General, even though General's closer.''

''That's to make sure there aren't any undesirables waiting as part of your welcoming committee,'' Rena supplied when Mike raised his eyebrows in surprise. ''If you wound somebody, you expect him to be taken to the nearest hospital. You're not hurt badly enough for that, so we can cover ourselves in case that sweetheart decides to come back and finish the job. Larry and Art Renquist are already there, along with their own welcoming committee.''

''I was wondering where Art was,'' Mike commented. ''I expected him to be here, ready to keep reporters away from the body. Rena, I want a guard put on Tanda, and another just as strong on her dog. That bloodhound got a good whiff of our killer's scent, which means he might be able to identify the man when he recovers. By this time the killer knows that, so have them work in pairs but not in a car, and make sure they don't separate for any reason, even to go to the bathroom.''

''And I'll make sure the Sweet Bunch is covered,'' Rena said with a nod as she straightened. ''We've got a good excuse for it now, but I'd do it even without one. I wonder how they'll take hearing that the blackmailer isn't the murderer."

"We still have to decide whether or not to tell them," Mike answered, wincing as he tried to sit up on the stretcher. "Along with the fact that our friend with the knife is a Messenger of God, complete with clearly heard capital letters. Ow—"

"I'm sorry if I hurt you, but you're not sitting up," Tanda informed him in the hardest voice he'd ever heard her use. Her hands had gently pushed him back down, and trying to resist the push was what had hurt him. "And I'm going to the hospital with you," she added in the same voice. "Do you have any objections to that?"

"No, ma'am," he answered hurriedly, trying not to grin that really stupid grin. "Not an objection in the world. I won't be staying there long anyway, so—"

"You'll stay as long as they want you to," Rena said, taking her turn at bullying. "If you think you won't, I'll give your gun back to Tanda. From the way she was handling it, I know she can use it."

"Outnumbered *and* outgunned," Mike said with a sigh as the second ambulance attendant came up to help. "Okay, people, I surrender. And I definitely need the time to think."

"We all do," Tanda agreed, stepping back to let the attendants lift the stretcher. "Not to mention that the field has now been narrowed."

"But only because the quarry has now become two people," Rena pointed out as she also stepped back. "Finding one won't automatically mean finding the other, which is a step back in my book."

"Maybe it is, and maybe it isn't," Tanda replied as Mike was lifted and carried toward the ambulance. "Mike and I figured something out earlier tonight, about who the murderer was, before this all started. Even if we find the theory is wrong, locating that blackmailer will be the answer to everything. We'd then—''

Mike didn't hear the rest of that as he was put into the ambulance, but he didn't have to. The same thought had occurred to him, and Tanda was right. If only they could find that blackmailer—and if only Tanda didn't change her mind about getting involved with him. She'd insisted on going to the hospital, but how would she feel tomorrow, once he was completely out of danger? Would she decide the aggravation and terror weren't worth it? That she'd had more of attacks in the night than she'd ever wanted in the first place?

Mike watched her climb into the ambulance and sit down beside him, and that was when the other side of the coin had its say. How did *he* feel, having drawn a psychotic killer down on himself with her only a matter of feet away? What if that maniac had killed her? Did he have the right to put her in that kind of danger, expose her to something that could conceivably happen again? He was a cop, and sometimes a cop's danger spilled over onto his family. Would he be able to live with that?

One of the attendants came over to give him a shot of something, and the interruption was a definite relief. There were a lot of things he'd have to think about over the next couple of days, and one of the items would be more painful than the wound in his side.

It was past eleven-thirty in the morning before Tanda, with her own set of police guards, got home. It hadn't taken them long to get Mike settled into a hospital bed the night before, and the doctor had relieved her mind almost at once. Mike's wound would be painful for a while, but it wasn't serious. The shock from sudden loss of blood had caused him to black out, but a shot of blood builder plus an undisturbed night's sleep should make him almost as good as new.

Tanda had been delighted to hear that, but she'd still spent the night in his room, eventually falling asleep in the chair near his bed. There was a police guard outside his door, but she still needed to know personally that he was all right. If that maniac had tried to come back before the police had arrived the previous night, Tanda would have shot him without hesitation.

Which was what had kept her from falling asleep as soon as Mike went out from the medication they gave him. Tanda wasn't used to thinking of herself as blood-thirsty; even the murder of her brother had made her thirst for the arrest of his killer, not for the death of the man. But with Mike it was completely different, so much so that she'd been willing to take another human life to save his. She wasn't sure she could do the same to protect her own life, but with his there was no question.

And that was a very unsettling way to feel, not to mention how Mike might take it. Would the cop in him enjoy hearing she would willingly commit murder? Would the man in him want to think a woman believed he might need her protection? How did you tell a man something like that with any hope that he would understand? Len had always insisted that men hated to be protected by women, especially women who were prepared to kill. In all other ways Len and Mike were completely different, but what about in this way?

She'd been there when Mike woke up, and had stayed until they'd told him he was discharged. But the conversation had been the least bit awkward between them, and it had been something of a relief to leave. Was it possible he already knew how she felt about protecting him, and was regretting having gotten involved with her?

Tanda didn't know, and also didn't care to think about it right now. She was surprisingly refreshed from the sleep she'd had, and there were things she needed to do today.

The first, of course, was to stop by to see how Robby was doing at the vet's.

When she hadn't been worrying about Mike, she'd been worrying about her dog, but the second patient was doing almost as well as the first. He'd come through the surgery without any trouble and was healing, and had obviously been glad to see her. Tanda had stayed with him for a while, stroking him and telling him what a good dog he was. If Mike hadn't been able to get off that shot last night, she shuddered to think about what might have happened.

Getting home at eleven-thirty in the morning made her feel as if more than half the day was gone, and having slept in her clothes made her feel grimy. Still, she took care of the other dogs while her two guards checked the house, and only then did she shower and change clothes. Once that was done she went to see about the mail—and for the second time found something unexpected.

"From the law offices of Arthur Weddoes," she muttered, looking at the return address. "Don's lawyer, the one who left town yesterday. And delivered by messenger. What could possibly be so important?"

She sat down with a cup of coffee at the kitchen table before opening the envelope, an act of cowardice she wasn't in the least ashamed of. So much had happened over the last few days, both good and bad, that she didn't know if she could handle any more. Taking even a few minutes to brace herself was an absolute necessity, and then opening the envelope became a little easier.

The contents was a considerable surprise. Tanda had expected the contents to have something to do with Don's estate, something she hadn't wanted to deal with now. His estate reminded her of what he'd done to acquire it, but the sealed envelope, with a short note from the lawyer's assistant, proved to be only tangential to that. The note read:

Dear Ms. Grail,
The enclosed envelope was left for you by your late
brother just before his unfortunate death. Mr. Weddoes, prior to his leaving town, asked me to have this
delivered to you immediately. If you have any questions, or I can be of help in any way, please don't
hesitate to contact me.

The letter was signed by the woman, proving Weddoes
hadn't taken the time to do anything before leaving. From
what Mike had told her, the lawyer might not have been
there when Don's envelope had been left at his office.
That would explain why nothing had been said about it
sooner; his secretarial assistant hadn't had the authority to
send it or even to mention it without talking to Weddoes
first.

And then Tanda turned Don's envelope over, and chills
suddenly tingled along her body. On the front of the envelope was scrawled, "To be delivered to my sister,
Tanda Grail, in the event of my sudden death." Had Don
had a premonition, or had he known something for certain
about the instability of one of his group? If it was the
second, maybe he'd written down his suspicions—

Without wasting another second, Tanda turned the envelope over and pulled it open. The flap was well sealed,
and part of it tore when she forced her fingers across.
Inside was a single piece of paper, and unfolding it
showed her two lines of writing in Don's hand. The first
line said, "Mom's personal bank account," and the second said, "Valerie's dream come true."

Tanda read both lines twice, but not because she didn't
understand them. Someone else might have had trouble
with interpretation, but not the person they were meant
for. Don had known she'd understand, but the question
was, how strongly did she dare hope? If she was misin-
terpreting after all, or if someone had gotten there first—

The sound of the telephone ringing made her jump a foot, which then made her feel stupid. Not many people were murdered by phone, at least not in the real world. And if it *was* the murderer calling, it wouldn't bother her a bit. Hanging up on him would be easier than shooting him any day.

"Hello," she heard in answer to her own use of the word. "I thought I'd—call to see how you were doing."

"But you're the one who got wounded," she reminded Mike, finding it impossible not to smile. "Don't you think *I* should be the one making this call to *you?*"

"Well, it did occur to me that you might be considering it, so I thought you ought to know *where* to make it. Being at home and out of touch began to drive me crazy, so now I'm in my office at headquarters."

"In your office!" Tanda echoed, outraged but not surprised. "And you must have been out of touch a good ten or fifteen minutes. No wonder you began to go crazy. I'm surprised you were able to stand it that long."

"I managed only because I have the strength of ten," he returned wryly. "Are you really mad at me?"

"No," Tanda admitted with a sigh after a moment. "It's part of your nature, and no one can fight their nature for long. But I *will* make you a solemn promise—if you overdo it and kill yourself, I'll never speak to you again."

"I can't ask for any fairer than that," he returned with a chuckle. "And since I wouldn't want that, I'll have to take it easy. So how are you doing, and how's your dog?"

"Robby's doing fine, and even has the good sense not to want to go back to work yet," Tanda couldn't help answering. "But I, hopefully, am doing even better than that. I was going to call Rena, but since you insist on being there, I suppose I might as well tell *you.*"

"What have you come up with?" he asked at once, a lot more strength suddenly in his voice. "You really are

remarkable, you know, but I'll go into more detail about
that after you tell me what you've figured out.''

"I think I *will* start to believe you're after me for my
mind rather than my body,'' Tanda teased, almost embarrassed at how flattered she felt. "But this time it isn't
something I figured out, or at least not entirely.''

She went on to tell him about the messenger-delivered
envelope from Weddoes's office, and the two sentences
Don had sent. Mike listened quietly until she was through,
and then he blew out a breath.

"Talk about your lucky breaks,'' he said, sounding excited. "That first sentence has to refer to the place your
brother left his key. Do you have any idea what the second
sentence means?''

"I think I do, and if I'm right, it's where that strongbox
is,'' Tanda answered, fighting against her own rising excitement. "But Mike, what if someone already found it?
What if we get to the place but the box is gone?''

"There's only one way to know that,'' he said, the old
Mike back again. Gentle and reassuring, but also determined. "Where do we go, Tanda?''

"Don's house,'' she answered simply. "It's the only
place it can be.''

MIKE'S SIDE felt sore, but as long as he took things slow
and easy he could almost forget about it. He wasn't allowed to drive his own car to Don Grail's house—not
with Rena around—but as long as he got there he didn't
care that it was Larry doing the driving. And as long as
Rena went to pick up Tanda, leaving the unit covering
her house *at* her house. No more surprises was his new
rule of the day, and he hoped he could hold to it.

He and Larry waited in the car until Rena and Tanda
arrived, then the four of them plus half a dozen uniforms
went inside. Mike had taken the precaution of requesting
a search warrant before leaving headquarters, and the war-

rant arrived two minutes after the women. Tanda was supposed to be her brother's heir and they certainly had her permission to enter and search, but there was no sense in taking chances. If they found anything that would be usable in court, Mike didn't want it thrown out on a technicality.

Tanda smiled at him as they entered the house, but Mike thought he detected a shadow in that smile. Was she worried that they'd find nothing, or was the shadow more personal? Their conversation in his hospital room that morning had been somewhat strained. He'd been waiting for her to say she'd had second thoughts about their relationship, while he still hadn't made up his own mind about putting her in danger. Could she have been waiting for *him* to say something, a something that would have let her off the hook?

"Okay, Mike, you sit down there," Rena instructed, pointing to a chair. They'd climbed the few steps upward, and were now near the living room. "The rest of us will either stand or sit as we please, while Tanda tells us what we're looking for. Simply searching this place would take a week."

"And would probably be a waste of time," Tanda said with a nod. "My story won't be long, but it will be a better idea if you listen to it sitting down."

"I'm glad *I'm* in charge of this investigation," Mike grumbled in surrender as he went to the chair and sat. "If I weren't, everybody and their grandmother would end up giving me orders."

"I'm just one pushy female, not everybody," Rena pointed out pleasantly. "And Tanda certainly isn't my grandmother. Can we get on with it now, boss man?"

Mike held up a hand to show he'd already surrendered, and that became a signal for everyone else to find seats. Tanda went to perch on the carved mahogany coffee table, and once everyone was settled she looked up.

"Do you remember me telling you about Don's favorite book, Mike?" she asked. "It was called *Trail of Gold,* and he even had a copy of it here, in his bedroom bookcase."

"I remember," Mike answered. "I also remember that we looked through the book, and nothing seemed to be in it."

"Nothing *was* in it, not in the way *you* mean," she confirmed with a smile. "What I didn't mention was that Don talked briefly about the book the night we had dinner. He told me with a grin that he'd always known I'd sneaked into his room and read it, but he didn't mind. He said he felt it somehow brought us closer now that we were grown, and asked if I remembered any part of the book. When I assured him I remembered all of it, he changed the subject."

"That means the Valerie mentioned in his note refers to a character in the book," Mike said, seeing the point immediately. "What kind of character was she, and how did her dream come true?"

"That was one of the problems I had with the book," Tanda answered, her smile paled. "Valerie's dream never did come true, but the writer treated it in a 'oh, well, that's life' kind of way. He did that with all the women characters in the book, sacrificing their aims and dreams so his hero could climb higher and higher toward fame and fortune."

"Sounds like the kind of men I usually date," Rena commented. "So what was the dream that didn't come true?"

"Well, the hero in the book was named Don, which probably explains why my brother liked it so much," Tanda answered. "The Don in the book left home young with nothing but his good looks and charm, and met a number of young, beautiful and wealthy women. Valerie was the second, after the first had taken advantage of his innocence and then had thrown him out. Since he'd intended taking advantage of her first, I always wondered why he thought he had the right to be bitter.''

''It's a law,'' Larry said from his place on the couch next to Rena. ''If you start out to clip somebody but they clip you instead, the law says you have to be bitter. And it's an equal-opportunity law, so it doesn't matter if you're male or female.''

''Well, by the time Don met Valerie, he was determined to get what he could out of life no matter what,'' Tanda continued, ignoring the interruption. ''Valerie was young and rich and all alone, and he moved in on her—and in with her—and charmed her out of everything he could think of. She bought him clothes and expensive presents of jewelry, and a car, and all she asked in return was his support for her dream. She wanted to qualify as an Olympic swimmer, something he considered stupid and juvenile.''

''Swimming means the pool,'' Mike said. ''Or at least somewhere around it. Could the box possibly be in the pool?''

''It's possible, I suppose,'' Tanda allowed, looking doubtful. ''I considered that myself, but then I realized the box would have to be watertight for that, and the very fact of its being watertight would give people a clue to its hiding place. It's more likely to be hidden somewhere around the pool, maybe in a special niche of some kind.''

''And since your brother had this place rebuilt, that's a very possible possibility,'' Mike said with grim satisfaction. ''After all, who would look for a safe in a swimming pool? Okay, people, the area of our hunt is out back, around the pool.''

As everyone got up and prepared to go downstairs, Rena said to Tanda, ''So why didn't Valerie's dream come true? Did she spend her time catering to Don instead of practicing?''

"No," Tanda answered with a sigh, not quite looking at the other woman. "Don wanted her to do that, and when she tried to explain why she had to follow her dream, he got mad and started a big fight. He also drank too much, then stormed out to take a drive in one of her cars.

"She followed after him, trying to smooth things over, and made the mistake of getting into the car with him. He was too drunk and too angry to drive, and there was an accident. He got a couple of scratches, but she ended up paralyzed from the waist down and presumably never walked again. I don't know for sure, because as soon as Don heard she was paralyzed, he packed up everything she'd given him and left."

"What a surprise," Rena said with a head shake. "But at least slobs like that don't only come in the male variety. If they did, I'd be tempted to feel sorry for the bums. Take it slow, Mike. If the box is there now, it'll still be there five minutes from now."

"Larry, can I borrow your gun?" Mike asked with an obvious, pleasant smile. "I'll only need it for a minute, and then I'll give it right back."

"Just to make sure ballistics can't point to your gun as the murder weapon," Larry said with a nod of understanding, glancing at his partner. "I sympathize completely, but there's a less messy way of handling it. Let's go, partner, we've got a scavenger hunt to get involved in."

He took her arm and moved toward the stairs, and Rena was smart enough not to argue with being dragged away. It was concern that made her pester Mike, but pretty soon that would make no difference at all. He'd snap at her rather than try to be funny, and then— Better if the trouble was headed off before it started.

"Being babied *could* drive someone to murder, couldn't it?" Tanda asked him with a faint smile. "I guess I'd better watch my step too."

"You're not in the same category at all," Mike answered with his own smile, starting to raise a hand to her face. Then the guilt rose to ask him what he was doing, why he was encouraging her. If she didn't have the good sense to stay away from him, shouldn't he have enough for them both?

"Mike, when this is all over we'll have to talk," she said with disturbance in those beautiful gray eyes. She'd seen him start to touch her and then stop. "This isn't the time or the place, I know, so—later?"

"Later," he agreed with a quiet nod, then joined her in going toward the stairs. He still wasn't sure he could bear to give her up, but if it meant keeping her safe— Better to have the pain be his rather than hers.

Once downstairs, they went out the patio doors to the pool area. It was a fairly pretty day, typical August, but there seemed to be clouds moving in on the sunshine. Mike wondered if that was nature trying to imitate human life, then dismissed the question. He'd find out for certain once this case was over.

Larry and Rena and the six uniforms were already inspecting the pool, but hadn't yet found anything to draw their attention. Mike thought about joining in, then decided that that would be childish. If his side hadn't been hurting, he would have automatically begun to use his head while others used their eyes. He chose a deck chair halfway down the long side of the pool, lowered himself into the chair, then proceeded to use his head as well as his eyes.

The pool was Olympic-size—probably not by coincidence—and the water was still clean and clear. If anything was in the pool—despite Tanda's excellent objection— someone would have seen it by now.

"Take a good close look at the two ends of the pool," Mike called out to those trying to spot a secret hiding hole. "Olympic swimmers dive in one end, swim to the other, then swim back. They're not usually concerned with the long sides.''

"Darn, just when I was about to volunteer to jump in and check them personally," Rena called back, dabbing at the sweat on her forehead. "I don't know what it is about cool, clear aqua water on a hot August day..."

"The electric-blue tiles in the design on the shallow end!" Mike said as he suddenly noticed the tiles, feeling excited. "I should have seen it sooner, so check them first."

"My brother's favorite color," Tanda said, just stopping herself from quickly moving forward. "Good idea, Mike."

Hearing the excitement in their voices, Rena and Larry began a serious examination of the electric-blue tiles. That color appeared among the other brightly colored tiles decorating the shallow end of the pool, but not at the deep end. And they seemed to cluster where they were, almost as if they were together for a reason.

Which they were. Even as Mike watched, Larry called out, "Found a seam!" and then he was pressing on the tiles. It took a minute or so to get the proper angle, but a section of the tiles sank in as another section popped out. It was a simple, rectangular door above the waterline, and inside the niche it hid was a heavy metal container with three locks.

"We've got it!" Larry called, holding up the box, triumph strong in the words. "And, unless we're more unlucky than ten Jonahs, we've also got *them*."

Them, Mike thought, staring at their prize. The blackmailer, the murderer—and the end of this case. *And*, his mind insisted on adding as he stood, *maybe the end of something else as well.*

Chapter Sixteen

Tanda sat in the conference room at police headquarters, Mike, Rena and Larry there as well. They'd gotten a judge's permission to have a locksmith force open the strongbox—another precaution to be sure any evidence was usable, Mike had said—and now they were examining the slips of paper from the box. Twelve pieces of paper in twelve different handwritings, and one of them was Don's. She kept her thoughts very carefully on those pieces of paper, to make sure she didn't think about anything else. Later...later...

"What a lovely portrait of a group of friends," Rena said in disgust, staring at the two piles the papers had been put into. "Murder, arson, multiple rape, embezzlement—and at least one possible loss of life in almost every case. If it's true the blackmailer has evidence that they *are* guilty of the crimes they were only accused of, it's no wonder none of them simply packed up and left."

"And it's no wonder Miss Baderlie is now demanding another lawyer, rather than talking to us," Larry said in agreement. "But if we had the evidence the blackmailer does..."

"First we have to identify the blackmailer," Mike pointed out. "Anybody see anything in those slips that might give us a hint?"

"Separating them into two groups helps, but only a little," Larry said, reaching forward to tap one of the piles. "This group admits to violent crimes, and the other, smaller batch to nonviolent ones. But how do we know if they're all telling the truth? What if every one of them lied?"

"I don't think they dared to lie," Rena said, leaning back in her chair. "Remember, they did this last year, and this year they were supposed to bring proof that what they said on the slips was true. Anyone who didn't have newspaper clippings—*with* pictures—would have been in trouble."

"That assumes they were right, and the blackmailer *doesn't* have a crime of his own," Larry countered, but he still nodded in agreement. "Aside from that, though, I concede the point. The only liar in the bunch, if there was one, is the blackmailer. So where does that take us?"

"To the point where we start comparing," Mike said when Rena didn't answer immediately. "We now have reports back on all the victims, so let's match them up to their slips."

There was a pile of report folders on the table as well, and Tanda watched them each take one and begin to go through the slips of paper. Five slips were matched to five folders, and then the three detectives looked at each other again.

"Okay, so some of them were only telling part of the truth," Mike said. "Jeffrey Styles—originally known as John Sorliss—just mentioned the money he'd walked away with, nothing about the deaths he was directly responsible for. We'll have to keep that in mind with the ones that are left. Which ones are they?"

"Richard Draper, our legal expert, ought to be first," Larry said. "He claims he simply covered up for one of his clients, a large corporation, by bribing various people.

Anybody care to bet that that didn't go so far at least one person ended up dead?''

"No bet," Rena said for all of them. "Our second upstanding citizen is Miles Rayburn, the one who likes to push people around. He claims he did nothing more than overinsure his late wife, and the insurance company is out to get him because they hated having to pay out all that money. *I* believe the poor dear man, don't you?''

"Certainly," Larry agreed. "As much as I believe Lawrence Ransom, the man who thinks so much of his own good looks. This poor guy is being persecuted by women, lots of them who are jealous that he isn't giving them attention. They *must* be out to get him, otherwise why would they all accuse him of rape like that? Of course, he doesn't say if there are one or more who are beyond accusing anybody.''

"Oh, I'm sure there couldn't be," Rena said, sounding oh-so-sincere. "And I'm just as sure that Jocelyn Geroux is suffering only because other women—and nasty men—are jealous of her. She had a private business giving silly men what they really needed, and one of them was inconsiderate enough to die. It wasn't her fault, of course, it would have happened anywhere the man happened to be, but bad luck made it happen at *her* place.''

"She was a hooker?" Mike asked in surprise. "I had the impression she lacked the proper—temperament—for the job.''

"She wasn't a prostitute," Rena denied with a head shake. "I'll admit I'm guessing here, but I'll put money on the fact that she's a dominatrix. You know, the kind who dresses up in leather and high heels, then puts dog collars on the men disturbed enough to come to her. What she does after the dog collar goes on is certainly what caused the incident that wasn't in any way her fault.''

"Obviously another gem," Larry said as Mike shook his head and sighed. "Pretty soon we'll be able to make a necklace, and the next link will belong to Howard Ullman. With that incredible voice of his I can believe he's a con man, but I don't believe he never hurt anyone. If he's too well known by the police on the West Coast for him to ever go back, he has to be wanted for more than a bunch of scams.''

"I'd say the same goes for Mark King," Rena agreed. "He supposedly scammed a mob big shot by mistake, and now spends his time looking over his shoulder. If it's true, I can believe he's desperately on the run, and from worse than any police charges. But that sounds good enough to be another scam, especially since it's unlikely there are any newspaper stories to cover it.''

"Which means he's a good candidate for being the blackmailer," Larry put in. "He might have decided that blackmail is nothing but scamming on a slightly larger scale.''

"But that's the point," Mike disagreed. "A con artist might not refuse to indulge in a bit of polite blackmail if the opportunity came his way, but they usually lack the temperament to go out and set it up on a large scale. It's dangerous, don't forget, especially when you're dealing with people who have already killed once. Why go to all that trouble, when there are hundreds of safer scams to bring in money?''

"Well, maybe and maybe not," Rena grudged. "You can never tell what people will decide to do. Like our last friend, Miss Baderlie. She apparently embezzled a large amount of money from a company she worked for, and when the head of her department discovered the loss, he had a heart attack and died. That wasn't her fault, of course, but the police refused to agree.''

"And there's no statute of limitations to run out when a felony death is involved," Larry added. "That's why there have to be deaths involved with all of them. With the number of years this has been going on, at least a couple of them would have passed the statute of limitations on their crimes by now. If you turn someone in and the police can't touch them, your blackmail threat loses its teeth.''

''But that doesn't fit in with what we decided about Roger Saxon,'' Tanda finally contributed. ''From everything we learned about him, he was a good cop and a careful investigator. He'd never have simply opened the door to someone he knew was capable of murder.''

''That might mean he didn't know the person was capable of murder,'' Mike said, obviously having thought about it. ''The blackmailer found a connection the police never did, and dug for the evidence to prove it. Sometimes if someone is under investigation for a small, unrelated crime, no one will see a connection between that and a murder. No one who isn't looking for one, that is.''

''The big picture,'' Mike said slowly, suddenly looking as though he'd gotten the strangest idea. He thought about it for a minute while the others stared at him in silence, all of them understanding he might have something. When he finally looked up, he smiled, obviously hoping he was right.

''Well, it does make a lot of sense,'' he began, then realized they had no idea what he was talking about. ''Who the blackmailer is, I mean, and how she tripped herself up in a lie. Maybe she thought a year would be plenty of time to fake some proof.''

''She,'' Rena echoed while Tanda and Larry made comments of their own. ''I seriously doubt if you mean Jocelyn Geroux, so that leaves Miss Alicia Baderlie. What makes you think it's her?''

''Something you said, Rena,'' Mike answered. ''You would probably have noticed it yourself in a little while, once you had the chance to think about it. After we tracked Miss Baderlie to her house and you caught her going out the back, you said something about the woman having worked at the library 'forever.' If she's been there that long, when was it she did that embezzling? And if she got so much money from her crime, why would she settle in a place like this? At the very least, people would notice a newly arrived librarian who lived beyond her means—and she does. Did you see all those very expensive items her house is furnished with?''

''But if she lived here all her life and suddenly got—oh, an inheritance, for instance, people would think nothing of it,'' Rena added excitedly. ''And unless I got it wrong, I was given the impression she *has* lived here all her life. Went away to school, got a degree in library science, then came back to establish her reign as queen. It shouldn't take more than an hour or so to check that.''

''And who would be better for digging up blackmail dirt than a research librarian?'' Larry said as Rena stood and headed for the door. ''It makes sense, Mike, it really does.''

''But something that doesn't make sense is why she was the one chosen to break into my house,'' Tanda said. ''Among the seven of them, surely one of the others would have been able to do a better job of it.''

''But the incident does make sense if you realize she *wasn't* chosen,'' Mike said, moving forward slowly to lean his arms on the table. ''You'll remember we wondered about the way the other six denied knowing anything about the break-in? Well, now I believe they were all telling the truth. Baderlie lives in this area and knew your brother, so it's almost guaranteed that she knew about you as well. What would be more natural than to decide your brother would hide his key at your house?''

''But why would she want the key that badly?'' Larry asked, also leaning forward. ''As the blackmailer she'd know she wasn't doing the killings, so what would be the point in opening the box?''

''The point was to *not* open the box,'' Mike told him

with a snort. "She and the others found out that the murderer, apparently by chance, had eliminated all the holders of one of the three keys. Where the other victims hid their keys was anybody's guess, but Don Grail was most likely to have left it with his sister. Get that key and eliminate it, and the box could conceivably stay closed forever."

"Which would keep the murderer from finding out who she was," Tanda said with a nod. "But that seems to suggest she doesn't know who's doing the killing any more than we do. If she did know, she would have released his information to the police by now. What better way to get out from under than to have the police do your dirty work?"

"There's a chance that isn't true," Mike said, "and I'm praying hard the chance comes out. My biggest fear was that the blackmailer was already dead, that he or she was one of the first five victims. That could have happened easily enough, and then we'd be out of luck. This way... If we can prove Baderlie was lying, then we should be able to force her to talk."

"But what would she talk about?" Larry demanded. "If she doesn't know any more than we do, all she can do is guess. Are you hoping she'll turn over her files to us?"

"I think Mike is hoping she was bluffing when she blackmailed the murderer," Tanda said slowly, having gotten the idea from Mike's hints. "She must have solid evidence against most of her victims, but what if she saw a definite pattern with one of them but couldn't actually find the evidence she needed? Mightn't she have decided to pretend she did have something? If it worked, she would end up wealthier, if it didn't, she would have lost nothing but a little effort."

"But the murderer believed her, and still does believe," Larry jumped in with revelation. "And he must have relatively innocent charges pending against him, which would be useless without that necessary linking evidence. If she throws him to the police using only the minor charge, he'll finally understand she never did have what she claimed. Since he's crazy to begin with, that would send him completely over the edge. He'd never give up until every one of the last six were dead.''

"But that's only a guess, so we'll have to see if it's true," Mike warned. "It could turn out that she *doesn't* know, and in that case we *will* need her files—which she might not be willing to give up. It would mean supplying evidence against herself, and I won't offer immunity under any circumstances. Blackmail is a filthy business at any time, but six people are already dead and she made no effort to come forward even anonymously."

"So what will we do?" Larry asked, and Tanda thought he looked downright desperate. "Without immunity, how can we get her to cooperate?"

"There's a way," Mike said, and something in the words made her want to shiver. He had also stopped looking at her, and that was even worse than his tone. "Yes, definitely a way, and she'd better believe I'm serious, because I will be."

Larry glanced at Tanda, possibly to see if she understood what Mike meant, but she didn't. From the way Mike was acting, the idea must be terrible, and she, at least, believed every word. Mike Gerard would do what he had to in order to catch a murderer, but what would he think of himself afterward? It would definitely be a problem, one more among so many others.

AFTER SEVERAL phone calls had been made in less than an hour, Mike sat in an interrogation room and watched Alicia Baderlie walk in. This time it was Rena rather than Larry who brought her, and the librarian was accompanied by a tired-looking woman in a suit carrying a briefcase.

The new lawyer, Mike thought as the two women chose chairs, leaving Rena to stand at the wall behind them.

"I'm Barbara Abbott, Miss Baderlie's new attorney," the woman opened, confirming Mike's guess. "What's being done to her is unconscionable, and if you don't release her immediately I'll file against your department with the court."

"Before you do your filing, Ms. Abbott, you should know that the charges against your client are being added to," Mike said. "It's no longer simply a matter of attempted burglary and unlawful trespass."

"Why is that, Lieutenant?" she asked with a sourly wry smile. "Because you knew your trumped-up charges would never stick? Without concrete evidence, the frame constructed by that vindictive detective of yours will just fall apart."

"Is that the story she gave you?" Mike said, seeing the small, nasty smile the librarian wore. "That Sergeant Foreman framed her because she was holding a grudge? That would be quite an accomplishment, considering that we do have concrete evidence. Evidence, I might add, that was obtained while Sergeant Foreman was nowhere around."

"How seriously would anyone have taken that so-called evidence if the sergeant *had* been around?" Ms. Abbot asked with a snort. "You have nothing at all linking my client with any misdoing of any sort, so—"

"Ms. Abbott, we're wasting each other's time," Mike interrupted, not nearly as patient as he was forcing himself to sound. He was probably going to have to do something really low, and he wanted it behind him as quickly as possible. "Let me tell you exactly what we have, and then you can be the judge of how trumped up the evidence is."

"He'll lie to you, of course," Miss Baderlie stated quietly to her attorney without looking at the woman. Her soulless stare was reserved for Mike, as though he were the one who had broken the law. "They all lie and support each other's lies, and no one has the courage to oppose them."

"Of course we do," Mike said before the Abbott woman could respond defensively. "As I said, we'll let your attorney judge."

Mike then began the story, giving the woman everything that had bearing and wasn't being kept undisclosed. After a few minutes the expression in Abbott's eyes changed, telling Mike she was in the process of realizing that her client had lied to her. She kept silent about that, though, and simply listened.

"...and our lab found traces of mud on the shoes that matched the casts we made," he finally wound up. "The shoes had been cleaned off, but not quite enough. That along with everything else says we do have a case, which I'm sure you've realized by now."

Rather than answer in words, the woman sighed, then turned to look at her client.

"Miss Baderlie, none of this agrees with what you told me," she said, her tone very neutral. "It might be possible to twist circumstantial evidence, but they even have statements from the other six people that you're one of them. Do you want me to ask for a place where we can talk privately?"

"To what purpose?" the librarian demanded impatiently. "I deny everything they claim, and that's all there is to it. I'm a respectable member of this community, and those others are strangers with extremely uncertain reputations—or supposed police with imagined grudges. There's very little doubt as to who the court will believe."

"But you still haven't heard about the new charge we're prepared to make," Mike said, giving Ms. Abbott no chance to tell her client things would not really go as she was picturing. "Aren't you the least bit interested?

Your lawyer should know about it, at least, so she won't be caught by surprise in court.''

''He's right,'' the lawyer said before Miss Baderlie could decide she *wasn't* interested. Her expression had said she was about to do that, but Abbott's advice changed her mind.

''Oh, very well,'' the librarian grudged, granting an underling a favor. ''Let's get this nonsense over with, and then we can continue to court for my release.''

''This—nonsense—starts in a very interesting place,'' Mike said, determined not to let the woman's attitude get to him. ''That strongbox you and your friends were so eager to open, well, the good news is we found the box and opened it *for* you.''

Suddenly, the woman was no longer uninterested. Her light-skinned face paled even further, and she sat frozen without moving a muscle.

''I see you understand exactly what that means,'' Mike said with satisfaction he couldn't hide. ''There were slips of paper in the box, and the one with your name on it says you embezzled a large sum of money and incidentally caused the death of someone.''

''I'm sorry, Lieutenant, but that can't be used against my client,'' Abbott said immediately, although somewhat on the mechanical side. ''It's self-incrimination without foundation, and Miranda also comes into play. A supposed confession like that is worthless, so your additional charges would be the same.''

''Ah, but I don't intend to bring charges on those grounds,'' Mike said, watching Baderlie's sudden relief evaporate as quickly as it had appeared. ''You remember what I said about how the group intended to find the blackmailer in their midst? Well, it so happens the blackmailer made a stupid mistake. She claimed to be guilty of something she couldn't possibly be, not when she took her job at the library as soon as she left college. When people are born and raised in a town, there tend to be those around who know all about them.''

The expression Baderlie now wore was the strangest mix of fear and fury. The fear came from having been found out, Mike knew, but the fury was caused by having been called stupid. The woman was obviously pathological, but she wasn't too far gone to be reached.

''You're accusing my client of being the blackmailer?'' Abbott asked, not as derisively as she probably would have liked. ''Simply because she supposedly confessed to a crime she never committed? Really, Lieutenant, just how far do you think you'll get with that?''

''At least as far as an arraignment hearing,'' Mike answered, looking straight at Abbott to make her believe him. They both had to believe, or his plan would never work. ''Miss Baderlie's attempt to break into Ms. Grail's house was a solitary attempt, one the others knew nothing about. There was no reason for her to act on her own if she wanted the same thing the others did, and considering her meager knowledge of housebreaking techniques, there was every reason for her to let one of the others do it. But she didn't let someone else do it because she didn't want Don Grail's key to become available. She wanted that box to stay closed forever.''

''Because then she would be suspected of being the serial killer?'' Abbott said, doing a little better with professional ridicule. ''If you're thinking of taking it that far, I couldn't be happier. My client had nothing to do with those murders, and I expect to have no trouble proving it.''

''Let me save you the trouble,'' Mike said gently, again taking faint relief from a still-silent Miss Baderlie. ''It was the group's belief that the blackmailer was also the serial killer, but that's been totally disproved. You see, I ran a small experiment yesterday, and got some results I wasn't expecting.''

"What did you do?" the librarian suddenly demanded, giving her lawyer no chance to ask the same question more politely. "Tell me, you fool! What did you do?"

"Unfortunately, I can't argue the fool part," Mike replied wryly, watching her closely. "I told the rest of your group that I knew who the blackmailer was, hoping to force one of them to come forward with useful information. The one who came forward instead was the serial killer, catching me in the dark last night and demanding to know the blackmailer's name. He left behind a slash in my side to prove I didn't imagine it all."

Miss Baderlie stared at Mike with lips parted, but nothing in the way of words emerged. He'd thought she looked pale earlier; right now her narrow face was so white, it was a wonder she wasn't down on the floor in a faint. Her thin neck moved as she swallowed twice, and there seemed to be a tremor traveling all through her body.

"Miss Baderlie, what is it?" Abbott asked her client. "Are you all right? Do you need a doctor?"

"I'm not a doctor, Ms. Abbott, but I can tell you what's wrong with your client," Mike said when it was clear the librarian wasn't going to respond. "We've decided that she knows who the serial killer is, but she can't prove it. You remember that the others of her group said three of their previous members had been turned in to the police, as a warning and lesson to the rest of them? That leads us to believe your client hasn't done the same with the murderer because she blackmailed him on a bluff. She doesn't have anything concrete on him, and if he finds out who she is he'll kill her with his dying effort."

"He will!" Baderlie whispered, the tremor now in her voice. "He's more insane than I ever imagined he could be, and he must have planned and waited for this all year. If he finds out who I am I'll never be safe, never!"

"Miss Baderlie, as your attorney I have to caution

you," Abbott said, and now *her* voice was trembling. "You were Mirandized when you were arrested, and you're now accompanied by an attorney. Anything you say can be used against you, so—"

"Oh, be quiet, you stupid little fool!" Baderlie snarled, her arms wrapped tightly around herself. "Don't you understand that my life is at stake? You have to make them protect me, even if they don't want to!"

"Certainly they'll protect you," Abbott said, trying for soothing but coming up instead with stiff and insulted. "It's what the police do, even though sometimes I question the wisdom of being that uncritical."

"Well, now, Ms. Abbott, it would be more accurate to say that the police do what they can," Mike said slowly, rubbing his chin with one finger. "As you pointed out earlier, a confession all by itself is considered without foundation. We can go for arraignment against Miss Baderlie with what we have—and we will—but the court could very well throw out the entire case. In that event she would be set free, almost completely on her own. We don't have the manpower to keep her guarded around the clock, especially when she's been less than cooperative and there's no case the man hours can be charged against. Our hands will be tied…"

Abbott looked faintly disturbed, as though her first instinct was to argue that stance, but was deliberately keeping herself quiet. Baderlie, on the other hand, was frantic, and she wasn't too far into instability to fully understand the point.

"You're trying to say you won't protect me unless I cooperate," she snarled, once again furious. "Do you think I'm stupid enough to believe that? Police always do their duty, especially when there's a lawyer around to force them into it! I know how these things work, so don't waste my time trying to lie to me!"

"Lady, you're not important enough to be lied to,"

Mike told her very flatly, finally out of patience. "And you seem to have spent too much time watching bad television and movies. The highest-paid lawyer in the world can't force the police to do something against their own rules, not when they don't want to. You could have gotten in touch with us anonymously after the first or second murder, telling us who you suspected even though you had no proof. If you catch someone in the act you don't need any other proof, but you didn't give us a chance to save the rest of the victims. All you thought about was yourself, and now you can pay for that stupidity. If you don't cooperate fully, you can try your hand at protecting yourself."

The librarian's still-pale face was expressionless, but her cold eyes were narrowed as she stared at him. Mike sat calmly under the stare, his own gaze steady with determination. She searched for some hint that he was bluffing, he knew, but she wasn't about to find one.

"You've made your position very clear, Lieutenant," Barbara Abbott said quietly. "If my client refuses to cooperate, you'll try to catch the murderer when he goes after *her*. Whether or not you'll be able to stop him before he reaches her depends on luck, I think, and I've learned it isn't wise to depend on luck. What sort of deal are you willing to offer in exchange for Miss Baderlie's full cooperation? Immunity at least, I should think—"

"No," Mike interrupted gently but firmly. The woman, although constrained to look after her client's interests, was now clearly trying to help *him*. "I don't believe in rewarding people when they deal only to save their own necks. Miss Baderlie will either give us everything we want, or we'll charge her as I said we would. Since we probably don't have enough evidence to go to trial, I'm sure you know what will happen next."

Mike had shifted his gaze to the attorney while he spoke to her, and when he looked back at Baderlie she was no longer staring at him. Her eyes were closed and her narrow lips were set, and there was nothing about her suggesting satisfaction or pleasure.

"Damn you," she whispered after a moment, with hatred and defeat clear in her voice. "I'll give you what you want, but damn you forever."

Under other circumstances Mike would have felt the twisting of guilt, but this woman aroused nothing of the sort in him. Some people ended up in trouble with the law by accident, but this woman had done exactly as she pleased because she'd believed she was untouchable. Now that it was time for her to pay, she regretted only that she'd been caught. What she'd done was, to her, still more than justified.

Mike exchanged glances with Rena, then turned his head to nod toward Larry and Tanda who sat behind the mirror. What they were about to hear would identify a multiple murderer, and then all the four of them had to do was think of a way to catch him.

Chapter Seventeen

All six of them were there in the large room, and Tanda found it hard not to stare at the murderer and shudder. As a matter of fact all of them made her want to shudder now that she knew the exact details of what they'd done. They were all cold-blooded murderers, and in every case but one the proof was conclusive.

Mike stirred in his chair beside her, almost as though he was going to make sure again that the uniformed officer was still behind her. He didn't seem prepared to take any chances at all, not after having gone through Miss Baderlie's files. If anything, he was more shaken than she was.

And they'd all been astounded. You would expect a research librarian to be really good at research, but Miss Baderlie had been incredible. She'd carefully clipped out the details of all suspected murders-for-profit involving those who had run away or hadn't been charged for lack of evidence, and then had kept a close watch on those communities catering to the rich. Sooner or later a newspaper item appeared about new residents in the area showing up at one of the parties, and most often there were pictures. When one of the pictures matched a similar photo in her files, she then went on to the next phase.

If the people were wanted somewhere under another

name, she used a hired hacker to break into the computer files of travel agents in the new community, to find out which one her victim used. Once that was known, she kept a list of all the places they went and especially the places they went most often, building up a pattern. With that she was able to threaten not only to expose them, but to direct the police to find them again if they ran. She never told them how she'd found them, but the threat of passing on her unmentioned method helped to keep them in line.

With those where the evidence hadn't been enough to charge them, her method was different. Taking a few days of the full month's worth of vacation due her, she would travel to the place her discovery had committed his or her crime, and then she would get down to the real research. It was incredible how much evidence was overlooked by the police during an investigation, things that were part of the public record. Too often the police had looked for hidden information, and the public sort went entirely unnoticed.

As with the wife of Miles Rayburn, for instance. Tanda felt helpless fury whenever she thought about it, and the way Rayburn had bought so much insurance on the woman a little more than two years before her "unfortunate" death. By all newspaper accounts she'd been a shy but pleasant little woman, who was very much in love with her husband. No one had been able to understand how she'd forced herself to take skydiving lessons, but one of her friends had speculated that she must have been trying to prove something.

Rayburn had told one reporter he'd considered taking those same lessons himself, but had never imagined his wife would want to join him. She'd been terrified of things like that, so terrified that it wasn't surprising she'd panicked on her first jump and had died because of it. He'd had no idea she was doing that sort of thing, and must have intended to surprise him.

Miss Baderlie had tapped into the computer records of the skydiving school, and had gotten a facsimile of the woman's application to the school. Since Rayburn's wife had shown up alone each time for her lesson, the police hadn't bothered to do the same checking. If they had, they would have discovered the signature on the form didn't match any other public-records signature from the woman, but did match Rayburn's handwriting. The slime must have used her love for him to bully her into taking the lessons, knowing there was an excellent chance she would never survive her first real jump. Even people who wanted to do what they were doing had trouble the first time.

"Well?" Richard Draper said after checking his watch for the dozenth time. "We were told this wouldn't take long, and it's already been twenty minutes without anything happening. If *you* don't have anything better to do with your time, I do."

"We were waiting for everyone to be here, Mr. Draper," Mike answered mildly from beside Tanda. "I know lawyers think time is money, but you're not a practicing lawyer any longer, are you?"

Draper made no effort to snap out an answer, and Tanda could see the sudden worry in his eyes. It was obvious Mike hadn't been guessing about Draper's past, and that wasn't a good sign as far as the group was concerned.

"But now that everyone is here, we *can* get started," Mike went on in the same mild voice. "At the suggestion of the district attorney's office, I've called you all together to give you some information—and to give some advice. I'm told the advice will eventually work to our good, and that's the only reason I'm bothering."

A stir went through the six, accompanied by nervous sidelong glances. Something unpleasant was coming, they knew, and they were very much afraid they also knew what.

"I've been authorized to tell you that we've identified the blackmailer among you," Mike said, slowly looking at each of them. "One of you, however, already knows that and was desperate enough to attack me in an attempt to learn the blackmailer's identity. I'm afraid that destroys your theory about the blackmailer and the murderer being one and the same."

A cloud of muttered exclamations arose, but not nearly as loud as it would have been with a different audience. These people were too frightened, Tanda saw, maybe almost as frightened as their victims had been.

"So who is it?" Lawrence Ransom demanded almost at once, his handsome good looks even more strained. "Not that *I* have anything to worry about. I paid only to keep scandal from embarrassing my family, not because I had anything to hide. You'll find that out when you check the file on me."

Two or three of the others began to say the same thing, but Mike held up a hand until they'd quieted down.

"Until I do see the files, I won't presume to disagree with any of you, Mr. Ransom," he said. "I can't say when that will be, exactly, but we *are* working on it. For that reason you're all being asked now to make no attempt to leave, and you're also strongly advised to seek legal representation. We expect that you'll soon be in need of it."

"You can't do that," Richard Draper said flatly, fear and desperation now strong in his face. "If you have no charges to hold us on now, you can't tell us not to leave."

"Oh, but I can, Mr. Draper," Mike returned, all but smiling. "I know for a fact that one of you attacked me, and as soon as we see those files we'll have corroborating evidence for the motive. Ms. Grail's bloodhound, who saved my life, is now recuperating some distance away from here. As soon as he's well enough to track, we'll put him on the trail of the person who attacked us both, and then we'll make an arrest. By then we'll have the files, so prosecuting won't be any trouble at all.''

"You're negotiating!" Jocelyn Geroux suddenly snarled, disbelieving fury on her face. "That's why you don't have the files yet, you're negotiating to get them! That slime has been sucking us dry, but we'll be the only ones who get it in the neck! If you think I'll stand still for that, you're crazy.''

"What you do or don't do is up to you, Ms. Geroux," Mike said, still amiable. "I'm sure the attorney you retain will tell you all your rights under the law. Right now I'd like to thank you all for coming, and the officers who brought you will see you get back to where you're staying. I, personally, have to get back to work.''

Tanda stood up when Mike did, and the two of them walked out and ignored the questions four of the six tried to put. Lawrence Ransom, Mile Rayburn, Mark King and Howard Ullman all seemed to want more information, but that was too bad about them. Mike had already said everything he was supposed to, and would not be adding one word more.

Larry and Rena waited for them in Mike's office, and as soon as Mike closed the door, Larry asked, "How did it go?''

"Hopefully just the way we wanted it to," Mike said, sitting down behind his desk. Tanda thought he looked tired, but he was apparently working hard to keep it from showing. "They're not stupid, after all, so it shouldn't take long for them to get the message.''

"That the only one among them who wasn't there has to be the blackmailer," Rena said with a nod. "But since we went out of our way not to name anyone, our murderer shouldn't be suspicious.''

"But he should try to take immediate advantage of our not having the files yet," Mike agreed. "If we don't get

them we won't have any concrete evidence to point to as
a motive for the murders, and having a bloodhound track
him well after the fact won't be enough by itself to file
charges on. He'll try to silence Miss Baderlie perma-
nently, and trust to luck that her files will never be found
without her.''

"Which means we'd better get moving on setting our
trap for tonight," Rena said as she stood. "You know, I
can't get over the woman's nerve in having her victims
come here, to her own hometown, and not once worrying
that someone would suspect her. Running her part of the
library with an iron hand was such a passion with her, the
others couldn't picture her being interested in anything
else.''

"She was also camouflaged by the presence of Don
Grail," Larry pointed out as he also stood. "She had a
month's vacation she could have spent elsewhere, so it
must have been coincidence that her hometown was chosen. In every other way, she was the same as all the others.
And this trap of ours had better work, or our murderer
will hide in the same way.''

"Only a lot more successfully," Mike said with a nod.
"You two get started, and I'll be there not long after you.
It will be dark in a few hours, and that's all our murderer
will be waiting for.''

The two detectives left without adding anything else,
and Tanda waited until they were gone before looking at
Mike.

"Shouldn't you have said *we'll* be there not long after
them?" she asked, trying to keep it light. "You're not
thinking of getting rid of me, are you?"

"That's what I want to prevent," he answered without
a smile, nothing of lightness in the words. "Someone trying to get rid of you, I mean. You've been too close to
the action too many times during this insanity, and now
that you're out of it I want to keep you out. He knows

Robby is being taken care of someplace secret and far away, so you're not even involved to that extent. Tanda, I don't want to take the chance of you getting hurt.''

"I see," Tanda answered, wondering how she was supposed to get hurt if she made sure to stay next to *him*. But that seemed to be the point, that he didn't *want* her near him. He must be remembering how she'd sat over him with a gun, and was finally feeling the humiliation. How could a man feel like a man in the presence of a woman who'd had to protect him?

"Look, this is almost over," he said, now sounding even more weary than he had. "Once it is we'll talk, and get things all straightened out."

"Of course," Tanda said as she stood, wishing he would stop looking at her like that. She would remember the way he looked at her till her dying day. "Now is certainly not the time, so we'll leave it for later. You'll let me know as soon as you have him?"

"The minute he's in cuffs," Mike agreed, also standing. "Let me find someone to drive you home."

She nodded and let him walk her out of his office, then went with the officer he assigned to take her home. She felt like running and hiding rather than quietly saying goodbye, but what good would that have done? And besides, that could always be done—later.

The officer let her out in her own driveway, and she waved to the two policemen still on duty before going into the house. They'd waved back reassuringly, telling her no one had gotten into the house while she was gone. But she already knew that, since the murderer had been getting into a car at police headquarters at the same time she had.

Tanda took care of the dogs in their runs, but trying to do paperwork proved to be completely impossible. Her mind insisted on thinking about the conversation she and Mike would be having later, and occasionally wondering if there would even be a conversation. What if he decided there was nothing for either of them to say, or that he didn't want an argument like the ones he'd had with his ex-wife? Tanda couldn't imagine him refusing to say goodbye in person if that was what he'd decided to say, but how could she know how deeply his painful marriage had affected him?

By the time she'd climbed out of her thoughts, it was full dark out. She'd begun her thinking feeling depressed, but the longer it had gone on, the more her determination grew to hear from Mike before writing off the chance of their staying together. She loved Mike Gerard, and unless he felt differently they still had a chance to work things out. She'd make something to eat and wait for his phone call, and then—

The knock at the front door came when she was halfway to the kitchen, and sent her to answer it. It had to be one of the officers from the patrol car, possibly with word they'd gotten over their radio. Tanda pulled open the door, more than ready to hear that the nightmare was finally over, but it wasn't a police officer standing inside the screen door.

"Good evening, Ms. Grail," Howard Ullman said quietly, his beautiful voice turning the words into poetry and song. "I hope I'm not disturbing you, but I wonder if you might spare me a few moments of conversation? It's about these terrible murders, and something I know that I haven't told the police. In point of truth I'm rather uncomfortable talking to police, but I don't mind talking to *you* and it's something the police really should know."

Tanda stood there with the smile still on her face, but how she managed it, she had no idea. This mild-speaking, plain-looking man with the beautiful voice was the deranged murderer Mike and the others had set the trap for, but instead of being *there,* he stood not two feet in front of her. And the two officers in the patrol car. If they hadn't stopped him, or at least come over to see what he wanted, they had to be—

And she couldn't possibly close the door fast enough to keep him out. If she tried that, it might set him off, which left her with no choice at all.

"Mr. Ullman, how nice to see you again," she said, fighting to keep from shivering and screaming. "Do come in."

Chapter Eighteen

"I was about to pour myself a cup of coffee, Mr. Ull-man," Tanda said as her guest closed the door behind himself. "Would you care to join me?"

"I'd be delighted to, Ms. Grail," the man answered, his beautiful speaking voice turning the decision into friendly thanks. "I take it black, if you please."

Tanda nodded and headed for the kitchen again, forcing herself not to notice that the man wore cotton gardening gloves. She *couldn't* notice anything out of the ordinary— or act any way but normal—otherwise she would certainly die as quickly as those poor police officers outside. Hadn't they gotten Mike's orders about not staying in their car? Didn't they know they'd be vulnerable when they weren't looking at each other? Mike...

"We'll drink the coffee here at the table, if you don't mind," Ullman said from behind her, obviously having followed her into the kitchen. "It's been many years since I last found myself in a real home with an actual, often-used kitchen. Not since I was a small child, in fact."

"I find myself missing the time I was a child too," Tanda said, primarily to keep her hands from shaking as she brought the filled mugs to the table. *Be careful of what you say, mouth, very, very careful.*

"Well, I can't honestly say I miss my time as a child,"

Ullman told her as he watched her get the cream and join him at the table. Once she sat, he did too, his gloved hands held casually in front of him. "I was a very *bad* child, you see, and my mother and father were careful never to let me forget that. It was constantly necessary for me to ask God's pardon for my sins, but I haven't had to do that for many years now. God is fully aware of the fact that I don't sin any longer."

His plain face looked peacefully pleased with that, the happiness of a child who has finally found approval in his parents' eyes. And his golden voice had been so gentle and loving, it made Tanda want to shudder violently.

"I've been spending my life spreading God's word, you know," Ullman continued, raising his coffee mug and sipping from it. "Many of the people I preached to could see I knew God personally—that I was His Messenger— and could therefore speak for Him, and they gave me quite a lot of money. The problems arose with those who were related to some of these people of vision, relatives who were themselves completely blind. They accused me of lying in order to steal the money and then called the police, and I was forced to move on. But that let me reach so many more people, that I almost didn't mind."

He sipped from his mug again, apparently not noticing that Tanda hadn't added the cream or tasted her own coffee, and then he smiled and nodded.

"This is really good, and just what I needed," he said, gesturing with his mug. "The coffee and the lovely conversation both."

Tanda simply smiled in return and tried to look pleased. It would have been better if she'd spoken, but what do you say in a situation like this one?

"Very often, you must understand, children are closer to God than adults," Ullman went on in a soft, benevolent way. "It's our duty to instruct our children, but we can also learn from them. If they say God has forgiven them their sins, we should make an effort to believe them. After checking in the prescribed way, of course. My father always checked, but he never believed me.''

Now the look in Ullman's eyes was far away, and Tanda realized he no longer saw his surroundings. His memory had returned him to what he spoke about, and she no longer had to worry about responding.

''The procedure comes from the Bible, in the story of Sodom and Gomorrah,'' Ullman said, almost dreamily. ''It was something the men did to each other all the time, even though it was evil and a sin. My father said he would know God had forgiven me when it no longer hurt me to be tested, but it never did stop hurting. Even when I *knew* I had God's forgiveness, it never stopped hurting.

''And that, of course, told me my father was doing the test wrong,'' Ullman added. ''Were you ever tested like that?''

Tanda nearly jumped when she saw he was looking directly at her again, waiting for an answer. Using both hands she raised the mug to her lips, her mind searching frantically for what she might say. She didn't dare lie, but could she chance telling the truth? The coffee was faintly bitter without cream, but the strength of it helped her to make up her mind.

''I don't think my father knew about the test,'' she ventured carefully. ''If he did, he never mentioned it.''

''Yes, some fathers haven't the strength to administer the test to their children,'' Ullman said with a thoughtful nod, letting Tanda breathe again. ''But it *is* God's test, and if their fathers haven't the courage, God appoints Messengers who do.''

Tanda suddenly discovered that it was perfectly possible to feel the blood freeze in your veins. She'd never felt so chilled in her life, or so helpless. Miss Baderlie's files said children had been savaged in every city Ullman had preached in, but no police force had ever connected up the two events.

"And it takes a great deal of strength to be God's Messenger," Ullman went on after another swallow of coffee. "The testing is a trial for everyone involved, but God's will must be obeyed nevertheless. How is your dog?"

"My dog?" Tanda echoed. "Which dog?"

"The one who was hurt the other night," Ullman answered patiently with a smile. "When I was young I really wanted a dog, but when I got older I discovered that dogs don't like me. Your dog is very well trained, but no one around here knows how to handle him, do they? If you weren't here, they'd never be able to handle him properly, would they?"

So that was it. Tanda hadn't thought it was possible to be even more frightened, but finding out the reason for Ullman's visit made it happen. Only she could set Robby on the murderer's trail when he recovered, and she couldn't do it if she was dead.

"As a matter of fact, my former assistant could handle him just as easily as I do," she forced herself to say, speaking the lie with as much casual conviction as was humanly possible. "He moved down to Georgia to start his own school, but we're constantly in touch. Why would a Messenger of God take to murder? I don't understand."

This time Tanda really held her breath with the question, knowing she had to keep the man talking or she was dead. She was certain he'd decided to kill her no matter what, but every second it was delayed was another second of life.

"Asking for enlightenment is a sign that God is prepared to favor you with his blessing," Ullman told her gently with a really warm smile. "Most often it's difficult for people to understand God's will, but that's one of the things *I'm* here for, to explain. Would you mind giving me another cup of coffee?"

"Not at all," Tanda answered faintly, struggling not to pass out. He was going to keep talking for a while, and the relief that realization brought made her light-headed.

"Thank you," Ullman said when she put the mug back in front of him. "Now, you have to understand that God wants to protect His Messengers, but sometimes there are human beings so evil who threaten His Messengers, that God refuses to have anything to do with them. That means the Messenger has to protect himself, and help God out in another way."

He paused to take a sip of the fresh coffee, then gestured with one hand. "Take those people I was forced to associate with, for instance. Every one of them was evil, and for a while I thought I was meant to show them the path to forgiveness. I tried over and over, but they all refused to hear me. They thought I was a charlatan simply bilking people of their money, and that turned out to be a good thing for me. If they'd known I was a Messenger of God, I finally realized, they would have tried to pull me down.

"And then, last year, your brother announced he'd thought of a way to unmask the one who held all our secrets close. The others all supported his idea, so I was forced to go along with it, but the longer I thought about it, the worse his idea seemed. Chances were excellent that when the holder of secrets was exposed, we, too, would be exposed. And I couldn't allow that, not when God was counting on me. I had to find the holder of secrets first, and take mine away.

"I spoke to your brother after we discovered the lawyer wasn't in town, hoping to convince him to take me to the box and open it without anyone else around. He had no idea of the real reason I wanted to do that, but he also didn't care. He spoke harshly to me and I'm afraid I lost my temper a bit, but all he did was thrust me away and stalk off. His shirt was torn and that had made him even more angry, and he told me not to come near him again.

"So, naturally, I began the necessary eliminations with him. I'm sorry to have to tell you this, but you're entitled to know. I thought *he* might be the blackmailer and his idea had been a way to divert suspicion from himself, but that wasn't the truth. He was just another evil one, and he confessed to me fully before he died. As did all the others. I had to find some way to choose who to take and in what order, so I chose the others who had been given the same key as your brother, in just the order they'd been given their keys. I'm surprised no one else noticed and remembered."

"But if Don told you not to come near him again, how did you get close enough to—send him home?" Tanda asked, letting her confusion speak. "And the others— weren't any of them afraid to meet you alone?"

"Oh, I told them all I thought I knew who the black-mailer was, but didn't know what to do with the information," Ullman answered with a faint smile. "They each insisted I come to them alone with what I had, and not tell anyone else in the group. I'm sure they meant to use my…'information' to their own benefit, but things worked out differently than they expected. And you should have heard their secrets! Right from the start I had to admit I admired them for being able to hide such evil from the world, just the way I was hiding goodness. That's why I left those notes on their bodies, to show God and man that I admired what they'd hidden. And the letter opener was, of course, symbolic of a device to open their secrets to God."

"Then it was *'secret'* admirer,' not 'secret *admirer*,'" Tanda said, finally understanding the note. "But I think the number of wounds was also significant, as well as the money that was taken. Would you explain that?"

"Of course," he answered amiably. "The money was,

of course, their donation to my holy cause, and each wound represented one of us in the group. I struck for all of us, you know, in an effort to cleanse those who needed cleansing. I'd certainly noticed our numbers matched those of the Last Supper, which was clearly God telling me what to do.''

''And Roger Saxon, the man you met twice when he was a police officer?'' Tanda prompted, wishing it wasn't necessary to do that. She was running out of questions, and once that happened...

''I think that poor man's death was the most necessary of all,'' Ullman said, now sounding faintly sad. ''He'd been there twice, in two different cities, when the relatives of believers called in the police. The second time he looked at me strangely, as though he was close to recognizing me as a Messenger of God. Sure enough, when he saw me for the third time here, in the library, the recognition on his face couldn't be missed. I'd gone there to speak to Miss Baderlie about the meeting the others were insisting on holding, and I turned around to see that look on his face.

''When I left the library, he was waiting for me outside. He pretended he didn't know my secret and only wanted to talk to me about what was going on in that town, but I knew better. When he invited me to come to his motel room the next day, I immediately insisted that it be that evening. The next day was the Sabbath, you see, so I had to do my duty before or after the holy day. He was favored to know me for what I was, but I couldn't allow him to speak of it to others. You do understand now, don't you?''

''Yes, I certainly do,'' Tanda answered with a sigh. Roger Saxon had recognized Ullman, all right, but just as someone who had been involved more than once with the police. His instincts had told him Ullman knew something about what was going on, and he'd undoubtedly meant to do nothing more than question the man. Unfortunately for him, his instincts had centered on the wrong source of information.

"And that, I think, just about covers it," Ullman said softly, words that made Tanda's heart thud painfully hard. "There are times when being God's Messenger is difficult, but it's a duty that's impossible to shirk. What you must remember is that you're being called home, and will arrive in our Father's presence in a state of grace. I *am* able to do that, you know, so you needn't be afraid."

"Killing me won't accomplish anything at all," Tanda whispered, helpless to move her gaze from the gloved hand that had begun to reach into his jacket pocket. "Robby will track you even without me, especially since they already know who and what you are. All they need is Miss Baderlie's evidence, and in a little while they'll have it. Killing me now would be murder, and God won't forgive you for committing murder."

"Don't say that!" Ullman screamed, suddenly transformed into someone else entirely. He stood up fast, knocking over his chair, and a stained knife gleamed sullenly in his fist. "*You* don't know God's will. Only *I* know, and I say He's already forgiven me for anything I have to do. First it will be you and then Miss Baderlie, and after that it will the lieutenant's turn."

Tanda was on her feet by then too, but suddenly her fear was mixed with something else.

"Not Mike," she denied with a head shake, sickened anger beginning to rise in her. "You're not going to hurt Mike. I won't let you hurt him."

"I knew you weren't a believer, I knew it," Ullman said, his face twisted and his voice vindictive, like a pettish child's. "You thought you could fool me by pretending you were, but it didn't work! *God* is on my side, and those who are against me are against God! When you get home, He'll tell you so Himself—which will be in just another minute."

With that he started around the table toward Tanda, circling to his left as he tried to come at her from her right. Tanda was terrified, but most of the terror wasn't for herself. He intended to kill Mike, and he was crazy enough that he just might manage it. But he couldn't do it until he killed *her,* and that wasn't going to be as easy as he thought.

Without hesitation, Tanda picked up her coffee mug and flung it at him backhanded, hitting him in the left shoulder and splashing him with still-warm coffee. That was enough to make Ullman shout and flinch, which gave her enough time to slip left around the table away from him. If she could keep the heavy wooden table between them long enough, she'd think of something to stop him.

"You think that did you any good?" Ullman sneered as he wiped an angry hand across his face. "Well, it didn't, and you're about to find that out. I'm God's Messenger, and *no one* can stop me."

"I think you'll find you're mistaken," another voice said, one Tanda hadn't even dared to pray for. "Now that she's out of my line of fire, you're directly in it. Drop that knife and put your hands behind your head. You're under arrest for murder and attempted murder."

As impossible as it seemed, Mike stood in the hall beyond the kitchen, a uniformed officer visible behind him. Ullman had turned to look at him, frustrated rage in his maddened eyes before Tanda could no longer see them, and then Ullman laughed shortly.

"God works in mysterious ways," he said, his beautiful voice making it sound like a prayer. "Obviously I'm supposed to send you home first, and the girl later. Thank you for keeping me from making a mistake."

And then the madman was racing at Mike with a scream, the knife up and ready to plunge into him. Tanda muffled a scream of her own, seeing the shock on the face of the officer behind Mike. If he'd been the one under attack by the madman, he would have died where he stood.

But it was Mike who was the intended victim, and apparently knives didn't frighten Mike. Ullman was less than five feet away when Mike fired twice, and the madman was thrown back with the force of the bullets hitting him. He crashed to the floor and lay unmoving, eyes wide and staring; as soon as Mike came forward cautiously and kicked the knife out of the loosened grip, it was finally over.

MIKE STOOD with his arms tight around a trembling Tanda, but he wasn't holding her that tight for her sake. He'd come so close to losing her that he couldn't bear to think about it, not without starting to shake, himself.

"Have I ever told you what a beautiful sight you are?" Tanda finally whispered, the first words she'd spoken since he'd shot Ullman. "I suppose I shouldn't admit this, but I never expected to see that beautiful sight. How did you get from the trap at Miss Baderlie's house to here?"

"Ullman finally made a mistake," Mike answered, stroking her hair. "If he'd broken into your house from the back, we never would have known he was here. But he must have been too used to walking right up to his victims, either outside or at their front door. It kills me that two more lives had to be lost for his mistake to count against him, but at least there won't be any others. When he failed to show up at Baderlie's house, I had my people call to check with the men on duty here. They would have responded if they'd still been alive, and when they didn't I knew what had happened."

"But I guess you left Rena and Larry at the trap, just to be on the safe side," she said, taking a deep breath and leaning back from him just a little. "If they were here, I know they'd be inside by now. But how did you get in? Every door and window in this house is locked."

"We broke in through your bedroom window," Mike answered with a head shake. "If you want the truth, I don't understand how the breaking-and-entering crowd stand the nerve-racking tension. We didn't dare make any noise that would set Ullman off immediately, but at one point there *was* a small tinkle of breaking glass. My heart stopped until I knew for certain that neither of you had heard it."

"I wish I *had* heard it," Tanda said ruefully. "What you told him about me finally being out of the line of fire... Until that minute, I didn't realize I'd been between you and him the entire time. But maybe it wouldn't have helped after all. It probably wouldn't have occurred to me to drop flat. How long were you here?"

"Long enough to hear him explain how and why he'd killed the others of his—group," Mike told her. "And to hear his plans for you and Baderlie and me. You never know what crazy really means until you come up against it in the flesh. I wouldn't mind if I still didn't know. Why don't you pack a few things, and we'll find you someplace else to stay tonight. Once all the mess is gone, you'll find coming back here easier."

"I suppose you're right," she said as she stood, but instead of going toward her bedroom, she turned to look directly at him. "Mike, where did you have in mind for me to stay?"

"Well, I was thinking about a friend's house, or a motel," he lied, knowing where he most wanted to take her. His place and nowhere else, where he could hold her close and thank God she was all right. But tonight she'd come closer to dying than anyone should ever have to, and it was all his fault. He should have anticipated which way Ullman would jump, or at least considered all possibilities. But he hadn't, and because of that he'd almost lost her forever.

"Mike," she said, and her sweet voice was very uneven. "Mike, please look at me."

He hadn't realized he'd been too ashamed to continue to meet her gaze. When she pointed out how far he'd looked away, he brought his full attention back to her.

"Mike, I'm sorry," she said, and for an instant he thought she was about to say goodbye. The pain of that was incredible, but if it served to keep her safe... "I'm sorry I embarrassed you like that, but I couldn't help it. I wish I could say I'll never do it again, but I'm afraid I will. Are you sure it isn't something you could eventually live with, even if you can't accept it completely?"

"Excuse me?" Mike temporized, the only words his sudden bewilderment could think of. "What are you talking about?"

"Oh, you know what I mean," she said, misery filling her tone as her fingers twisted in front of her. "The way I embarrassed you twice by wanting to defend you. Last night when you were unconscious was bad enough, but tonight— I threw that mug hoping to crack his skull, something that would have kept him from going after you. I know you don't need anyone to protect you, especially not a woman civilian, but I just couldn't help myself—"

"Tanda," he interrupted, holding her arms. "You can't possibly be apologizing for *caring* about me? Everybody needs help at some time in their lives, and if they're very lucky there's someone there to give it. How could you possibly imagine I'd be bothered? All your bravery does is make me love you even more."

"Then why are you pulling back away from me?" she demanded in a whisper, no more than a shadow step away from tears. "If what I did really doesn't bother you, why are you trying to end what we had?"

"How can I do anything else?" he countered, blurting what he hadn't meant to say. "Don't you realize how close you came tonight to being killed? And it was *my*

fault! I should never have said that about Robby tracking
the man who'd attacked me, or if I did, I should have
realized I'd involved you as well as a safely hidden dog.
We don't have madmen running around here all the time,
but I'm a cop. If it happened once it could happen again,
and next time I might not make it to you until it was too
late."

He turned away then, torn apart by voicing a decision
he hadn't even been able to admit to himself. She'd be a
thousand times better off without him, but only his intel-
lect was willing to accept that. His emotions—his emotions couldn't, and there just weren't any words.

"Now *I'm* the one who doesn't understand," he heard
from behind him, and she did seem to sound confused.
"You're making it sound as if I would have been completely uninvolved in this mess if not for you, and that
doesn't happen to be the truth. If you want the real truth,
meeting you is probably the only thing that kept me from
being listed among the victims. I'd just decided to launch
my own private investigation, when you talked me out of
it."

"Oh, you had too much sense to go off on your own,"
Mike said, turning back to her. "I know you tried not to
mention finding that key, but—"

"Mike, I was completely determined," she interrupted,
putting a hand to his arm as she looked up into his eyes.
"I didn't want anyone else to be hurt because of me, so
I would have stuck to the decision. But there was something about the way you talked to me—not what you said,
but how you said it—that made me trust you. Are you
saying now that I was wrong to do it?"

"No, of course not," Mike said, all but coming apart
under that steady gray gaze. "I was deliriously happy
when I finally knew you trusted me. But—Tanda, I was
wrong to want that from you. I don't deserve your trust,
not when I keep putting you in danger. Associating with

me could get you killed someday, and I couldn't live with being responsible for that."

"I love you for worrying like that about me, but there was no way you could have guessed that Ullman would think getting rid of me would neutralize Robby. The idea is insane, but that's exactly what Ullman was. Are you going to blame yourself for not being insane?"

Mike couldn't quite answer that, and then he suddenly discovered that he didn't even want to. He realized that throwing away his happiness for something that might happen *was* stupid. His arms had somehow found their way around Tanda, which proved they were smarter than their owner.

"And I love you, Ms. Watson," he said, never having meant anything so much. "Why don't you go and get packed now."

"To spend the night at a friend's or a motel?" she asked, faint worry in those beautiful gray eyes.

"Not on your life," he answered, leaning down to brush her lips with his. "There's this fool of a cop I know, sometimes called Holmes by his intimates, and you'll be spending the night with him. And, if he's very lucky, it will be the first night of all the nights for the rest of his life."

"That cop's not such a fool," she answered with a laugh that drove away all worry. "No one called Holmes ever could be. But he *is* hurt, so this first night we'll let him get his sleep. After all, he'll have all the nights for the rest of his life to make up for the loss."

"We'll discuss that later," Mike said with a grin as he reluctantly released her. "Don't forget, you can't know if you can do something unless you try."

Her delighted laughter trailed her out of the room, and Mike hesitated only a moment before following. That fool of a cop had almost made the biggest mistake of his life, but that was all behind him now. What was ahead was life with the woman he loved, and he couldn't wait to get started.

The romantic suspense at

HARLEQUIN®
INTRIGUE

just got more intense!

On the precipice between imminent danger and smoldering desire, they are

When your back is against the wall and nothing makes sense, only one man is strong enough to pull you from the brink— and into his loving arms! Look for all the books in this riveting new promotion:

WOMAN MOST WANTED (#599)
by **Harper Allen**
On sale January 2001

PRIVATE VOWS (#603)
by **Sally Steward**
On sale February 2001

NIGHTTIME GUARDIAN (#607)
by **Amanda Stevens**
On sale March 2001

Available at your favorite retail outlet.

HARLEQUIN®
Makes any time special ™

Tyler Brides

It happened one weekend...

Quinn and Molly Spencer are delighted to accept three bookings for their newly opened B&B, Breakfast Inn Bed, located in America's favorite hometown, Tyler, Wisconsin.

But Gina Santori is anything but thrilled to discover her best friend has tricked her into sharing a room with the man who broke her heart eight years ago....

And Delia Mayhew can hardly believe that she's gotten herself locked in the Breakfast Inn Bed basement with the sexiest man in America.

Then there's Rebecca Salter. She's turned up at the Inn in her wedding gown. Minus her groom.

Come home to Tyler for three delightful novellas by three of your favorite authors: Kristine Rolofson, Heather MacAllister and Jacqueline Diamond.

HARLEQUIN®
Makes any time special ™

TEXAS CONFIDENTIAL

Penny Archer has always been the
dependable and hardworking executive
assistant for Texas Confidential, a secret
agency of Texas lawmen. But her daring
heart yearned to be the heroine of her
own adventure—and to find a love
that would last a lifetime.

And this time...
THE SECRETARY GETS HER MAN
by Mindy Neff

Coming in January 2001 from

If you missed the TEXAS CONFIDENTIAL series
from Harlequin Intrigue, you can place an order
with our Customer Service Department.

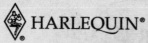 **HARLEQUIN®**

makes any time special—online...

your romantic life

—Romance 101—
♥ Guides to romance, dating and flirting.

—Dr. Romance—
♥ Get romance advice and tips from our expert, Dr. Romance.

—Recipes for Romance—
♥ How to plan romantic meals for you and your sweetie.

—Daily Love Dose—
♥ Tips on how to keep the romance alive every day.

—Tales from the Heart—
♥ Discuss romantic dilemmas with other members in our Tales from the Heart message board.

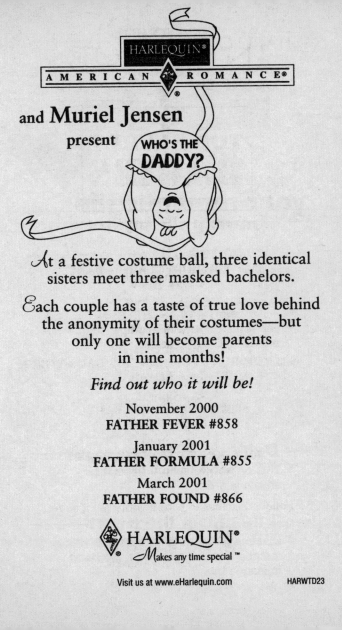

HARLEQUIN®

AMERICAN ◆ ROMANCE®

and Muriel Jensen

present

WHO'S THE
DADDY?

*A*t a festive costume ball, three identical
sisters meet three masked bachelors.

*E*ach couple has a taste of true love behind
the anonymity of their costumes—but
only one will become parents
in nine months!

Find out who it will be!

November 2000
FATHER FEVER #858

January 2001
FATHER FORMULA #855

March 2001
FATHER FOUND #866

HARLEQUIN®
Makes any time special ™

HARLEQUIN®
INTRIGUE

opens the case files on:

TOP SECRET BABIES

Unwrap the mystery!

January 2001
#597 THE BODYGUARD'S BABY
Debra Webb

February 2001
#601 SAVING HIS SON
Rita Herron

March 2001
#605 THE HUNT FOR HAWKE'S DAUGHTER
Jean Barrett

April 2001
#609 UNDERCOVER BABY
Adrianne Lee

May 2001
#613 CONCEPTION COVER-UP
Karen Lawton Barrett

Follow the clues to your favorite retail outlet.

HARLEQUIN®

Makes any time special ™